Edge of Memories

A NOVEL

By

GINNY LEVA

VILLAGE HILL PUBLISHERS

2003

PUBLISHED BY VILLAGE HILL PUBLISHERS

EDGE OF MEMORIES

Library of Congress Cataloging-in-Publication Data
        Leva, Ginny
        Edge of memories : a novel / by Ginny Leva
        p. cm.
        ISBN 0-9723907-0-7

        1. Ghost--Fiction.   2. Father and daughter --Fiction.
        3. Happiness--Fiction. 4. Supernatural--Fiction
        5. Love stories. I. Title
        PS3612.E823E45 2003   813'.6
                    QBI33-1227

        Co-editor: Jacquelline Leva
        Cover Editor: Jean-Paul Leva

Printed in the United States of America

Author's Note

I've had the gift to receive the insight about a universe which is ethereal but also very tangible, leading me to believe in the eternal relationship of soul mates. There's a reason why human beings befriend some and not others, why we feel comfortable trusting certain people, compelling us to get closer and solidify relationships. It's our soul, growing with us, living and moving us forward. Trust the gut feeling compelling you to act and beware of the senses that deceive and distort the message from inside.

My practice of medicine has grown into two New York offices, one in Queens and the other in Northport, Long Island. Sometimes, I sense the spirit inside my patients and a bond is established between us, carrying us forward, compelling them to trust me, to find comfort in my touch and through my words I have evolved in medicine, not just evaluating with the knowledge that comes from books and scientific study, but also with the intuition that makes me a better physician, guided by the soul inside me.

As a mother, I raise two wonderful children, my twins. I have tried to show them to look at life with the same believes guiding me through a world of experiences. My husband is a kind and understanding man, who I know from other life times and who will be my companion forever.

Throughout my life I have searched for reason, for the purpose of why some things must happen, and I have discovered there is no such thing as coincidence because every action is linked to another, sooner or later.

On Valentine's Day nineteen-sixty-one, my family and I discovered the plight of political immigrants when we left our homeland in Cuba. From prominence and wealth, my parents, sister and I discovered destitution and struggle when everything we owned, business, home and family, were taken away when I was only three years old. Although I was so young, the burning memories remain, a brutal reality set in, and we fled through the island of Jamaica, where we awaited the paper work that allowed us to enter the U.S. I have known hunger and poverty and out of them I forged the inner strength that guides me.

Seven years ago I lost a daughter, and through my despair I found the calling to write. Through my pain I gave hope and although I lack the wisdom to see the global picture of my existence, I believe everything that happens, good or bad, serves to enrich my soul. I have learned that from my deepest anguish and my greatest hardship, I must take out something positive, and although this may seem very hard at times or too altruistic to accomplish, I give you — my reader — the means to triumph in the journey of life.

I always felt a calling, the restless wandering to be fulfilled but not until the moment when one of my patients came to say goodbye at the exact moment when she died, that I *understood*. I awoke from my dream at five in the morning. The call from the hospital to tell me she was dead never came, an oversight, but Agnes delivered enveloped in a blinding brightness to leave me with the message that there is no pain, no hardship on the other side, and that it's fine to surrender into an end. She was the messenger, the voice that gave me the news. I knew our relationship had survived death, and that I, too, will be well when my time arrives, because now I can see in a way I never saw. Of course, there have been many special dreams. Dreams that are different from other dreams because of their vividness, and lingering memory through the years, dreams that are never forgotten.

In my humblest experience I hope to spread a belief through my writing. This book is forged by a will and long-time dreams, and will be launched with the guidance of the kindred spirits that inspire me.

But foremost, the reason why I write is to spread the news that death is not the end, but a door by which to cross.

I dedicate my book to the people who have lived a dream with me. Through their encouragement and support, I have leaped into the future.

To Paul, my husband, who has allowed me the time to write, to my children who have listened and involved themselves with my creation, and to my office staff in Northport, Daphne, Janice, and Candice, dear people who believe in me. Also to Laura, my niece, who's been there from early days.

A special thanks to my friend Glen, my favorite English professor.

May God bless you all.

1

Snoqualmie Pass, Washington State 1989

Elizabeth held her breath when she saw him ready to take the challenge of the mountain. Skiers avoided Kensington Peak because years ago six deaths made it known as a dangerous terrain. Lawsuits followed, and a slew of injuries lead to the final calamity, the rumor that the mountain was haunted.

Dark moonless nights brought forth a mysterious cry coming with the wind, a moan sounding like a wounded man stranded on a slope. Guests at the lodge were caught by a chilling swirl of air that made their hair stand on end. Innocent conversations, rumors inside the village, and after a while there were more vacancies than bookings and for that reason, Elizabeth and Claude were alone.

Some people can see the dead. Others can hear them or say it's a powerful feeling taking over, a silent voice inside the head, shadows caught from the corner of the eye, noises cracking in the silence of dark but in Claude's case, she knew he didn't believe in ghosts, in much of anything else, and as far as danger was concerned, extinction was just a word.

"Stop daydreaming and meet me at the bottom," he said.

Claude dropped down, propelling forward with a swing of the poles. Death be their friend. A fall — a clumsy twist of self-induced fate — would end the predicament. She took off, knowing she was pregnant with his child.

She slid over the loose powder like the wind riding the mountain, flying with the air. Claude was far ahead of her with no thought but a challenge and its conquest, but it was more complicated than that. Through her faith in God, she believed in a soul that lived eternal, but now she wondered, at what stage does it settle into the chosen body? Was it at the moment of birth, or earlier in the fetal life? Mother and fetus sharing the energy of the host, just like blood and nutrients are shared. Then, severing the umbilical cord, another soul comes in, into the body that has been made, without doubts, without fears, ready to take its first breath, and traverse through its destiny. Who was she to deny life?

No.

This was not a time to die but to live, for herself and her child, regardless of the uncertainty in the future.

Snow sprayed at her sides as she carved through the bends in the terrain, taking dangerous speed. At times she crouched to avoid low offshoots from smashing into her face while her hands pooled wetness inside the gloves, despite the cold. One last run. With steady concentration she used the poles to gain momentum. The wind rode behind her as she jumped over the edge of the inevitable cliff.

Claude waited at the bottom, tall and handsome, smiling as she stopped in front of him. She thought to scream, maybe burst out of her suit and roll in the snow, shocking her senses into something other than the sheer torture of her thoughts.

"That was fun, wasn't it?"

"You're always so sure of the outcome," she said with flat refrain.

"For a while I thought I was going to walk down with you."

"It was too dangerous."

"Hmm, but exciting."

"It's the thrill of overcoming obstacles, isn't it?"

"I'm a winner, not a loser." He led her through the snow. "Don't you know me by now?"

"Didn't it worry you that I could get hurt?"

"But you didn't."

Claude's dimples marked the hollow of his cheeks, and his smile warmed the blood in her veins, warmer than any furnace ever could. His face, chapped from the wind, made her alive with want. The five feet, eleven inches of cerebral testosterone rushed in with the excitement of love, but her life was shadowed by the incipient unrest. She was going to drop it. He had made her pregnant.

"I'm tired, Claude." She took a deep sigh. "Let's head back."

They had been at it all day, and now the sun was coming down on the horizon with magenta hues that made the sky ablaze. Mixing business with pleasure on a weekend away from the pace in New York was his way to unwind. She knew he didn't have the luxury of taking off more than a day or two from work. On this trip, he had traveled to the West Coast seeking the technology of Silicon Valley for his new business, pursuing the young minds that could make his firm successful. He snatched people eager to make a better income, paying them more because in turn they brought back greater returns. He was used to getting what he wanted; he was used to buying people like everything else.

"One day I'm going to own a mountain." His laughter filled the valley in his boast. "Maybe not this one, but I'll find my own, secluded from the rest of civilization. For today this one did well."

"You want a lot out of life. It's scary when I think you're serious about the things you say."

"Hmm, you're moody."

"No, it's just that my needs are more basic than yours."

She agreed to this weekend knowing it a mistake. Every second together she wanted to tell him about his child. Instead, she kept silent because a baby compromised his plans and she didn't want to lose him. Fear swallowed her, cluttering the ability to chose the right moment to voice that after a lot of soul-searching, she had decided her baby was conceived out of an act of love, not to be destroyed.

He had invested all his money in a new company and his mind was set on building a financial future, not a family. She fantasized too often that he would be pleased to discover they shared something precious and rare, but these were her thoughts, not his.

She saw the clouds in the sky, pushed forward without choice, not because they wanted to go anywhere, but because the wind moved them onward.

"What mountains do you want to conquer?" Gliding slowly over the snow, he turned toward her. He removed the goggles from his eyes to look at her with the blue steel of his eyes. "Do you want your own art gallery, or perhaps to be the curator of a large museum?"

"I love you, Claude."

Surrounded by his careful silence she heard her voice come back in echos.

He couldn't see behind the shield of her own goggles, but her lacrimals clogged with the tears burning with stunning pain. She knew she was there to enliven the dread of his routine. Her hair clipped into a ponytail, her figure covered by a one-piece bright blue suit, accentuating her slender shape, was enticing, but soon her pregnant state would be unquestionable. Therefore, she was aware her options were limited by time.

A shared love of art had brought them together two years ago when he entered the small gallery in Soho where she worked part-time. He asked her about one of the art pieces and his smile touched her; his flirtatious attitude seduced her.

"I've been thinking."

"What about?"

"About you and me, about us."

"And?" He turned to look at her. "What about us, Liz?"

"We hardly see each other, I'm so afraid of losing what we have."

"I'm not going anywhere."

She saw his cautious smile.

"Neither are we."

"That's because I'm working, but we've talked about it. Why are you dwelling on it again, while we're here? I don't want to talk about the same issues every time we get together."

"Oh, Claude." Her voice shook. "It's not easy."

"I'm not in the mood." He stopped moving forward as a frown formed over his forehead.

"I want you. I love you *enough* to want to settle down, to raise a family by your side. I feel like I know your soul even better than you do. Unfortunately, because I do know you, I realize these thoughts are foolish."

"Let's drop it, all right?"

"Don't push me away."

A crude reality settled. Triumph moved him and anything that stood in its way was an undesired impediment. She knew they met at the wrong time in life and that her love was a hindrance if she meant to tie him down, but in her heart she knew they were meant to grow old together, if only he could figure it out, too.

"Would it bother you if I left you? I should go away, you know."

"You're in the mood to pick a fight and I don't want one." Taking hold of her arm, he forced her to meet his eyes. "Why the hell are you complicating our relationship? I don't need your guilt trips."

"You don't understand." She jolted from his grasp.

"I asked you to come along because I wanted your company, but not to argue."

"I need more than just the good times. When I start to talk about my feelings, you brush me off."

"It's about getting married, isn't it?" The glare of the sun against the white background made him squint.

Tired, she looked back toward the abandoned mountain behind them. A glimmer of pain betrayed her smile.

"Don't get upset. I love you too much to force you into marriage. I'll make your choices simple."

"Simple? I liked you better when I thought you understood me."

"You see, I still do."

"I hate when you're irrational," he said.

"This weekend, you assumed I wanted to come, calling me, telling me rather than asking for my company, while I hadn't seen or heard from you in weeks. You come around, you take and then you leave me with the pain of missing you, of wanting more than you give."

"I can't slow down to become a complacent partner for you."

"It's your first million or bust, right?"

"Nothing is more important than success."

"Would you marry me if I asked you?" Elizabeth held her breath for a moment and then went on to answer in the wake of his silence. "No, you wouldn't. I told you, I know you so well."

"You refuse to understand."

"Then enlighten me," she said.

"I come from nothing, but I want a lot better from life — it's that simple. Feelings can mess it all up."

"You're blind, Claude. You can't see beyond your greed."

"You're bright, sophisticated and one day you might make a great partner for life, but right now, I can't say what you wanna hear." His voice turned softer, like a gentle caress. "You've got the fire which fills me with the want of you, but I can't marry you."

"You can't or won't?"

"My life is too complicated."

"It's never simple. Do you think you're the only one with problems?"

"I would be a terrible husband, traveling as much as I do, coming home late . . . while you'd find yourself lonelier than you thought. No, you can't expect me to slow down, and I can't expect to make you happy."

"You're right, Claude. My choices are clear. How can I expect you to stop for me?" She walked a few paces ahead as they approached the village.

"I'm not about to change my lifestyle."

"You're a fool," she said. "Love comes once at its very best, and you either chose to retain it or give it up. If you let it go, you'll forfeit the chance to be happy and with second best, something will always be missing. I assure you, no one will love you the way I do."

"You could be right, but I'll take my chances."

"At any other time it would be easier to deal with your choices, but not now that —"

"*Not now* that what?"

A white clearing surrounded them.

"Seems so pure." Elizabeth looked down at the snow, lost with the thought of something much deeper. She knew he would never understand why she had to keep the baby. Abortion seemed so sensible and he didn't understand anything that was impractical. "I'm going home, to my parent's house. I'll drop out of school for a semester for the business I need to take care of."

"Business?"

"It's different from the one you're used to. Mine has to do with commitment, about feelings."

"Are your parents ill?"

"First time you've asked about them. You don't even know where I come from, do you?"

"Well, I'm asking."

"You're a man blinded by himself." She took a deep sigh. "My parents are healthy, but right now, the way you're making me feel, I'm not very much in the mood to tell you anything that has to do with me."

"What is it, dammit?"

"You have a superficial affair with life, with me. Isn't that enough?" She formed a grin. Their time together seemed like a million years of nothing. "I've been waiting for a while. I guess I've been waiting much too long for you."

"Look, don't lecture me."

"You're all about action and outcome, aren't you? It's better that I leave you." She wanted to yell, this was the time to forget him, but how could she run away from herself or from the life beating inside her body?

"I thought things were going well between us," he said. "If you're going because you think I don't care, you're wrong. I find myself thinking about you more than I'm willing to concede, but I don't like to talk about that stuff. I thought you and I had it all figured out."

"I thought *we* were important."

The glance in his eyes devoured her with ire.

"In case you haven't figured it out yet, I'm not dating anyone else because I'm content in our relationship, but I never made promises. Take me or leave me. This is who I am."

"Stop it," she said. "I'm not going to let you hurt me any more."

"I want a lot out of life," he softened the tone of voice. "Today I can only offer you a ton of debt, my student loans, and my uncertain business venture. No, I don't have very much."

"When have I asked you for more?" Money didn't seduce her, nor could it buy her. She didn't have to own an art gallery to find happiness. A lot less would be fine so long as they were together.

"You're too romantic, too naive."

"Call it my sin."

"I grew up in poverty, but that's not the way I want to die." He took a deep breath. "I know I'm blunt as hell, but our marriage would asphyxiate me. We have a fabulous time together, but I can't complicate my life any further than I have. You're right. It might do us well to see other people, to take a break from each other."

They were almost by the lodge. She could see the smoke from the chimney over the roof, staining the sky gray under a red sun. The smell of burning logs filled the air. Claude trailed behind her. She raised the goggles over her head, stooping to remove the skis while the fatigue of her mood sunk in, flattening her desire to do much else.

"You're dead serious about your plans, aren't you?"

"We're at a point in our relationship where I need more," she said. Without raising her head she released the skies, while he towered in front of her.

With a gentle gesture he made her stand up again, placing his arms around her waist. *How wonderful their intimacy could be*, but she lacked something much stronger, something elusive yet firm in its roots, something she needed to hear that he could never say. Love and its commitment were forbidden in his world.

"The warmth of your body seeps into my skin," he voiced, in his deepest tone. "You look great. Don't leave me, because if you go, I'll miss you."

She looked into his eyes, wishing he could find the secret hidden behind her silence.

"Remember when I'm gone that I love you," she said.

"A man needs a woman. I'm not the type to dwell in the past, nor on people who are gone. If I date other women, we will distance."

"I appreciate your honesty."

Her cheeks flushed; the air from her lungs seemed to disappear. She had to push away from his hold in order to reserve the truth within herself. In his arms all her plans grew weaker as tears threatened in her eyes.

"It's your choice, go." He grabbed around his neck, yanking off the chain and ankh she had given him as a present. "Take them."

"They're yours. I don't want them back." She clutched the jewelry inside her hand. "They were your Valentine's Day presents."

"I wear it because you gave it to me, but I don't believe in their symbolism. When we die, it's the end of everything. There are no soul mates, no life after death. We make our own luck, our own future, and it's better if nothing reminds me of you or your ideas."

A twist of fate was going to end it all. Nothing in life could stop her from loving him, but she had to go. She was due to give birth in September, but she'd be back. She was twenty, he was twenty-five, both of them old enough to understand the consequences of their actions. The raucous call of a crow pulled her from her thoughts as she walked away, leaving him behind but knowing that whatever happened, she would never forget him.

2

New York City, 1998

"You disappoint me, Jack," said Claude. He sat with cold resolution behind a glass desk, in a suite more the size of a tennis court than an office, studying the face of his employee as the man bit the outer corner of large lips.

"I worked hard to pull the account, but Mc Dougal is a cheap bastard. The economy is slowing down, and he figures in six months he'll get a better deal. Competition is tough, and people are waiting for prices to come down. You know we're at a peak in tech."

In the arrogance of his genius, Claude had devised a communication software that tied discordant computer systems and linked them to those of any other by the power of a programming language.

"My product is a solid investment. I'm on my way to Camp David this afternoon because our government couldn't get better than what we have to offer. My prices are not coming down. I thought I could count on you."

"You know you can." Jack squirmed in his chair.

"How many accounts did you bring in the last six months?"

"Dallas, that stuff was mine."

Claude pushed back from behind the desk, eyeing the man in front of him as though he were a bug on a wall. He turned to look outside through the wall of glass rising behind him, discovering his own reflection. Aging had carved lines over his forehead, like roads that splintered into rivers of silver, crowding at the temples. He worked in a world of steel and concrete, of buildings that were built to soar above the clouds, of technology that launched the future. For a few moments he sat without a word because he scorned effortless arguments. Taking in a deep breath, he swivelled back.

"I brought Dallas. I chased after Peter Crawford for three years and when

I knew he was sold on my technology, I handed you the grand finale."

Beads of sweat crowded Jack's upper lip.

"Mr. Aumont, I work hard for you."

"I'm not saying you don't, but you're not as effective as you led me to believe when I hired you. I've been keeping an eye on you, and your deadlines are late. You've grown comfortable. Your secretary had the good sense to divert Mc Dougal's call to Pilar Haydig when you instructed her to avert all calls because you where going on vacation and didn't want to complicate the day. Damm, the man means a lot of money for this firm and if I'm paying you, you take calls whenever and wherever you are. Pilar Haydig managed to convince Mc Dougal that the economy is not as dismal as he believed."

"Pilar met with him?"

"She did."

"I didn't think."

"You're too laid back, not hungry enough to work for me. Productivity, Jack. I don't mind paying if I get full returns . . . but when you don't bring in a return, I can't carry you."

"My wife, she's pregnant," Jack's voice was a trail. "We moved into a new house to accommodate the baby."

"You should have thought about it yourself. I'm not good with charity. My nurturing instinct died when the plant my secretary gave me wilted."

Jack got up and looked at his boss. He cleared his throat and said, "I've worked a long time for you."

"Possibly too long. Nothing personal, Jack. You'll have to excuse me now, I'm on my way to Virginia and I have to wrap up before I leave. "

Jack stood under the shadow of his doom, smitten by the vile fate that forfeited his future at the firm. His hands had a fine quiver when he picked up the copy of Newsday among the other magazines on the side table beside his seat. Claude Aumont's face stared back from the cover as it read "A Man Of His Time." The dry smack of pages slapped over the cold surface of his desk while Jack surrendered a final glance of revulsion. With the hopelessness of the facts, Claude saw him walk out through the double doors of the suite.

*   *   *

Tonight Claude moved forward, conquering a perilous road that lead to his cabin retreat. Burned out from stress, he was trying to stay alert but his shoulders weighed like boulders, too big to carry anymore.

He had come upon these parts traveling from Northern California's

Silicon Valley, Everett, to a spot near Seattle. When he couldn't stand it any more, when he knew he was at the breaking point of sanity, this was his well-deserved getaway.

Thunder tore the skies open. He thought of nothing but the pavement ahead while the windshield wipers flagged in a poor attempt to improve vision. Up on the high ground where his cabin overlooked the ocean, there was no chance of flooding, but mud slides along the way made the slippery ascent treacherous.

Out of nowhere, the ethereal vision of a woman ran in front of his vehicle.

"What the hell," he cried out.

Escaping an accident by a few inches, he swerved into a mud bank. When he looked again, she had disappeared. He threw the gear into park while the beams of the headlights cut through the thick black of the surroundings. The cold drops of water lashed against his face when he climbed out of the truck. Upset at his own resolution, he set out to follow after her, catapulted by the thought that she might be in trouble. He looked, around but no one came from any direction, and at that moment, he realized he was unarmed.

"Where are you?" he yelled out, disregarding all danger.

He heard the response of the wind as it rushed through the branches of the enormous pine trees: a haunting song that forewarned. Off the main road the vegetation was wild, difficult to push away. Anyone could ambush him from behind. Larger limbs swung with violence as though they were small twigs, and he realized the real threat came from above.

"Damn," he said. *Who could possibly wander on foot in the midst of such a storm?*

Conscious of the uneven surface that grabbed at his feet like cadaverous hands raising through the soggy earth to make him trip, he advanced in the dark. Then, with the light from another bolt of lightning, he saw her there, still, on the ground of the forest. He stared, knowing this was crazy. Dressed in a blouse and jeans, and a parka over them, she was drenched to the touch. He picked her up, intent on reaching his vehicle, but at moments, feeling the weight of the girl over his arms, fearful his knees were going to buckle. His boots sank deeper into the mud with the weight of the woman as the chill of that night filtered through his bones.

After placing her inside the vehicle, he reclined the seat on the passenger side, remembering somewhere he had learned about establishing blood flow to the head with postural recumbency. From the back of the truck he retrieved a blanket and covered her with it. For seconds he stared forgetting the storm, disregarding the freezing water that dripped from his chin. Pushing back the strands of wet hair covering the hollow of her checks, he saw that she was breathing.

"I hope you don't die on me."

He was talking to himself because she was unconscious.

As he drove again toward the cabin, his house appeared a long awaited refuge. After parking beneath the carport, he brought her inside and up the stairs that led to the main bedroom, knowing he would spend the night on the couch.

He undressed the limp figure, dressing her in his own warm clothes as she remained unconscious. There were no bruises, nothing that was an obvious injury. With a layman's basic medical knowledge he spread a few wool blankets over her body and lay beside her counting her shallow breaths, exchanging his warmth for the glacial cold of her flesh. The chill of death crawled into his own skin as he pressed to give her life.

Time stood still, immersed in the noise of silence. He listened, as the raindrops banged against the roof like the tom-toms of many tapping fingers. When she felt warmer, her breathing resumed to a more synchronous rhythm. In this weather it was impossible to go for help, but he could get logs for the fireplaces. He managed to gather enough dry wood to light those upstairs and in the den. The crackle of the fire filled the empty night as he pushed to store perishables in the refrigerator and other victuals into the pantry.

Uneasy about the girl, he tried to forget about her by the physical burden of his chores. However, it was impossible to dispel the thoughts about the woman upstairs. When he came back to his bedroom, he touched her arm.

"Now you're much more alive," he said.

That night while he slept, he saw the stranger in his dreams. Once again she was in the deep of the forest, but the sharp brightness of the lightning now embraced her, making her glow in her aura. She drifted through the air rather than walk. His heartbeat grew quicker, but he knew she meant him no harm.

Her lips were still, but he heard the woman draw him near; a voice without words, and he felt compelled to come closer. Through the eyes offering hope he sensed her, peace and his mind acknowledged what had to be a telepathic message, as clear as though sentences were uttered; she summoned. Although he walked toward her the small space between them was insurmountable. Soon the pain of longing filled his heart, and his vocal cords released a guttural moan sadder than anything he'd heard before. Suddenly, the darkness swallowed him into the emptiness that made him sink. His loneliness became a living hell.

With the sensation that it was she who tried to save him — rather than reaching out.

*   *   *

The disturbing dream followed into the morning when the details remained vivid in his mind, his pajamas drenched in sweat. Even though he was awake, the sensation remained of being trapped inside the dream. He shook his head, looked around twice to realize he had awakened in the den. With one toss he pushed away the blankets, rising from the sofa and shuffling across the Indian area rug, heading toward the windows. The haze rose, drifting slowly from the oceanfront, and once again he was compelled by the unusual magnetism in the land. Long ago he had stood over the cliffs near his cabin knowing he had to build here. Price didn't matter when he bought one thousand acres of forest.

He used the bathroom upstairs because all his toiletries were there. On his way to the kitchen, he peeked into his bedroom, reassuring himself that the experience of the night before was real. He couldn't help to speculate about the possibilities that brought the woman to the moment in the forest where he came upon her. She slept in peace.

He left the bedside and went to the kitchen. Soon the smell of bacon and eggs mingled with the aroma of a fresh made pot of coffee. Thirty-five years of life had brought him to the zenith of his career. With his laid back appearance, far from the poise of his demeanor in the city, he was a different man. Living alone he knew how to fend for himself. Before having the money to hire servants, he worked in the kitchen of his uncle's restaurant, helping the cook, cleaning, doing whatever had to be done, but today seemed far from there.

When he turned to place his plate of food on the table, he saw her standing before him as though she had materialized out of nowhere, wearing his oversized plaid shirt and jogging pants.

Barefoot, she came closer, quiet like a leaf gliding through the air. They stared in silence for a few seconds, eyeing each other. Natural soft waves tangled as her hair fell beneath the shoulders. Large brown eyes stared at him like the core of an unknown universe, her presence full of the mystery that stirred his stomach into leaps.

"Good morning,,"he said."How do you feel?" When she didn't answer he went on. "Please, sit with me and have breakfast." Claude motioned her to take the seat in front of him and she obeyed, pursuing each of his movements. "I usually stay here by myself. This is my vacation place," he said. "It's great to get away from work and everything else."

Although he was trying to establish a conversation, she looked as though she couldn't care less. For all he knew, she was a creature from outer space studying a rambling idiot. Perhaps a more reasonable explanation: she was deaf-mute.

He finished setting a place for her and then sat across. "I found you last night, in the woods. You were half frozen."

He took a sip from his coffee and started to eat, trying to pretend indifference when everything about her arose a flutter inside him.

"Am I wearing your clothing?"

He heard her voice. *She has vocal cords after all.*

"I grabbed the first warm thing I found. I got here just last night, so I had to pick out of my suitcase." He saw her fold her arms over her chest. "Are you cold?"

He got up and went toward the closet by the front door. From a perch he grabbed his hunting vest, giving it to her.

"I'm afraid there's nothing other than my clothing in this house." Saying that, he placed more wood into the fireplace of the dining area. "The rain forced landslides along the road, so we're temporarily stuck with each other, but if you want to call somebody, I have a cellular phone."

"I don't need to call anyone." She walked over to where her clothing was hanging. On the fireplace screen her jeans and shirt were drying. Her boots were also near by, taking heat from the grate which burned the wood, but everything was soaking wet. She grabbed her bra and panties, slipping them into the pocket of her pants before coming back to the table. "Do you live alone?"

"I'm by myself, yes," he smiled. "Don't worry, as soon as the weather improves, I'll drive you into town."

He lost eye contact when she held her breath, long enough that he thought the woman would pass out.

"No, don't take me into town."

"Then where do you want to go?"

"I'm not sure," she said. "I would prefer to stay away from people."

"Did you kill someone and you want to hide away?" His statement was meant to be funny.

She gave him an unpleasant stare.

"I'm sorry. Just kidding," he said. She seemed gentle, not the violent type at all. Her eyes filled with an odd melancholy, and he was lured deeper into her puzzle, enveloped by the the glance she gave him. "Are you hungry? I'm not the greatest cook, but it's edible."

At first it was a small bite, but soon they were three pieces of bread spread with butter and then another two pieces with orange marmalade. He sat back to watch her devour the food. If it wasn't for decency, he thought she would have had more toast. She took slices of pineapple served on a dish, savoring the sweetness of every bite. The girl finished one cup of coffee, helping herself to a second.

He understood that she was hungry after the ordeal from the day before, but she ate every morsel of food without haste, chewing for the extravagance of the pleasure in her taste buds. He was tempted to ask how many days she had not eaten, but it seemed more than that. As impossible as it could be, he was sure she had discovered the magnificence in the sense of taste after years of abstinence. Indeed, maybe she was an alien from outer space, attempting to mix in with the population of the planet, but if she was, she had chosen the perfect body parts because she was beautiful. He smiled, humored by his own thoughts.

Wanting to learn much more about her, it dawned on him he had bypassed a simple introduction.

"My name is Claude-Phillipe. What's yours?"

When she replied her voice was hardly audible, "*I don't know.*"

3

Claude combed back the rebel lock of hair that brushed over his eyebrow. Dressed in blue jeans and a thermal undershirt, he stood up from the table. Amnesia was a familiar concept, but it didn't happen to people he knew. This was a fantastic notion.

"What do you mean, *you-don't-know?*" His voice knifed the words.

"I can't remember who I am. Everything before this morning is gone."

He stood up in disbelief, but by the tone of her voice, she wasn't teasing.

"I found you running in the middle of the woods. For the life of me, I can't imagine what you were doing there, running on foot through this miserable weather." He raised an eyebrow. "You seemed unreal in the darkness, almost like a ghost that came from nowhere. I would say you crashed on earth through one of those bolts of lightning, but it's not possible, is it?"

"Was I alone?"

He sat down again.

"There was nobody else and no one seemed to chase you."

"I'm sorry. I can't recall anything." There was a tremble in her voice.

"Are you kidding me?"

"I don't lie."

He rubbed over the stubs of beard on his face, watching her, trying to focus deeper into the truth behind her. If this were true, then she was at his mercy, with no one to turn to. The girl blinked, and the calm in her face lost itself in the uncertainty of the world in front of her.

"I guess I'll have to believe you."

"Did you undress me?"

"Who else could have done it? You were out cold, and if I left you wet in your clothes, you would have caught pneumonia."

"Or, so you thought."

"Logical deduction, and common sense. I would not take advantage of you." He had used people to get where he was in life but he never abused a woman. The blood rushed into her face, into her lips, color of red poppies that made him giddy with desire.

"Somehow, I do believe you," she said. "Are you a doctor?"

He made a subtle smile. "No, not at all, I'm just an ordinary man living in the seclusion of a few days away from my job."

Her face reminded him of someone, but he wasn't sure who this was, as though his mind too, had forgotten. A feeling of having found a long lost friend took over, but his curiosity climaxed in vain because she had no answers to any of his questions.

"What do you do for a living?" she asked.

Is she scrutinizing me in a cunning sort of way?

He was going to be vague about himself because one of the richest men in the world, his cybernetic network controlled transportation and national defense. Claude-Phillipe Aumont was CEO of a multi billion-dollar industry, trading in the stock exchange worldwide and employing over ninety thousand people. Silicon Valley uttered his name with respect, but wealth had many tradeoffs, and anonymity was one of them. Everyone had secondary gains, as he hated the calculating hypocrisy within his circles.

"Computers, I work in the computer business."

"Ah. So, do you fix them or do you program them?"

"I design software, but I don't want to talk about work. I'm here to get away from it."

"Then we won't talk of it."

Her unforseen disinterest set him at ease.

"A terrible ordeal must have left you stranded," he said. "Forgetting can be merciful."

"Can it?"

For him, forgetting undesirable moments was the only way to survive the past.

"Although you seem hesitant to leave here — after the storm clears — the answers might be in the coastal town near by," he said. "The population is small so I'm sure we can find a husband or family living in Everett."

"Oh God! I don't remember anyone and I don't want to stay with anybody." Her words trampled out of her mouth, and then trailed off to say, "I feel safe with you. Please, don't take me back."

"You can stay for a while, but inevitably, I have to go back to the roof over her head, but he had to make it clear. She couldn't expect to stay with him too long.

"If you let me, I would like to stay until you leave. I'll be out of your way. I'll cook, clean, help you with whatever you have to do, but don't send me away. All my instincts tell me I can't go back from where I came, at least — not for now."

Her predicament was understandable, but he didn't need her servitude and, least of all, companionship.

What she didn't know was that he had come to Washington to get away from people, and the reason why he was there without caretakers was not that he couldn't pay for them, but because solitude was his best friend.

Her reaction was peculiar or perhaps not, understanding the fear of the unknown. She looked scared, with circles under her eyes and in need of his patience.

"Well, since some of the roads are blocked off, we're stuck with each other for the next few days."

They sat in the kitchen a while longer, and without exchanging further words, she went upstairs. Later that morning, he could hear her coughing from everywhere he went in his cabin. When she didn't come down for lunch, he brought her a bowl of clam chowder, and a plate of the rigatoni pasta he had fixed for himself. He walked in and out, with only a brief exchange but leaving the door open, in case she needed something, but bundled under the covers, she didn't call him.

Maybe it was the stillness of her face when he came to get the empty tray or the equanimity of her movements, as though she belonged in his home, that excited his heart beat all too fast. He wasn't able to concentrate or relax with the uneasy and awkward sensation filtering inside with the knowledge of her presence — something that was most uncommon for him. Despite their casual encounter, the feeling of deja-vu grew stronger and the more contact he had with her, the more it crept in that she was familiar.

By the evening she had exhausted a box of tissues filling up the waste basket by the bed. He brought another box and was emptying the garbage into a trash bag, when he caught from the corner of his eyes the flush in her cheeks and the raw skin under her nose.

"You look ill," he said.

He didn't wait for her to answer, placing a hand over her forehead. She was burning and then he realized she was shivering with a temperature.

"Damn, why didn't you say something?" He went to the bathroom cabinet and took the bottle of antibiotics given by his private physician had he gotten sick while he was away. She had a glass of water by the bedside. "These should make you feel better. Take one tablet twice a day and the ibuprophen for your temperature every six hours. Don't be so self sufficient next time. It's a bad character trait."

"I don't want to bother you."

"I pulled you out of the storm to keep you alive, not to die afterward." He sat on the edge of the bed. They stared at each other and he understood that she was all alone in the world. "Make sure you drink plenty of water," he softened his tone. "I'll bring you another bottle from downstairs."

She shrugged. "Maybe you should have driven away. Now that I'm here, you have to deal with me."

"It's fine. I know about having nowhere to go."

The loudness of her silence stumbled over him.

"I have books downstairs, if you want one —."

"Tomorrow," she said.

"Call me during the night if you need me. I'm a light sleeper, so I'll hear you if you call."

He saw her nod, agreeing to do as he proposed.

"Fate brought me to you." She spoke in a low hush, hiding her eyes from him.

"Interesting thought but I was driving and you were lost."

"There are acts that can change life forever." Her voice came soft and gentle, like a melody trying to tame the fierce distrust between two strangers. "This was supposed to be your unspoiled retreat."

"I'll survive."

"Where do you live outside of these mountains?"

"In New York. Have you been there?"

"I don't know." She took a moment, as though searching in the depths of her mind.

There was no sense prying into her memories, he thought, because she had none, and if there were some, she was not going to reveal them.

"Well, if you ever think of pizza, or a hot dog, that's the place to eat them. None better."

"You're a food connoisseur," she said with a lopsided smile. "I know about French people; they have a way with food."

He stood by the door, glued to the face that meant to make him laugh. She seemed like the honest, ingenue type. No, he couldn't imagine too much malice behind that face.

"I was born in Vancouver, not in France."

"Why did you leave?" She looked down at the bed sheets. "I'm sorry, I shouldn't ask so many questions."

Without hesitation he went ahead with a response.

"I like the fast pace of life."

"You got it all figured out."

"That sounds about right."

Downstairs, he sat in front of the fireplace watching the dance of the flames upon the logs. Dappled shadows moved against the walls of the den while his heart lit with the dull twisting of a yearning, prompting him to be somebody he wasn't. He was a man who felt nothing, who never got involved because he had learned to disconnect from the rest of his body. But for this night he wished he could surrender the memories that made him.

His mind took him far into the past, to the time when he was six. A night like any other night when his father stumbled over the walls of the trailer, seething, uttering sentences that made no sense but which frightened him into unmovable silence. He hid under the covers, praying he'd be forgotten at the other side of the doorknob.

With the weight of elephants sitting on his chest, fear pressed over him. Marcel's violence was unpredictable. Twenty minutes later, counting with the accuracy of his Big Ben, his mother's footsteps made him feel at ease, knowing she was home from work. Blonde and lanky, eyes steel blue like his own, she moved around the kitchen being easily heard. The walls were paper thin.

His mother liked tea and every night she made a batch before retiring. Innumerable times she told him how the brew of chamomile helped her unwind because as tired as she was, her body lay in bed, staring at the ceiling, unable to find rest.

With eyes wide open, he remained in his room, listening to the tic-tac of the clock, thinking chamomile had to be a magic potion. His father had disturbed his rest, and he knew in the morning he would be exhausted. He imagined a bunch of Indians dancing under the moon, lifting the dry earth every time they stamped their feet, waiving their hands up and down into the dusty air, letting out a rhythmic chant over a large cauldron of chamomile. He wanted to aks his mother for some of her tea tonight, because like her, he couldn't fall asleep and now his bladder was full, as though he really had drunk a tank of it.

On his way to the bathroom he caught sight of his parents from the hallway, through the carelessness of an open door into their bedroom.

The sight of Marcel's pinning his mother against the wall, paralyzed him. Slumped in the ferocity of alcohol, Marcel slid a hand inside the blouse which stuck onto his mother's skin with sweat. Nicotine stained teeth peered through the lustful grin of a monster. He pushed, bit, mauled with impudence everywhere he touched and every once in a while an icy cry of pain from her.

His father slapped his mother's face when she pushed away. Unable to go on and overpowered by his brute strength, she let it happen. On her fours, bent over the bed, with the skirt of her waitress's uniform raised, she let Marcel spread her panties with his fingers — hands like paws — showing the mound of pubic hair between his mother's legs.

Watching from a distance, like a movie on TV, he stares at everything with burning eyes glued to the floor because he couldn't run away. He held his breath hoping to pass out — perhaps the thud of his body as it collapsed could halt the scene — but he was weak, allowing his breath again when suffocation crammed. The taste of salt entered his mouth as silent tears slid over his face. His mother's rape went on. Intimately, he knew he was too small to win if he intervened. He'd tried it before, but it was always worse. Much worse. The pain.

Pants off, his father grabbed a long piece of flesh, tumefied and engorged, and came in from behind with brute aggression, thrusting many times. Unbalanced on his feet, drooling from the mouth, he fell over her. Marcel was motionless over his mother — asleep — not dead.

His mother pushed out from under, sitting on the edge of the bed, adjusting her blouse when her blue eyes caught a glimpse of his small body in the limelight. She had defused the drunken anger with her offering. They both looked at each other, saying nothing while she covered herself faster.

Scared that his mother was mad at him, he waited for a word. His heart ran faster but it had been doing so for the last half hour. She waved him on with a languid arm and he understood she didn't have the strength to get up from where she sat. The kettle blew like the deafening whistle of a train skidding toward them. He ran to turn off the water on the stove.

Moments later in the kitchen, listening to the gurgling inside the pot a warm liquid ran down his legs, making an amber pool at his feet. With a kitchen towel, he squatted over the linoleum to clean up his mess, taken by violent shivers, soaked by the urine on his pajamas.

Images, flashes — his memories of Vancouver.

4

The woman wasn't very talkative. She avoided him much of the week, something amazing considering they were indoors, captives of the weather because it still rained. In what he thought an effort to be unobtrusive, she talked only when addressed in a speech that was soft spoken. The after dinner evening found them clearing the table and doing dishes together. She was wiping the sawbuck table when her eyes found his stare.

"I have my rough spots, so don't take offence if I seem harsh," he mumbled.

"I won't."

"I cherish my private time, but you don't have to walk out of a room because I come in. You're beginning to make me feel as though I had a dreadful disease that should be quarantined."

She laughed at his remark and he fixed into her eyes, with a direct and steady gaze.

"I appreciate everything you've done," she said in a voice that melted him. "I can't take your bed again. I'll be fine down here."

"Are you sure?"

"I'm much better." After a silence, she said, "You saved my life."

"Anyone would have done the same thing."

"It's easier to look away. Knowing that too often heroes lie in graves."

"Behaving any differently would have been murder." His words carried the passionate hold of a feeling. The sadness in her eyes took him by surprise, making him realize how much he wanted to discover this woman on his own.

"Nonetheless, I thank you for being so nice and for being there. Your presence reassures me everything will work out . . . somehow."

"You make me sound like some kind of hero, but I'm just a man made out of the flaws that make so many other men. No, I'm no hero."

"You're too modest."

"Modest?" He laughed out loud. No one had ever called him that.

She moved by the fire, and her face glowed with the light that warmed it.

"You don't have television or radio. Don't you get bored here?"

"I eat when I'm hungry, sleep when tiredness takes over." A white patch of skin over the left wrist marked the absence of his watch. "I don't need time, either. My cellular is the only touch with an outside world. I guess my mountain is my refuge of peace."

Walking toward the wall unit, he browsed through a stack of records. Minutes later an alto saxophone filled the room with the melody of a jazzy tune.

"I can offer you my music."

"The past seems to have a place in your present. Not too many people have a record player," she said.

"I have old favorites, sort of like a treat when I'm here."

"Then you agree that it's a shame to throw away the past."

Saying that, she closed her eyes while the song played. For him it was irrelevant as only the future could modify his life and yes, he liked some old songs, but that was about it. When she looked at him again, he was still watching her from a distance.

"There's a lot of sadness hidden in your music, Claude."

"Perhaps. Sometimes I like to surrender my moods into the songs."

"Are you an artist? I saw an easel and canvases piled up against the walls upstairs." She took a hand and pushed her hair behind an ear. "I couldn't help looking through them. You haven't finished them, but they're quite good."

"It's an amateur effort. No, I'm not an artist, but you are certainly an inquisitive woman."

"They show talent."

"I disagree," he said very matter-of-fact. "I always wanted to paint, but somehow that feeling was cast aside in the complexity of my life. The inspiration fails me and they are half way done. I couldn't make a living from my paintings, no."

"That's your first mistake, you should paint oblivious to its financial merit."

"That's all great and well, but I have to eat, pay for the roof over my head, that sort of thing."

"Expression in the form of art can be a great cathartic. You should pursue it, at least in your spare time."

"I'm an art collector," he said. "I can afford to buy what I like."

"*Creating* can hold a different pleasure than buying."

Her dark eyes burned into his soul. She was clever.

"To create, one must have a special sensitivity. I've hired models. Even in the surrounding of this countryside, I can't finish what I start," he said, looking down.

"You're too pragmatic to dwell in an impulse."

"My world is a mathematical expression of life, and to paint, one must be abstract."

For an intense moment he admired the charm with which she had discovered him. She was better than any shrink he ever paid. Painting was his unfulfilled passion because he was caught in an every day world, full of practicality.

"There's talent in your hands."

"Sure," he said.

"You haven't found the right inspiration."

"It's too late for me."

"Is it? Sometimes to succeed you must be one with your theme. Your eyes must capture the essence of what you feel, not of what you *see*."

Her words were intuitive, but he was consumed with technology. His goals filled him with solitude, which like a demon devoured all his sensitivity. But standing in front of her, he wanted to forget. He wanted to tease himself with everything about this woman, because he enjoyed her beauty, the profoundness in her thoughts, the wit and careful direction in the lead of her analysis of a man she did not know.

The opposite sex always attracted him, but he wasn't a womanizer. Beautiful women had found his fancy, but none enough to marry, and too many of them sought out his wealth. Love as a sincere sentiment was lost, just like his ability to paint, because genuine feelings were near impossible.

Desire.

Never love.

A distraction from work, but never leaving a mark.

His assets in the range of fifty billion dollars was in itself an irresistible allure. Women noticed him, but in the last few years, it was hard to believe in the sincerity of emotions underneath this polished exterior. In the presence of a gorgeous woman who had no idea of who he was, he treasured the thought, knowing her conquest could be a most delectable challenge because pleasure derived from a woman had become a superficial pursuit.

Unlike the others, he found her poised in her sexuality, so much that he was overcome with the urge to explore deeper into the primal sensation growing inside. This was as close as he could get to a spiritual self. With this woman he was tempted to be the dealer of a deck, but he wasn't sure at all if he had the right to touch the vulnerable void inside her mind.

When she moved to the couch, he seized the opportunity to throw logs into the fireplace. As he opened the screen to stir around the ashes, he was careful not to dirty the floor, and when he turned to look at her, she was looking at him.

"You're an attractive man," she said, reading through his thoughts. "There's no reason why a woman couldn't want you for yourself, but you know that, right? Maybe one of them might even fall in love with you."

Her forwardness took him off guard, catapulting his stomach into major leaps. He was surprised that she could be so blunt. Was she coming onto him, or was she being polite?

"It would be interesting to discover who you are," he said, " . . . a woman with no past to write about, intriguing, even romantic at that. Would I be pretentious wanting to fill some of those pages?" He leaned against the log-and-mortar that made the walls of his cabin. "Why are you here?"

"Why?" She looked at the fire and then back at him.

"Yes. There's something about you, something so unusual that I can't figure it out."

"It could be that I'm here because you helped me, or perhaps . . . to help us both."

The girl smiled as though she kept a secret and he was the fool, not figuring it out.

"You think I need help?"

He was sure there was something overlooked in the content of her statement, because obviously he was fine.

"It's not easy to look upon oneself," she said. "We learn by the reactions of others toward us. It could be that our meeting will have a positive outcome, no matter who you are."

He liked her game.

"And who do you think I am?"

"I'm not sure. I hardly know you — " she said.

They were alone, and the music played soft and sensuous. She was arousing every fiber of his manhood. The drizzle outside added to the mood of comfort within the space of his cabin. Although she should look devastated by the incertitude of her life, she was composed. She didn't look ill anymore, and he was getting drunk with the *pique* behind her gorgeous eyes.

He frowned because his keen sense advised him she was an uncommon woman. Everything about her pulled him to come close, and for some unknown reason he liked her. For a moment he wished that she could stay forever, but even a few days was a welcomed interruption. He was spellbound by the temptation of her unknown past or maybe by the inner strength gushing out of her as she walked toward an unpredictable future. Regardless of what it was, she challenged his existence like no other woman had.

5

Monday afternoon marked the beginning of their second week together. Claude leaned against the railing of the open hallway, closing the buttons on his shirt. His hair was wet and combed to the side after his exercise routine and a shower. She had browsed through his books, and a pile of them lay on the floor, books on art, sculpture, painting, and its technique. Now she read a volume of Tolstoy's *Anna Kareryna* and had been doing so for a while. Literature was there for his leisure — nothing on computers or the technology which involved him.

She was light on her feet, invisible at times, and he remembered her promise to stay out of his way. But she was there, and some time during that day — without his knowledge — she had made his bed and picked up around the house. He was going to tell her straight that he didn't need her gratitude nor her services in exchange of hospitality.

"You like to read?" He stood before her, now downstairs.

"I do. I'm glad you have these books." She returned a smile.

"Listen, I told you I don't want you doing any more than I do around here. Don't think you have to pay me back with your labor."

"I mean to help."

"I'll pick up after myself."

"Then I will do the same that you have done for me."

He thought her tone of voice was too enthusiastic.

"What can you do for me?"

"*Save your life,*" she said

Composing the features of her face into a sublime expression she made him believe in her power over fate. A moment later she teased with her giggle, releasing him from the seriousness that took over.

"I don't plan on having an accident."

"Most people don't."

"Okay, okay, if you want, you can save me, but don't become my maid. Got it?"

She smiled, so big that he could see the row of upper teeth inside her mouth. White, pearly, each one next to the other, aligned without spaces, an expression that seemed to come from heaven. He thought she was pleased with his bewilderment. Everything about her served the purpose of drawing him closer, compelling him to know more about a woman without memories. He thought she had become a peculiar dilemma, and he was fascinated by her gentle eyes, and a careful smile.

"You must be bored to death cooked up in here with me. I'm not good at small talk." He noted with sincerity. "I wish you could remember something about yourself, so I could learn something about you."

"But we can talk about you, since I can't tell you very much about myself."

"I'll fill your ears."

"So far you haven't. As a matter of fact you spend a lot of time in your room."

"I'm supposed to be relaxing, but in truth I'm always working. This is as close as I get to vacation. There's a suitcase ful of paper work in my room. "

"You're a workaholic," she cut him off. "A perfectionist?"

"Yes, I guess you could say that." He smiled. She had caught on fast although these character traits were less than desirable by the condescending tone in her voice.

"I've been thinking a lot about what's happened. There must be a reason why I came across your way."

"Coincidence — "

"No, I don't believe in chance."

"You don't?"

"Every action brings forth reaction," she said, oddly profound. "Nothing is coincidence, as people choose to explain what seems unsynchronized. People call it chance when their senses can't explain a circumstance."

She propped her posture in the couch, leaving the book on the side.

"Interesting philosophy."

"Often our intellect can't rationalize an outcome so we call it an inexplicable coincidence. Everything around us triggers some kind of reaction, as simple, or as complicated as we allow it to go." Her voice was steady. "Chance is too abstract to be real."

"So, I ran into you for a specific purpose? Would you mind telling me what it was or do I have to guess?" he said, smiling more deeply.

"I have no idea why it happened. I'm a player just like you, but we have been touched by each other."

"Ah, destiny — it brought us together. You really believe there's a definite purpose in all of this?"

She didn't answer, holding up to his scrutiny without a blink.

"I wish I could share my recollections the same way I offer you my thoughts."

"But obviously you can't."

"How old do you think I am?"

"You must be much younger than I, venturing to say early twenties?" He couldn't help speculating if she had a boyfriend, or maybe a husband. Somehow, she didn't look too motherly.

"How old are you?"

"Hmm, thirty-five going on much more," his voice trailed. "Sometimes I feel like I've seen it all, like I've lived too much."

He ventured out on the front porch leaving her behind. His lungs filled with the sogginess that clung in the air.

"Does it ever stop raining?" she asked. She was standing behind him.

"I like the rain."

"Don't you ponder about the consequence of living, Claude? About death and what happens afterward?"

The wind brushed the trees back and forth. He gazed into the forest and the soggy grass in front of his home.

"You should know that I don't dwell on death or the afterlife."

"Most people have thought about what happens afterward."

"Why bother with fantasy?"

"We finish where we start," she said. "Living is all about love and loss."

There was a warning or perhaps a promise but whatever it was, her thoughts provoked a sultry undertone which left him wanting more.

He took her by the arm and brought her inside with him.

"I'd rather love."

"You're making fun of me but . . . every person experiences both," she whispered, too serious to tangent off. "Sometimes, even a child must suffer in order to discover the meaning of life."

"A child?" *What do you know about me?* He fixed his eyes on her.

"The rape of innocence is the cruelest trespass. Pain is a memory that lingers even beyond life, but it's all chosen by the spirit as a means to learn. Our spirit knows the journey's end before it starts. The chosen lifetime *is* for a particular experience."

Claude held his breath baffled by the riddle in the content of her mind. He leaned against the wooded beam supporting the upstairs. She had evoked visions of his childhood, a brutal reality where he forged a way of living. Sentimentality was an obstacle, he knew about people, and he didn't like them much. It was difficult to imagine tragedy and evil having a greater purpose, such that she spoke about.

She sat again, oblivious to the repercussion of her words, and he sat across from her on the sofa.

"A woman leaves her lover and many years later they meet again," she said. "What does it mean? Is it coincidence without a purpose?"

For a moment he held his breath, trying to remember something forgotten, a face, another place, but he realized they had just met. Again the feeling that he knew her came from nowhere, but it was impossible; she didn't remind him of anyone else, and his memory was excellent. And then he noticed: hidden under her hair when she turned her head to look at the fire. He discovered the brown mole on the right side of her neck and he realized he must have noticed it before because he knew it was there.

"Come on, what do you know about me?" He shook his head, full of suspicion in the undertone of the mood she had produced.

"Nothing, I've told you I don't remember anything about the past."

But then why did he feel as though she knew more than she let on, that she knew about him and people in his past?

"Two lovers," she said. "They run into each other after a long time."

"It's not coincidence if she meant to run into him on purpose," he went on to say.

"Aha, you're skepticism."

"Your concepts are interesting but I don't believe in very much."

"How can you hope to explain all the secrets of the universe? We are owners of free will and sometimes, our free will fills an unexpected script into the karma of our lives. Free will is the small curve ball in God's plans. I certainly wonder about a purpose, about the fate that brought me here."

Claude inched forward toward the girl who sat legs crossed. For a moment the arm chair seemed like a throne for the high priestess of a remote civilization. Her talk was strange, and he sensed her urgency to enlighten him.

Why does it seem important considering it's nonsense talk? Is she a messenger allowed in the deliverance of my soul? As human as she was, her presence seemed fantastic. The certainty of her words allowed no doubts in her conclusions. Inexplicably, he found himself more and more charmed by the voice casting a mesmerizing incantation, and although amused, he could not ignore the passion that lit her eyes.

"You promise to be a most interesting woman. I guess, as you said, you're touching my life and hence forth, coincidence is bringing forth reactions."

"These are my thoughts, nothing more."

"Controversial at that. Who taught you these things?"

"I told you these are ideas inside my head, feelings that charge my mind and they come as fear comes or hunger crawls, only . . . convictions go deeper than sensations."

She sighed, closing her eyes.

"What else do you know?" He wanted more. The serenity of her dissertation made him feel ashamed to take her so lightly.

"Do I bore you?"

"You do anything but that."

It was unusual that a woman without memory could retain these thoughts. He wasn't one to '*believe*' but he had to accommodate because the fervor of her expose was irresistible.

"During the evolution of our souls memories imprint within us." Her voice was a murmur, drawing closer, forcing him to tune in on the pitch of her words. "Pain, anguish, interpersonal relations, they all help the growth of our spirit in a process of learning. We come back through many lives, many times — until we have achieved close to perfection."

"So then I'm here to learn. I'm the reincarnation of a spirit, absorbing knowledge from the people I meet. Are you supposed to be my teacher?" He rumbled with laughter.

The room turned airless and he sensed she had been hurt by his mocking.

"Please understand me," he said. "You believe in the immortality of the soul. I don't. Death is the end to all I know. I live the way I choose for my own sake, not for any plot of enlightenment."

"I don't mean to make you feel uncomfortable.".

Brought into an unusual plateau, a world where old souls meet over and over again, a new feeling urged inside him. Like branches of one trunk, he felt linked to her destiny. Perhaps this was his deja-vu sensation. Could the past reside somewhere other than the mind? A past not born from the experiences of childhood, nor the genes that are inherited, but instead from previous ventures of the soul? According to this woman, past lives were a dynamic force.

"I believe in love at first sight and the instant affinity for someone that I've never met." She smiled at him, reaching inward.

"Love at first sight is just lust."

"Are you so sure?"

"You're a silly girl," he tittered. "Obviously, you don't know much about life and men if you think so naively."

"You've never felt the inexplicable chemistry, compelling closeness?"

"No, I can't say that I have." He lied, because from the moment he met her, he was never the same. An invisible energy kept him alert to her presence as it drew him closer than ever.

"Then I'm sorry."

"And have you? Fallen in love head over heels?"

"I would hope that I have."

"Well, if you did, then I'm sure you discovered the pain of love."

He imagined her in his arms, stretched out over his bed, forged with intense want. Swallowing, he controlled the sweet dizziness that invaded.

"I'm luckier than you," she said.

"Than I?"He had money, a future and all of his memory. Pleasure came easily, and he could own anything or anyone. How could she presume to feel sorry for him?

"Because I believe."

"Believe?"

"That love survives death, that death is not an end, but merely a phase in the process of *living.*"

"Like a door — " he said.

"Yes, a door to go through, from one state to another." Speaking almost inaudibly, she commanded his attention. "The body is a vehicle, a tool, like a car that wears out. People get another car because they need to travel. In a more sophisticated fashion, our souls must continue their journey. We are reborn into many new lives."

"You want me to believe I might have known you in some other life of mine?" He drew a breath, and each one measured the other. It was hard enough remembering some of his lovers, and she expected him to remember other lives.

She drew a smile, enticing him to taste from the soul of which she spoke.

"The senses can distort reality," she said. "Our body is the imperfect tool accepting the stimuli of out surroundings, and the mind must protect us from the things that are too difficult to assimilate. Our mind is underutilized."

"Hmm, like seeing what we want to see."

"Like disregarding what is right in front of us to avoid madness."

"You're in front of me," he smiled.

"You want to see me."

"No, I see you because you're in front of me."

"It could be that you have found me through a pathway awakened in your brain, allowing you to see me."

"Too sci-fi for me."

"It would be foolish for mankind to limit the size of the universe only to what we can see, hear or touch." She stood up, coming by his side. "You wonder about me, but who are you, Claude? Your universe is too predictable, too safe and convenient."

"I'm a man who finds fiction entertaining but far from reality." Wishing he could believe, the only god he knew was his intellect. "Heaven or hell are what we make of life, and God is simply a lot of good will."

"What could make you believe there's more to life than the obvious?"

"You would have to cross through death, returning with the proof."

He smiled, pleased with the impossibility of his challenge. Despite their philosophical differences — she was a sublime woman, with intelligent arguments and a quality that made her sound so sensible, so in tune with what she had to say. It was as though great secrets were revealed to her in exchange of memories about her life. The mystery surrounding her had become even more engrossing. *Are you a witch or just bewitching?*

Her smile was an invitation to explore the alchemy of her universe. They played with words, and he was glad to come upon her, and the opportunity to deepen more. Despite the dreary weather outside, the days were passing full of the excitement discovering a woman without parallel. The night cast them into a tranquil rest, or so Claude wanted to believe.

6

This was another time, a place different from anything in Claude's reality. Sand mountains rose in the distance, the land of pyramids and pharaohs, remote from any place he'd ever been. From afar, the sound of the river reached, wide and long. The Nile was the river of life. Irrigation came from its flow, through the channels dug by his workers, and standing by the terrace of his home, he watched the vast open field, green with exuberance. In this dream he was a landlord, a warrior who had conquered, and all this was part of his bounty.

A healed scar on the left side of his chest served as a reminder of a battle fought long before to preserve their way of life. His jet black hair brushed over his shoulders, his skin bronzed to a deep tan by the ardent sun over the Egyptian countryside. He knew his eyes were darker and more oval. This was not the body he knew.

And then he saw her too, Tizara, the love of his life, untouched by any other man but him. This was his wife. Her skin soft and warm, lips the perfect tracing of pleasure, turquoise beads draping over her hair flirting with his fancy, and now his body filled with desire just by watching her walk out of their house. The children near her belonged to him, a boy and a girl. Happiness clung to this life because he had found his soul mate and identified her as part of his karma.

Contentment came believing in the afterlife, knowing that they would remain together, beyond death. Anubis — the God with the head of a jackal — would guide their journey through the underworld, reuniting them for all eternity.

When he awoke to silence, he looked at the walls of his room, at the pale blue bed sheets over him. His heart and mind filled with the feeling that touched him in a dream, so strange because it was so vivid, but unlike the other times, the sense of loss was gone. He felt her inside of him, in the place where life is summoned.

Egypt, the Nile River. He had traveled to the memory of a past encounter, but he had never been to the Middle East. The interplay within his mind impressed him for the details, for the taste of reality which lingered afterward. He figured it had been all the talk from the day before, because the dialogue between the girl and him had taken a strange twist. The conversations, all so staggering, impressed his subconscious into the keen experience of a fantastic place, and at that moment he realized that he had no name for his new friend.

Claude went to look through the window. The ocean was visible from the second story of the cabin. The skies remained gray but without the threat of rain because the clouds had lifted and the storm moved away. He stretched his arms in the air and let out a lazy groan from the bottom of his throat. Papers in a briefcase reminded him of the work that was pending.

He walked around the room looking for the leather case with his reading glasses, and after he found them, he took out the documents from a leather portfolio and sank into a cushioned armchair to read, reviewing contracts and technical details about the software of his industry.

Four hours passed yielding to concentration. He remembered breakfast and that she had called him a workaholic. His cellular phone was at hand's reach recharging in its holster, but on at all times, in case one of his associates had to reach him, but they were warned: it better be emergent. There were times when he left before an anticipated date, but he hoped it wouldn't happen this time.

He stopped working. Between his fingers swung his reading glasses as he pondered with the thought of calling the police station. This was the devil inside him urging him to move forward. Unlike his normal state of resolution he had been passive, unearthing the girl's identity. Now his fingers moved over the keys, cursed by his practicality.

"Police department," said a man's voice at the other end.

"I would like to know if anyone has reported a missing woman from these parts."

"Is there a problem, sir?"

Claude heard telephones ringing at the other end.

"No, I mean, I ran into a woman who needed help. I'm afraid I don't know her name."

"Are you reporting an assault or an accident?"

"No, I don't want to make a report. I just want to know if anyone is looking for a young woman, brunette, long hair, about five-five."

"Hold on," said the voice and then he heard silence at the other end.

The noise of the telephones told him he was no longer on hold.

"Your description is generic, but we're not a large city where people can disappear and go unnoticed. Nobody's missing in Everett, but we have a list of folks from Seattle and other parts of the state if you want to come in and look at pictures." There was a silence at the other end. "The best thing is to come here and look at the photos in our data base."

"Very well, I'll think about it."

He wasn't interested in looking through hundreds of pictures, let alone getting more involved than he had. Close to noon he tired of his paperwork and looking out the window once again, he noticed her, sitting in the Adirondack chairs, taking in what little sun there was.

Her eyes were closed as though she slept, looking more voluptuous, as her figure came through, dressed in her own garments, not his oversized clothing. His heart leaped, his blood filled with her the want of her. He remembered the fantasy his mind created during the resting hours of that early dawn.

However, different from a dream, she was there, real and not inspired by his imagination, with her beauty staggering with all its might. He acknowledged the definition of coincidence as she had explained the day before. A smile drew over his face. For a man who was not susceptible to outside influences, he'd managed to be touched by her. Briefly he was downstairs, finding it impossible to stay away.

Interrupting her peaceful rest, he greeted her in a friendly voice. Her eyes opened reciprocating his welcome. Down the cleavage of her blouse, he noticed the freckles that were floating like cinnamon over a milky surface.

"You slept the morning," she said.

"Not at all. I was working."

"Wouldn't it be nice if someone else could take care of those details for you? Doesn't seem like you get a chance to relax, even though you're here for that purpose."

"There is nothing more important than my business."

The garden was blooming with peach and yellow daffodils and dozens of red tulips that grew in clumps through the beds that were manicured with a careful hand. An allée of white pines and pink dogwoods formed the edge of an opening leading to the woods, while against the house viburnums crowned with clumps of white flowers like giant powder puffs. The bushes in the borders had been trimmed, and river stones were used to contain the outline of the garden. The patio furniture was surrounded by an iron pergola crowned by a ceiling of white wisteria. The grass in the backyard was a deep green surrounding gravel paths, reminiscent of a French countryside.

"Did you do the landscaping yourself?"

"No, but I supervised most of the initial work," he said. "When I step out here, I want to get drunk with the scent of jasmine and the color floating into my eyes throughout the season. I have people from town who come every so often to renew the planting."

"Your yard is an emotional sanctuary," she said, "yet you want to show me the austere side of you."

She had sneaked up on him again, disarming the cynic and he liked the way she came upon him.

"You're going to be reading Tolstoy for a while." The book was lying over her legs. "It's a long story."

"Interesting you should own a book like *Anna Kareryna*."

"Why is it remarkable?"

"Seems out of place with your art books. You're not the sort of person I expect to dwell on the story of a woman who renounces everything for the love of a man."

He looked somewhere over her shoulders. "The book belonged to my mother. When she died, I kept it."

Her eyes focused into his, and for an unexplainable reason he found them full of understanding. When her eyelids dropped, they turned into the languid sweep of a willow forced to bow by the weight of an ache, and he understood that she meant to escape the same feeling that had trapped him into the memory of his mother.

"The sun is shining." She got up, leaving the book over the lacquered chair. "Would you like to take a walk in the woods?"

The temperature was cool and the ground was damp but that would not stop them. They walked toward the white pines and into a narrow trail that led away.

"You left me thinking about you."

"I like that." She smiled and waited for more.

"I even had a dream about you."

"Hmm, you dreamed about me?"

Their pace was slow, walking side by side. He couldn't imagine her without romantic ties.

"You're an intriguing woman, and we've met under unusual circumstances, don't you think?"

She kicked a pebble with her boot, and the noise of the rock bouncing off over the ground scattered his thoughts. She slowed down, looking to kick it again, like a child lost in a game but unable to further her intent because it disappeared off the trail, lost in the vegetation at the sides of the path.

"Peculiar," he said, trying to corner her attention. "We were in another time, a place very far away. You and I looked different from what we do, but I knew we were these people. The dream was like a window to look at the past, our lives together and you were . . . my wife. We had two young children. Can you imagine that?"

"I believe in dreams." She raised an eyebrow, turning to look at him. "They are a way to learn. Like this particular dream of yours, they can be something easy to decipher or they can haunt with their symbolic message."

"Dreams are part of the sleep cycle and nothing more."

"And yet they puzzle you."

"You're an exquisite dilemma so I dreamed about you. I have always enjoyed decoding computer programs."

"But I'm not a computer."

He regretted his unpoetic words.

Yearlings sprouted from the ground. Moss covered the north side of most trees, and the sky was partly covered by the foliage of the evergreens which formed a roof over their heads. The timid sunlight filtered down over some spots as he heard his boots crushing through the bark of fallen twigs. Larger pieces of wood had to be skipped, but he was finding it hard to take his eyes away from her. He noticed that his heart was racing with the need to tell her about himself, but this feeling was absurd.

"It's peaceful," she said."I can see why you come here."

She swished her hair back and it filled him with her beauty. He thought her personality was like these mountains, majestic and full of natural wisdom.

"I realized this morning that I don't know what to call you," he simpered. "I thought Natalie would be appropriate. It comes from the Latin root to be born and you are seemingly just born, having no memory of the past, just the future you choose to follow."

"I like that name." She turned toward him, breathing out a smile.

He saw her focus back on the trail ahead.

"I envy people like you who see further than their eyes can seize."

"I must seem strange, though." She looked away. "Not knowing anything about myself and coming on with such talk. Forgive me."

"You give me nothing to forgive."

The sounds of the wooded acreage came, forewarning that the forest was alive despite its deceptive calm. Natalie was there, conjured from the same substance as his life source, like the woman in his Egyptian dream, filling him with the same tumultuous feeling to posses her.

"I wish I could reciprocate your kindness," she whispered, searching for his eyes, "but I doubt you'll ever be as lost as I am."

If only she knew that sometimes, he too felt misplaced in the space he occupied. He learned to live without family, apart from the warmth of a true friend, being so because he himself chose to live in the web of life he had created. But grabbing on to his thoughts, these were debilities he was not about to divulge.

"What do you see when you look at the world around you, at me?" His voice was a raspy return.

"You're a man, wrapped up in a microcosm, who perhaps forgot to live beyond the grasp of the physical. If you're able to discover the intangibles of life it's a fascinating talent, but I think you must be brave to unearth the world of feelings."

"Emotions are erratic."

"But they intensify the experience of living."

Natalie slowed down the pace, looking over the forest floor, searching in the foliage until she saw the hairy worm inching its way up a birch tree.

"Look, nature gives us the caterpillar to understand the concept of metamorphosis, a modification of death." She allowed the hairy creature to crawl on to her finger. "The caterpillar doesn't die in the cocoon, she emerges more graceful. The clumsiness of the caterpillar is purposeful as well as the agility of the flying insect."

"Then you must be the graceful butterfly," he said.

"I'm more like the clumsy caterpillar, saying some of the things I do."

"If I were any different, I would accept your concept of life after death."

"Believing is advancement for the soul." Natalie left the caterpillar back where it was. "It's sad when one two soul mates fails to recognize the other for whatever reason and the opportunity to converge gets lost for a lifetime. Their own life force will bring them very close, but they must connect, and if they don't, neither one will be happy because they fail to meet destiny together."

"That was free will leading two lovers into the wrong choice,"

Silence came and then he thought he heard someone, a voice coming from the forest, a message reaching from nowhere: *She has loved you from the beginning of time and she is bound to you, but you too are linked to her. She's here for you.* He turned around, but no one came in sight. These thoughts were inside his head, they had to be, but for a few minutes he felt surrounded by the dance of invisible beings, like butterflies in flight — aerial.

"There's a parallel world which surrounds us," said Natalie. Stretching her arms to touch someone, as though she had tuned to the message of the breeze which blew past him, and as she spoke, he was convinced that somehow she had read his mind again. "There are life forms all around us, but they move much faster. We can't see them like we can't see the animals in this forest, camouflaged by their colors. We think of them as the dead, but they are alive. Death is just a gate by which to travel, by which to evolve like the caterpillar."

"I can only believe in what my senses show me."

"It's pure physics," she dared with her voice. "Matter moves at different speed depending on its state, solids of course the slowest. The essence of a spirit is the lightest. Our senses are ill equipped to detect their dispersed atoms. Like some gases, this fourth state can be invisible, but it occupies space. We can't touch it but we can feel it like we feel a breeze. Environmental factors change matter, like water to solid, liquid or gas. The power of natural phenomena like heat, cold, or the electrical charges in thunder control the gate dictating forms, therefore, the possibilities within a storm."

"You're a beautiful scientist, but I don't believe in ghosts."

"One day you might. Energy can neither be created nor destroyed. The energy inside us can not end — this is our soul, a fourth state of matter."

He blinked twice when his vision grew hazy, her figure blurry and he rubbed his eyes, thinking it was a trick from the light trickling through the branches fading away the contour of her body. Could she be the product of his tired mind, breaking down from fatigue and overwork? Every time he retreated to his mountain it was at the brink of physical collapse. This time was no exception. Their situation was peculiar. His dreams were even more fantastic. But if Natalie was a figment of his imagination, she seemed awfully real.

"It would be nice if death was not the end."

"I assure you it is not."

"Buddhism, Moslem, Hindu, where did you learn this?" he challenged.

"You missed Christianity, Judaism." She looked at him. "They all believe in life after death. Why can't you?"

"It's the wish of men to live beyond the span of their bodies. I believe in myself, in the here and now."

"You have eyes, but you can't see. Faith gives you sight: love gives you the fortitude to search and find." Her words were low and intimate. "The subject is in front of you, but you're blind."

"I can see you, can't I?" he charged.

"You're missing the point," she said with a broad smile, wiser than he expected. "Are you so sure I'm here, walking, talking to you? You're the only one that's seen me."

For a moment her words cornered him. Of course she was real, even if no one else had witnessed her. Closer to the end of the trail the land dropped onto the coast, revealing an open mouth of blue. Seagulls flew above them, raking the sky with their wings.

"Sensations are the tools of an artist," she went on in the mid of his silence. "You can't paint because you haven't learned to see. To paint you must be guided by your soul and not your mind. It's the feeling that comes inside, filling with itself day and night. The only way to rid from its maddening effect is to express it."

"You tempt my existence, but I'm a lost cause."

"I disagree."

"I'm not an impulsive sort of guy." Claude embraced her with a look. Having fulfilled all of his material needs, he was unable to find the human touch to satisfy the loneliness within. "The passion of your words is more than I could ever entertain."

"Find the key to unlock the feelings trapped inside you."

Claude stopped her, grabbing her by an arm.

"Let me help you with the medical expense of having your amnesia checked out by a doctor."

"I couldn't take your money. You have extended your hospitality already."

"But I want to," he insisted. "Leaving you at the mercy of a street corner is not exactly the right thing to do. I could drop you off at police station, but what's going to happen? No, I don't want to do it that way. I hope to know you one day with the awareness of what you left behind." Claude lowered his eyes. "I won't take advantage of you in exchange of anything I've offered. My hospitality and my friendship have no secondary intent . . . other than perhaps your company."

"I'll think about it."

"You're a superb person, and if fate brought you to me, it must have been important."

"I'll remember one of these days."

"I'm sure you will, but in the mean time — " Saying that, Claude realized he was reaching out, getting involved more than he ever did. He took a deep breath and the smell of the ocean filled his lungs.

"Claude?" As though she had been thinking about the appropriateness of her question, she asked. "Are you married?"

"My family consists of an uncle to whom I haven't spoken in ages." His voice held a glimmer of tedium. "He lived with my mother and I while I was growing up. My mother is dead, my father for all I know is alive, but I don't know where he lives. He left us when I was very young."

"You have scars, but it's much easier for those who meet you to skim over the surface. People prefer to look from afar, over the table rather than under it."

"You're not like those people, are you?"

"Sounds like you bartered feelings for survival."

"I did okay."

"Did you really survive?"

"I've done fine," he said, cutting her off. She had touched a nerve.

"Will you tell me about your mother? All I know is that she read Tolstoy."

Claude took a few steps forward, reaching the edge of the land. His eyes dropped to the precipice below, and his jaw tightened. Crests of white foam exploded against the wall of rocks with violent anger.

"An angel living in this rotten world." The grinding of his teeth made a noise. "She was a high school dropout married to an alcoholic with enough common sense to survive for the two of us. She said books could teach me everything, and she was right."

"That's a wise thing to tell her kid." Natalie's voice sounded neutral in her observation.

"She dropped out of school, not life."

"I didn't mean to put her down."

"Nobody gave her credit." Neither of them said a word and then his voice came out in a deep retort. "She put me through school on her own, waiting on tables but never re-marrying because no man was good enough to be my father. One day, in the precocious intuition of a boy, I asked her if she ever felt as though she needed more than we had. She smiled at me, caressed my face and told me I was all she ever wanted out of life."

"She must have loved you very much," said Natalie.

"Amnesia can be kind." Claude turned to look at the woman who was sharing with him the intensity of a memory.

"I don't think you should ever forget." Natalie came by his side, putting her arm around his. Her touch entered into his body and by the way he felt, he thought she had always been there.

"Don't worry. I was an accident for a lot of people, and it's unlikely that I will forget any of it," he said in a hush. "My father drank to forget, forget about the responsibility of life and his family."

"Your mother is a limb from your trunk; you and she have journeyed through the ages," she said, touching with her voice. "When you smile because she enters your thoughts — in a moment out of nowhere — it's because her spirit has traveled close to where you are. Souls come and go, just like people do because love keeps them bound to their earthly relations. One day you will meet again. Be certain that death is not the end."

The wind was messing up his hair. Her body touched his and the promise of her world felt as powerful as life itself. She took his hand and he let her lead the way back.

A wish awakened. If only her reality were true.

7

Colossal granite boulders covered the waterfront with salmon hues splattered of black. Yards away the Pacific pounded against a cliff lined coast, but here at the beach the incessant punishment was overcome by calm. Claude sat on the shore, a few feet away from Natalie, breathing the salt air from the ocean. He watched Natalie explore between giant medallions of rock, in the reefs exposed by low tides at this time of day. They were dangerous spikes out of the ocean floor, because the algae growing on them made them slippery and the sharp jagged edges were sharper than a knife over raw meat.

"You're going to get hurt," he yelled from the shore.

He saw her smile, like a child without regard to danger.

"Come over here," she said. "This is great!"

The rubber soles of his sneakers slipped over the uneven formation, throwing his body off balance when he avoided a nest of sea urchins.

"I'm the one whose going to break his head," he grumbled between teeth.

"Don't worry, there's iodine and bandages at the cabin. I'll fix you up."

"Looking into these tanks of water bores me."

"There's a neon-blue fish over there." She pointed to his left. "I've never seen anything so beautiful. Come, let me show you."

For a moment he envied the sunlight that touched her smile as she walked toward him. By his side, she made him take her hand and follow to the puddle on the rock. Indeed, the graceful sea creature went back and forth in the water, majestic with the splendor of its color. Natalie looked into his eyes, but she went past them, deeper than anyone had looked.

"I'm not in the mood to limp back, that's all."

She took a step ahead of him and then led the way toward the sand.

Once there she stopped by his side.

"Love, friends — the artist who's a dreamer — you displace them without much thought. You shy away, thinking it's the only way to survive."

He moved next to her, and their faces came so close that her breath was almost his, and he realized it was impossible to hide from her. He could have taken her lips right there, he could have breached a longing at the bottom of his heart compelling him to take her in his arms, to surround her with his own embrace, but he realized her undisclosed past made her untouchable.

"How can you know so much about me?" His voice faded and a clumsy silence followed.

"I"m a careful observer."

With a small gesture she waved him on, back toward the house. The temperature had warmed up as the days were promising to get better. Natalie was wearing his vest over her clothing and it made him content to know it gave her comfort.

"You're very different — "

"I have two eyes, two ears — not so different." She laughed with an intimate tone as they walked together.

"Your mind is different." Claude cleared his throat. "I want to listen to you, to share my day, to find out everything about the woman you are."

More than half a day was spent and it had gone too fast.

"Your uncle — " she jumped in to say, as though she had forgotten to inquire days ago. "Why didn't you go back?"

"I said it before, you're a curious woman and I don't know if that's good or bad."

"The consequences will find me, won't they?"

"Too much pain in my memories, so I dismiss them when they are too complicated. Makes life simple."

"I don't think your life is as simple as you want me to believe. Love brings pain too often, but without it, we'd miss the most intense part of our lives. You never went back, did you?"

"After Mom's death I had no reason to stay in Vancouver."

"Your uncle is a relative."

"I hate everything about the life from which I came. When my father abandoned us, we moved into the apartment upstairs from the restaurant my uncle owned. Mom worked there, and I did too, with little time for anything but work. The only goodness in my childhood is her memory. Once she was gone, there was no reason to stay or — "

"Or to go back," she finished his sentence.

"You got that right."

"Maybe things changed."

"I told you, I dismiss unpleasantries," he said plagued by his thoughts. "Why should I give anyone a second chance? I never got any. The rotted core of an apple gets more rotten with time, and I'm sure he's a bitter old man."

"It sounds too easy."

"It is."

"Then I'm sorry."

"No need to be sorry about something which is alien to you for the sake of being polite," he noted curtly. "I hate the formality of pretense."

"Claude, I care . . . about you. Nothing I say is pretense."

They didn't talk anymore, and almost by the house, he remembered food. The hike made his stomach grumble. When he went into the cabin, he grabbed an apple without thought and his jaws crushed the succulent fruit. She stayed behind in the garden. From the kitchen he saw her come in with a handful of tulips. While he made sandwiches, she found a vase for flowers and afterwards, she came to help with the meal. When her hand touched his, grabbing for the jar of mayonnaise, she looked at him and he realized Natalie was tempting like forbidden fruit. Forbidden because he didn't know if she was married, nor her commitments to the past.

"Aren't you hungry? I hope you are because I'm starved."

"Maybe not as much as you," she laughed.

They ate in the den instead of the kitchen, and he watched as she kept her eyes on him. The scent of the fresh cut flowers found him.

"Go ahead, ask me."

"Ask you?"

"Yes, whatever you want." He smiled because he was figuring her out too. "Your eyes are asking what your lips are too shy to utter."

"As a woman, it's not good to be so transparent."

"But you are, and I like that. Most of the women I know are professionals at hiding behind a look but that's not you at all, is it?"

Her eyes had a zeal of their own; her silence, the thunder of a storm.

"Why do you live so alone, Claude?"

"People are a handicap. No commitments equals no disappointments."

"Don't say that."

"Why not? This mountain is my deserted island, away from those who want something all the time."

"I'm an intruder in your mountain."

"You should be, but you're not."

The distance between them appeared very short. She sat across the coffee table, but at that moment she felt much closer.

"Have we met before?"

"I'm sorry to think you have forgotten me. I have very little recollection of anything that happened before we met." Her lips formed a pout.

"There's something about you, as though you had been with me for a long time. You pry into my past as though you were a long time friend. But the most interesting part in the equation is that I like letting you into my life, and I haven't done that in ages."

"I think you're too cunning to forget someone unless you wanted to forget them," she said.

He smacked his lips, slipping his tongue under the upper palate.

"I certainly wouldn't want to do that with you."

"Then, you answered your own question. I can't tell you about my memories because they're all absent, but I share yours. To me, you seem like a generous man. Your kindness has made me feel comfortable inside your house."

"I'm a man . . ."

"Someone I can trust," she said. "Perhaps we have met, not in this life, but in a distant past. If only we could look into a greater realm. Our senses confuse us, they accept the illusion of time and the space we occupy. That gut feeling which makes you feel comfortable around me is untouched by those senses. It's the raw power to see beyond the physical input."

"Do you really think you can reach me with your way of thinking?"

"Intuition can make you succumb to the intangible message reaching from the soul within. Surrender," she said. "You allowed yourself to chase me during the storm, it was your will to find me against the common sense that beckoned your indifference."

"You say such things."

"Your common sense is the poison to the silent message which yearns to be acknowledged. Learn to trust the instinct speaking out. Maybe you're right, we must have met before."

His mind dealt with the uncommon content of her thoughts and he realized it would be great to play a game of lust and passion with her appetizing body.

The den of the log cabin was an ample room with the fireplace as the center point. A hand woven rug defined the area of the living space where they sat. Everything was simple, reflecting the existence he yearned. Nearby, a rack held multiple rifles, and heads of hunted game adorning the walls of the room. There was a buck, a moose, and a wild cat.

"You hunted these animals?"

"I did," he smiled with subtle pride.

"I don't think killing for sport is right."

The roar of his laughter was great. "That's because you haven't felt the adrenaline of the kill!"

"Destroying is a false pleasure. It's cruel to corner something defenseless, to snap away its life. You sneak up on innocence, mutilating trust. That's why man is such a treacherous animal." Her face filled with the flush of her spirited words.

"I thrive on the power to overcome an opponent. You can't understand the thrill of a chase, but it's something which fills me with an eloquent emotion," he said in complete control. Although she disagreed strongly with his sport, he had no intentions of changing for her or anyone else.

Having finished eating, she walked back into the kitchen, leaving him alone. He heard the sound of running water in the sink drowning her disappointment. When she came back, he was spread out over the sofa. In his careless abandonment he wasn't ready to get up, and it was obvious she wasn't going to pick up after him. She took the same seat again, the leather couch across the cocktail table, and he was surprised she had returned to sit with him at all.

"How did your mother pass away?"

"Why do you want to know?" Her question took him by surprise.

"I would like to learn more about her."

"Stomach cancer," he dropped. "The doctors said she had a bacterium that produced the malignancy. Antibiotics could have spared the illness but she avoided doctors, saying it was the greasy food from the restaurant that gave her heartburn. She took over-the-counter antacids, cheap stuff. According to the doctors they said people who live in low socioeconomic groups are predisposed to catching this bug. Well, we were low all right."

"A bacteria?"

"Yes, crowded living arrangements, unsanitary habits. She spent a lifetime saving money for my tuition. When the doctors recommended tests, she turned them down because they were too expensive. My uncle thought she was a substance abuser when bottles of pain killers showed up in the house."

"Were you in Vancouver when she got sick?"

"No, at U.C.L.A.. studying art through a scholarship. She called two weeks before Christmas and life changed."

"You dropped out?"

"I had to."

"And you lost the chance to go back?"

"I got caught up in her illness, and my life went on hold." Without flinching he looked away, toward the beams of the ceiling. "Mom waited until she couldn't handle it alone, so by the time I found out, her disease was far advanced. Have you ever seen anyone drenched in a cold sweat because their body hurts so much not even morphine can stop it?"

He paused and closed his eyes tightly.

"No, I guess not. I hated my uncle because he thought of his business to the very end. First, he didn't want to close the restaurant so he had the nerve to say she had a nervous stomach. I remember bottles of Maalox and what-else-not on her dresser, but not until she collapsed over a table did he acknowledge her emaciated look. There were two waitresses and Mom was one of them, so it was convenient to look the other way.

"Two weeks after I took her to the doctor we found out her cancer had spread to the bone. When she had to be hospitalized for chemotherapy, my uncle wouldn't travel to see her because he didn't want to close the kitchen, see — he was the cook, and visiting hours were in the afternoon, during peak rush.

"You think he would have been different after she slaved for so many years in the joint. Damn, he had the money but instead, my mother went to a hospice because he didn't want her back in the apartment when she was too sick to take care of herself. He was a royal prick."

Claude got up, went to the kitchen, and returned with another beer. This time he stood against the mantel of the fireplace with his eyes lost somewhere outside the realm of vision and gulped down half the bottle with one swig.

"I'm so sorry, Claude."

"I hated my mother for not seeking medical help," his voice rumbled. "She must have known something was very wrong, but instead she worked, day and night, so I could follow my dreams, dreams that turned into nightmares. But I loathed no one worse than myself for being dumb founded, going about my business without paying attention to her."

"You're too harsh on yourself," she said, breaking in. "How could you know?"

"Mom was always a thin woman, but for months she had been losing weight. That year I came home for Thanksgiving, and her clothing hung like sheets over a stick. I should have pushed her for the answers; instead I took a passive stand. She told me she was fine, and I believed her because it was the easiest thing to do. What an asshole: all I wanted to do was paint, and be the artist."

"People lose weight."

"But not forty pounds in six months," he wilted his voice. "At the very end of her life, I understood that it was just the two of us. People around us — the doctors, the nurses and my uncle — they were like furniture in a room. They were there, but their presence was meaningless. My mother lived for me and here I was for her. Life faded in the agony of her death."

"You're intense with your love," she said, probing into the blue of his eyes. "However, there's a shyness, as though you were afraid to surrender into the experience of discovering an intimate part of the whole."

"You seem to have me all figured out," he said, in an angry tone.

"No, but I see you were generous putting your life on hold for her. Your uncle didn't do it, your father wasn't there to help. You were the only one who gave up his routine. Don't you see that you gave your mother what she needed the most?"

"You don't understand," he said, filled with melancholy. "She was there a million times for everyone, how could I abandon her when she needed me the most?"

"There's always a choice. You could have stayed in L.A."

He took a pause in the flow of his thoughts and then went on. "The doctors, hospitals, the chemotherapy, God, they tortured her. I realized too late, love is not enough."

"You did what you could."

"Did you know that when a scorpion gives birth, the mother sacrifices herself? Her offsprings feed off her body until she dies." His face distorted by a grimace. "I was that kind of animal."

"She had the best, she had her son." Natalie's voice trembled.

"Money would have been more practical. That's when I swore to change my life, I swore to change myself and never stop for sentimentality or love. "

"Her time on earth was done. Remember what I said before? Her spirit chose the life it led knowing how it all would end, and when you were born, you chose her, too."

"What gift gives you the insight to say the things you do?"

Claude's tone was defiant.

She never answered him. Instead, as though she were a surgeon, careful with the blade that carves into an ulcer, she dug so that healthy tissue could replace the decay that made him rot.

"Where did you go from there?"

"I moved to the East Coast, went to college at MIT, became one of the nerds who can't get a book out of their face," he said. "When I finished my career, debts drowned me. I often wondered if studying was worthwhile, but I kept walking forward, closing my eyes to doubts, working eighty-hour weeks." Claude took a seat again, his semblance grave. "I swore on her deathbed that I would be rich one day."

"And are you rich?"

He had gone beyond his expectations; Claude-Phillipe Aumont was the envy of many men for the goals he had achieved. For the first time in his life he didn't feel mortified allowing his inner memories to surface. Exorcizing them felt natural, not in the least diminishing, and on the contrary, the knot that tightened around his throat at last had come loose, accepting her sympathy for what it was. His eyes landed on her as though she were the soothing balm to make his hell more bearable.

Shy steps delivered her to where he sat and then he saw her hand come up toward his forehead, sweeping a lock of hair that brushed over his face. As her hand came down he caught her wrist in mid air. He turned her palms up, looking as though he aimed to find something written on them.

"Delicate fingers, long and gracious, hands that have a steady grip." He fixed his gaze into the brown of her eyes and asked her, "Would you pose for me?" She looked at him with the surprise of his whim, saying nothing. "I can afford to pay you."

"I can't take your money," she murmured.

"Please, let me." His voice came out as bold and gentle as the caress offered by the hand he held. He had never felt compelled to paint the way he did today.

"Why me?" She took her hand back. "I don't know anything about posing for a painting."

"Do you trust me?"

She thought for a minute before answering. "I told you I did."

"And you said you never lie," he said, remembering another conversation and the solemn look in her eyes when she uttered such a statement.

Getting up, she reached the far side of the cabin and stood looking out a window, he thought, pondering, searching within herself. He went by her side. He sensed the inner beauty of her soul, and for the first time he saw beyond the facade, and into the essence of a person.

"You have opened feelings that were locked. It's your fault the way I feel," he said, trying to persuade her. "I would like to capture an unforgettable woman into a painting."

"You confuse me. I'm not sure." Not the thinnest paring of a wary smile curled either corner of her mouth.

He squared himself in front of her, forcing her to look at him.

"It's an impulse that has taken over, a different side of me. I'm as baffled as you might be." He hesitated for a moment and then he said it. "Besides, when we go our separate ways, I'm sure you could use the money."

Again a silence.

"Very well, I'll do it," she said, toying with her fingers.

They stared at each other and he found it difficult to ignore a greater purpose to their meeting rather than a fortuitous encounter. Inside his heart a feeling had awakened, a metamorphosis ongoing, and Natalie was his catalyst.

8

Claude brought her upstairs to the empty room where he kept his easel and paints, the study adjacent to his room where he began to draw her that same afternoon, using a charcoal pencil over a white drawing pad. At first it was the circumference of her head, then going down the vertical line of her torso, into the legs.

For hours she was plagued with the immobility of the job she'd assumed, inexperienced and naive about the pain of muscles stiffening. She did it for his sake, for the possibility of advancing his ability to create. Creating was a feeling which had to be encouraged, and he was as much an amateur in the field as she was with posing.

"You're too tense, relax," he said. The noise of paper ripping out of the spiral notebook followed as he crumpled the page inside his hands.

"I'm tired of sitting on this wooden stool," she said, squirming.

"Sit still. Can't you see my hands are awkward?" His voice came with roughened exasperation and saying this, he smashed the charcoal pencil against the wall. "Maybe you're right, what's the use of this?"

"Don't, please go on. I've seen your work and you're better than you think."

He stopped to open up a window because the room asphyxiated him.

"You don't know about the complexity of emotions that has to go into a painting." He was lashing out at her, angry with himself for failing. "I can haul you into the paper and that's easy, but if my work is to be any good, energy must live within it. My drawings are lifeless because I don't know how to grab the moment between two of your breaths, the movement frozen so briefly that all of you is there."

She went behind him, and he felt her hand on his back, gentle like the air coming into the room.

"Don't paint me from your eyes, look through your heart."

"It's a stupid game between us," he retorted.

Her voice was soft. "Imagine that you're the master of your hand and your fingers are your slaves. They will do as your soul commands if only you will trust your instincts, rather than your mind — I'll sit still for you."

Natalie went back to the stool. She dropped the shoulder of the shirt just like it was before. The difficulty was inside himself because he couldn't dwell in her psychological plateau, but he knew once she left him, these paintings would be all that would remain of her, and he either did it now or never.

After a while, she managed to loosen up, uninhibited by the eyes that worked her over. Madness compelled him to capture beyond her beauty, into the realm of feelings growing inside him, swelling, bursting to be let loose at every breath he took.

"You seem to understand me with a depth that prompts me to chase a strange concept of life," he said.

"I have a different way of looking at life, at you. If you stop being at war with yourself, you'll feel better."

"What gives you power over me? Are you trying to psychoanalyze me?"

"I don't think I hold the medical degree to do it." Untouched by the harshness of his tone, she kept a steady voice. "These are my simple observations."

"Your comments about me are far from being simple. What is so important about me painting? You make it seem like a matter of life and death, and it's nothing, totally unimportant."

"I don't mean to disturb you."

"But you do, and that's very unusual for a man like me."

"What have I done to make you angry?"

He was contrite because he was losing control, surrendering to a novel feeling. She was taking on importance, despite the absence of her past, and he was fearful of missing her because he didn't want to live with the emptiness of loss and grief.

She sat for hours and after a while charcoal was replaced by oil paints. The composition of the picture took shape from the intensity of pigments as he feverishly worked, not on paper but on the white cloth. With the passing of the hours the looseness of his brush strokes brought him forward, and in a bold adventure the artist rose from the grave of apathy. At the end of the day her figure stood ablaze against a bold display of lights and shadows, a mass of color in a field of red and yellow flowers. In the strange passion which drove him, he felt free, and if thoughts could touch, his would have embraced her.

"Do you want to break?" Claude discarded the content of a jar full of tainted turpentine. The pungent smell floated in the air when he replaced a clean batch, stirring his brushes into the fluid.

"I'll go downstairs and fix us a bite. Should I bring you something?"
He wiped his hands on a rag. The light of day was dead, and he had kidnaped her all day. The cool evening air made him close the open window.

"A drink would be fine."

Natalie buttoned the top of her shirt and then crouched down onto the floor twice, stretching out the stiffness of her legs, moving all her muscles from the stillness in which they had been fixed for hours.

"I'm the culprit of your pain."

"I agreed to the punishment," she smiled forgiving.

When she left him, the room felt empty, as though a spell were cast invoking him to miss her. Inexplicably, life was turning into the experiment of possibilities and feelings, something long forgotten. Interrupting the scavenging of his mind, she showed up with a tray and a bottle of wine. Two pieces of chicken scratched up from leftovers, tomatoes, lettuce and a roll served in a plate.

"Did you hear me ask for food?"

"I'm sorry, I thought you'd be hungry," she said with a nurturing voice. Leaving the tray on a desk by the far corner of the room, she moved away.

Hungry and tired, his mouth watered. Betraying himself he sat to eat while she walked around the room. When he turned around to see what she was doing, he realized Natalie had been looking at his work.

"It's far from being finished," Claude said in an unfriendly warning. "You should wait until I'm done."

"It's excellent." She turned a disobedient smile.

"You're not an art critic so stop humoring me."

"I have eyes — "

"Stop idealizing me." The harshness in his voice forced her to step back. "I don't need your praise, nor the generosity in your eyes."

She believed in his ability and it scared him to live up to her expectations as though she were the mirror on which to look at himself, divulging a frightening self image.

"Who are you behind your arrogance?"

"Don't worry about me. Work on remembering, because I won't need you once I'm done," he muttered.

"Did I do something to tick you off?"

"I'm the type of man a woman should keep at a distance. I don't allow deep relationships. They are the idle contemplation of a feeling, and I don't believe in love or sentimentality. To me you're very trusting."

"Is that why you offered to pay me? Was it to keep your distance or because everyone has a price?" She stood barefoot over the pine floor, her shoulders tilted back, her head high.

"I pay for everything I have." His voice sounded hollow.

"Then you must have little, because the very best comes for free. I'm not posing for the money, but because I care about you. Without being presumptuous, I think you need me."

The cold slashes of her words wounded, but he deserved it. She was young and beautiful, vulnerable, yet wiser than he handling the situation between them. The truth was he said these things to remind himself of the man he used to be. He was striving to sequester the susceptible self which wanted to be shared with a woman who was superb.

"Don't get confused, I need myself and nobody else. You're urging me to find a world of fantasy as ridiculous as the thought of painting you."

He couldn't imagine loving anyone or sharing life with someone else but she was right about him, although he didn't want to admit it. He needed her; for the first time someone had entered into his solitude.

"Hate me if you must, but don't stop, not now that you've started." She was pointing at her image. "Do it for yourself, for the feeling which makes no sense but can bring happiness."

The fire of her words burned inside his marrow. He took a drink, straight from the bottle of wine as though the liquid could calm the blaze that burned his skin. Then he stared out the window and into the dark void outside. The terror of another empty night filled his soul.

"What are you afraid of, Claude?" She spit out the words. "Are you afraid of me or of the feelings inside yourself? Is it the devil in a man, or the fear of being conquered by the intangibles which have always lived inside you?"

"You don't know me enough to make such judgements," he said.

Natalie had hit on a nail, and in turn, he was pushing away like he did whenever someone came too close. Nonetheless and despite his efforts, she seeped through his pores with invisible tentacles of love, reaching to free his soul.

"Don't be afraid of living for the full experience. Otherwise, you'll miss the very best."

Again he drank, wanting to dull his senses, holding his stance and realizing how easy it would be to be a man like his father. No, never like Marcel. Alcohol would never drown his pain.

A few feet from him, she stood by the easel and the can where he had his brushes, a bottle of linseed oil to mix the paints, and a few rags with which to wipe his hands.

"Are you this brave or an incredible fool, wanting to pry open the gates of hell?" he asked, taking a deep breath. "It would be a mistake for you to walk this close."

"You're not an antrum of evil."

"I would hurt you, destroy a woman like you."

"You might, but what makes you think I would let you?"

"There's no one more vulnerable than a woman in love."

"Do you think I plan to fall in love with you?"

"Yes, you might," he said, ". . . because you have romanticized our fortuitous meeting and because you trust me."

"There are men who know how to trust, who love without forgetting. There are those who love once and never again."

For a moment as though he were the one falling in love, as though he were the one being mauled by an attack, he couldn't speak. Defenseless, she confronted the world, she confronted him, and he was unprepared to duel with such courage.

"You're afraid to look, but you want to find. Aren't you looking for the answers? This is what it's all about. Look — " She was pointing at her portrait. "Do you think an animal could do that?"

Silence grew between them, and when he looked into her valiant eyes, he felt insignificant absorbing the inner strength that reached him.

"Emotions are erratic, unreliable, and far from being practical," he answered in a miserable tone of voice. "I would never want to be guided by the insecurity of my impulses. I don't know what came over me when I asked you to pose for me, but obviously it was a mistake."

She moved to the mattress in the far corner of the room, looking out the window unadorned by curtains. Her heard the faint sound of her sigh enrapture the loneliness of her soul. She was lost in the same night without stars, in the misery of her ache, and he had pushed her there.

The incandescent light of a lamp offered clarity through the shadows rushing to kidnap the room and his easel.

"What gives you the right to come upon my life to teach me anything at all? Who do you think you are?" he said, following her to where she sat.

"You're the man who stopped to help me," she whispered. "But I'm nobody in that man's life."

Her large brown eyes looked up at him and he felt the sting of the rebel tear that blurred her vision but it was obvious she wasn't going to give him the satisfaction of seeing her cry.

Aware of the wounds he had inflicted, he was afraid to turn back because softening his attack would mean she had entered into his heart. There could be no soft spots for anyone.

"Yes, I'm the man who found you, I brought you here because I had no choice, but I'm no mother Theresa — too inconvenient. I live for myself and no one else. Don't confuse yourself about me."

Her breath quickened under and he loathed himself. Taking a deep breath, her face took on a stunning beauty, and he understood that it was impossible to belittle her because she was above his petty flaws. His intuition told him she was there for the survival of his soul, his last chance.

"It's going to take a lot for me to hate you, Claude," she said. "You're like one of those animals you corner in your hunt, but you have nothing to fear from me. I'm not a hunter."

He admired her faith in life, in him — and at that instance he could have sworn he loved her. Natalie's voice entered, touching in a way that took his breath away. Was she the fallen angel sent to earth with the purpose of redeeming his lost cause, or was she the soul mate he had never found?

"You're clutching onto me because there's no one else," he whispered as though explaining to himself. "Let go. Don't idealize the concept of someone because he helped you."

Then he heard her voice again, "Don't worry, I'll walk out of here and you'll never see me again. I'm not going to keep you. I'm an acquaintance who can be left behind. Just remember when I'm gone that it's fine to feel with the intensity of all the life inside of you."

The rapid chase of his heartbeat flushed the blood into his face. Kneeling in front of her, he took her arms.

"Woman, why have you come into my life? What secrets live inside your mind that make your heart so wise? I don't want to hurt you, not with my words nor with my actions," he said. "You disturb me, you bring me in, in from the edge on which I stand. I helped you, but here you are wanting to save me from myself."

Her lips parted and he thought she was going to say something but her voice died somewhere deeper than her vocal cords.

His hands were dirtied by dry paint. Natalie took one of them as her fingers traced over the lines of his palm. It was a careful and gentle action over the outline of the creases, soothing the restlessness within.

"What are you doing?" he asked.

She looked into the black abyss centered in his eyes. "Maybe I was meant to find you. I could be here to introduce alternatives — it could be there are better ways than yours, but it could be that I'm too awkward showing you the road ahead."

"I have never made anyone happy except myself. I'm too self centered to be good for anyone else. Sometimes I wonder even if I'm good for me."

"You're not evil, Claude. Perhaps a little lost inside yourself — "

She had become his need.

"Don't let me come any closer than I have. I will damage you and I don't want to hurt you."

"I can take care of myself."

"Tempered by the right kind of man your passion is delicious. You're the type of woman who surrenders without putting on the brakes."

"I'm not afraid of you."

"You should never become a challenge in my life. If you do then I will try to conquer, and I always aim to win no matter what you think of me. I told you — I'm not the type of man who settles in your heart."

He leaned closer over her smaller body, skimming against her side and noticed that all her muscles tensed in anticipation of his next move. She was at his mercy, so small under his larger mass.

"Let your hair down."

She stared at him.

"I want to sketch you there, like this," he said.

She did as he asked, and her hair fell with inebriating sexuality. Her respirations grew deeper, her eyes fixed on his.

"I find your thoughts and your beauty the inspiration that my life was missing." His fingers tangled in her hair. He guided her into recumbency, gently moving her to how he wanted her to pose. The touch of her skin warmed, inviting him to be daring. It would be so easy to take her under his body. *What kind of lover are you?*

"Open your shirt," he whispered.

She clutched the shirt and her modesty touched the very essence of his manhood.

"You have nothing to worry about, I'm not going to seduce you," he said, caressing with the tone of his voice. "I don't know if you're at my mercy or I'm at yours."

Yes, she was safe tonight — safer than she imagined — because she had become a feeling in his heart. When he stepped away, she unbuttoned the shirt and through a slit that grew wider, the milky white of her breast was an offering. Enthralled, he stepped away to look at her nudity from afar. Pink nipples stood erect touched by the chill of the night. His actions could have filled with the naught inside his thoughts but convinced he was insane, he rejected the pleasure of her body for the silence of his work.

The hours passed, and midnight found them there. The satisfaction of creating in the image of this woman had known no other rivals.

After two hours, she had met with exhaustion and curled into the fetal position to fall asleep over the mattress. Natalie gave freely for the purpose of allowing a different side of him. If she had refused to pose, he would have understood the many reasons why, but instead she gave into an offering.

He brought out a comforter from the linen closet in the hallway. Rather than wake her, she could spend the night on the cot.

"What kind of a woman are you who seeks and gives so readily in the life of a lost man?" He spoke in a low voice, crouching over her. "Why are you moving me into a world unknown? It's been a long time."

He, too, was tired.

In the darkness that had devoured the day, lying down in his bed, he remembered another woman, and it was just as strange to have such thoughts.

Elizabeth.

He didn't think about her very often, but she was someone who meant something long ago. He had messed up royally. Tonight, after so many years he was missing her. Where could she be? Oddly, the feeling aroused by Natalie resembled that other, the one who had been . . . forgotten.

9

He walked through the downstairs, but it became apparent that he was alone inside the house. A rainbow of caked paint under his fingernails reminded him of the day before, and an oppressing thought took over as he pondered about her whereabouts. He ran outside, but she was nowhere near. She was gone. A vacant feeling settled in his heart looking at the Adirondack chair, and he mentally kicked himself for his rash outburst the day before.

His fingers ran through his dark brown hair when he felt the loneliness of his world, like a man drifting in the emptiness of outer space. Then he realized what he knew already, that caring could be dangerous.

Sprinting in the direction of the waterfront, he made it in no time to the other side of the forest and to the cliffs by the water's edge. Not too far away from the end of the trail he stopped to catch his breath, and then he saw her, about a hundred meters away, staring out to sea. He'd memorized every dip, every voluptuous curve of her figure. Red highlights gleamed through her hair like rivers of fire stolen from the sun. Everything she'd said was an echo in his mind and now he knew how her words had the power to crush his heart and how her smile could make him soar above the skies.

He called out to her, unable to repress the voice coming out of his throat and when she turned, her greeting was an open smile. He knew she had forgiven his rudeness.

"It's so peaceful out here," she said.

"It's early and the sun hasn't warmed the water front." He was taking off his windbreaker and slipping it over her shoulders. "How long have you been here?"

"Oh, I don't know, about an hour or two."

"I like when your eyes are happy," he said in a deep voice.

Natalie crossed her arms over her chest, warming herself.

"I made coffee," she said. "Did you have any?"

"No, I'll have some when we get back."

"You thought I had remembered?"

"I thought you had gone." He looked down. "When you leave I will miss you."

The fury of an ocean colliding against the rocks broke under the cliffs.

"I will miss you too," she whispered. "Will you sit with me?"

He squatted down by her side.

"I'm sorry, sorry about yesterday," he blurted out. "If you want to go, I'll drive you. The roads should be pretty good by now."

"Is that the way you feel?"

"It's better this way."

"Then why are you here, next to me?"

"I had to know.

"You're a hypocrite," she said.

"And you have character!" He laughed. "I bet you broke a few hearts."

"If I did, it wasn't on purpose. I don't like to hurt people, unlike — "

"Unlike me."

The girl shook her head while she looked toward the horizon.

He didn't answer right away.

"Why do you make me feel as though I have to apologize for so much of what I say? I don't want to hurt you. I don't want to lose you either."

"Then what do you want from me?"

Claude almost managed a smile, but to do so would have divulged his inadequacy. He tightened his jaw instead. She confused him, he wanted her more than anything else in the world, but at the same time he was afraid to reach inside and touch the woman by his side.

"I envy the man who falls in love with you. He would be fortunate. Last night it happened and now again, I don't know how to deal with the formidable feeling you inspire."

"As a man, you're a dichotomy," she said. "There's two of you, one who chooses to live marginally to his sensitivity as though it were a sin, the other — warm and caring."

They sat at the edge of the world, connected by the breeze that came inland, warmed by the sun above them, speaking through the soul that lived always. Her body was next to his, luring with the want that rushed. Her eyes werevery big, her voluptuous lips parted slightly, inviting him with obvious blessings.

"It's all about holding on to what I've found, isn't it?" he asked.

"And what have you found?"

"A beginning." His voice, deep and virile, filled the air.

"It's a good place to start."

"Just remember that I'm damned," he said. "The thought of dying in my loneliness never dawned on me, but after meeting you, it seems like an unhappy ending."

"Am I suppose to feel sorry for you?"

"Absolutely not. I don't want your pity."

"Then what?"

He could have told her that he wanted her passion, all the love that he could conjure. Searching into her eyes, he admired her integrity and the clear strength channeled in her voice. His fingertips dared to touch her cheeks, moving away the strand of hair rushing over her lips.

"You're the best thing that has happened in a long time," he told her.

"A friend — " she said softly.

"Would you dare reach further?" His voice embraced her.

"You and I are the horizon, very close but far apart from each other. We will distance as we get closer because I won't be able to stay with you. Too many pieces missing, so much incertitude in the future." She let out a sigh. "My stay will be a brief one."

"I'm laughing at myself, Natalie — or whoever you may be. I'm a fool if I can't tell you that I don't want you to go. Should I be selfish about you?" Claude took her hand. He didn't want to scare her, but he was dwelling in desire. "You're everywhere, even in my dreams."

"You said to stay away." She held her breath and her eyes vanished from his sight.

"But you're here, giving of yourself." He was so close that her body brushed against his own and then he took her in his arms. His words were just a whisper. "You're as intense as the crack of dawn and as dramatic as a sunset — a dangerous woman — but I'm terribly tempted."

"Claude . . ."

"What is it like to kiss your lips?" Her face came closer as she lowered her eyes in an offering.

Over and over he tasted her pleasures, feeling drunk with the contact of her body. She gave into his desires, trembling under his touch, feasting in the same sweetness invading him but when he least expected, she pulled away gently, leaving him with the want for more.

"My past . . ." she said in a low voice, barely speaking because tears threatened in her eyes.

"My God, Natalie! I hate the unspoken omen of your words."

"Too many pieces are missing, and my presence is all so strange."

"You said I should take more chances with my life."

"Who will hurt the other first, you or I?"

Claude laid her back over the granite rock making her rest over his outstretched arm. He brought her closer, wanting to banish the aftertaste of her reality. Her breath was in his mouth.

"Don't think, darling. Feel the bond forcing us together, compelling me to trust you. Like the waves bathing the shore, you have the effect of slowly but steady, chipping away my unyielding heart. Know that you have broken through someone who is as hard as the rock beneath us. I can paint because you made me search inside myself for the soul I had forgotten. You have released feelings and passions asleep inside a heartless man. Don't be afraid of me, because if you are, then I'll kill the beast that hurts you."

"Oh Claude." Her voice was a just a hush. "You're not evil. I like the man I see, maybe I like him too much for my own sake."

There was passion and want, but something more, unspoken by either one, something filling with a stronger tie than either one could comprehend, tumbling all his common sense. The world stopped in the dawn of a newfound feeling, unexpected as it was overwhelming.

"I could take you, I could posses you and you wouldn't know how to resist me with the desire I would awaken in you, but I'll wait for your memories because I want you to be sure this is what you want."

"Am I part of your metamorphosis?"

"You can very well be the woman to remove my blindfolds."

"I would like to be your friend, your lover, everything in life that could make you content," she said in a sultry voice.

"You're all I need, Natalie, my Natalie." Claude smiled full of contagious euphoria. "I know I'm a fool thinking there's no past to dampen the present but suddenly everything else seems unimportant. I own today, and every day that you spend with me. But don't ask me to explain why it's so intense, so wonderfully crazy, just know that it is."

"Promise me that only the truth will come between us, nothing more, nothing less." She said it in his arms, her voice touched with emotion.

He sealed his end of the pact with another kiss, lost in the moment that came. This was theirs, and it was true.

For the first time Claude forgot the complications of his money and the rancor that froze his heart because Natalie had halted the hollow pursuit of life.

They walked back to the house, thinking of nothing but the new feeling between them. So sudden, so unexpected in the strength with which it came.

10

Pilar Haydig sat at her desk when the intercom rang. She pressed a button, and her secretary announced Mr. Shearson at the other side of her door.

"Give me a couple of minutes, then send him in," she said.

Busy with the papers in front of her, she didn't lift her head when the door opened. Then she felt the weight of his stare, the hazel eyes meandering into the cleavage of her blouse. Brandon stood in front of her, tanned in the impeccable cut of his navy blue Armani. She pressed her lips together and glanced directly at the challenging figure in front of her.

"I didn't know we had an appointment. What brings you here?"

"I brought these documents, and I thought I'd stop in." He was holding an accordion folder in his hands.

"Claude is still on vacation," she said. "I guess I'll review them for him."

"There's no hurry."

"So, then?"

Brandon was one of the corporate lawyers employed by Transworld, and she was used to seeing him around the firm. But in the last few days, he was everywhere. A week ago she ran into him at The Food Emporium, and he walked her home, carrying her bags. Now he was taking a seat in front of her as though she had invited him to settle down.

"It's not business. I thought I'd say hello." He moved his eyes around the room as though to scan behind the art work hanging from the walls, looking for intruding eyes. There was a Joseph Crilley and a Ben Badura suspended under a spotlight and a 1940 street scene behind her desk.

"You bought these?"

"No, they were a gift from my boss. He surrounds himself with art, and sometimes it spills into my office. One of these was a birthday present, the other two were for some other holiday."

"I like them," he said. His voice was even, and he sat one leg squared over the other, spreading his arms over the back of the love seat.

"I'm very busy, Brandon. What's up?"

"I know you're all business within these walls, but . . . how about dinner tonight?"

Pilar smiled and got up from her seat, coming to the other side of her desk. A white blouse tucked inside the black skirt right above the knees smoothed over her curves.

"I'm sorry Brandon. I should tell you, so you don't waste time with me that I'm not your type."

Brandon looked at her from head to toe and afterward stood up, taller than she, even with the three inch heels on her black patent shoes. A smile cornered his lips. They stood so close that the scent of his cologne flared in her nostrils.

"And whose type are you, Pilar?"

"What do you mean by that?"

"I'll cut to the chase." His voice came, still patient and even. "I think you're very attractive, but it's more than that. You're right about my type, smart women don't attract me, but you, you're driving me crazy. You're brainy, and it doesn't stop me from saying you're beautiful."

Pilar smiled back.

"Haven't you heard the rumors about me? I devour men for breakfast."

"I think you devour men, all right. It's okay if you want a taste of me."

Pilar didn't blink, trying to steady her face to match Brandon's.

"I'm not interested in romance, and I'm too busy to connect with you."

He stood up, taking her by the waist and before she knew it, he was pressing over her lips, one hand sliding over her breast. She pushed away, and by the pale expression in his face, it was obvious he was baffled by her reaction.

"What's wrong?"

"Don't do that again, don't you ever corner me like this again," she said. "I don't like men who flirt with every skirt nor do I want cheap thrills. I don't appreciate getting manhandled by you."

"Are you playing hard to get? If you are, we're not in high school any more?"

"Of course not, I'm too worldly for that sort of thing. You're so swollen with yourself you probably think I liked it."

"Let's get together." He tried to come close once more but she went ⁺ steps back. "You're not one of those silly women who regret adventure."

"I don't like you, Brandon. Can't you get it?"

"You're after a much bigger fish." He looked at the art work.

"You're insulting. Leave my office now, and I'll try to forget your arrogance."

Brandon fixed his tie and closed the buttons of his suit. He stood a moment longer in front of Pilar, steady as an ice block.

"If you get lonely, I'm always around."

*   *   *

Claude knew the coast, and Natalie became the subject of all his pieces. For the last three days they came to the same place for the sake of indulging in his work. They were painting in a secluded cove surrounded by seagulls who were as whimsical in their actions as in the screech of their sonnet. He had noticed the red glow over her fair skin and knew the sunburn was going to be unbearable if he kept her here anymore.

With the boat loaded, they were ready to leave, but she insisted on collecting small sea shells to string in a necklace. He watched from a distance until he decided to chase after her. The birds scared away, taking to flight when she ran from him. Like children chasing in a game, this was part of the rapture in their idyll. The sound of her laughter carried through the shore line as he ran in pursuit of her treasure, until he caught up to her, tumbling over the sand.

He found himself lost in the soft curves of her body and in the taste of her mouth, but he remembered the refrain of his promise, holding back what seemed unstoppable. She seemed like a wave upon a beach, enamored, reaching — embracing like the ripples of water which teasingly came and went. They were the sand and the ocean, one perfect with the other.

And when they left, he smiled, looking back at the shore line, with the paintings on board and Natalie by his side. He had learned to use light and colors as the expressive tools of the artist. The harmony within reflected in the composition, rich in human emotion because he had accepted the inspiration of the woman who no longer was a stranger.

At the cabin she changed into one of his T-shirts because her sunburn made it impossible to wear anything else. When she came down, he was making dinner, and tempted, she came with a spoon near the crème brûlée he had prepared.

"Pass me two wine glasses, and don't eat dessert," he said. "I haven't torched the sugar on top."

"Ouch!" She pulled back when he touched her shoulder.

"You're going to be my favorite snake, shedding all that skin in a few days."

"Live and learn, what can I tell you." She was savoring a spoon full."This is my last disobedience. It tastes great even without the caramel but dessert after dinner and yes — use your sun screen. I think I got it."

"I like my meat medium-rare so you're just about right." He laughed, full of indulgence while she refrained a smile.

"Here." Without thinking, she retrieved the glasses from the cupboard while he flamed with a lighter the sugar on top of the desert. Afterward, he placed the dishes inside the refrigerator to cool.

Natalie wore her hair high in a pony tail. Kissing the back of her neck she scrunched with the tickle of his affectionate outburst and then she slid away.

He went to the rack of vintaged wines and pulled a bottle.

"Cabernet Sauvignon?"

"Yes, absolutely perfect."

Claude twisted the cork with the opener, dragging it out with a pop.

"I'm due at my firm in a few days. Come back with me."

"Has it been two weeks?" she turned around to look at him.

"More than that, my sweet. It's been nearly a month."

"I have to think about it."

"What's going on inside your sun-stroked head?"

"Nothing, I just want to think about it."

"Where would I leave you if you don't come along?" He placed the bottle on the table with the wineglasses and the plates.

"Maybe I should give you space to think about us."

Whether she remembered the past or not, he wanted her by his side. He cornered her against the counter where she had been leaning, touching the side of her face with his hand.

"I'm not offering charity. My invitation is compelled by a lot more." There was a hoarseness in his voice. "I want you with me, that's why I'm asking you to come."

"Tell me who I am, where I come from and whom I left behind. Then I'll go with you."

"You know I don't have a crystal ball to give you answers, but we'll work it out."

"I don't want to depend on you for everything, because I'll stifle you after a while. Here, far away from everyone, it's easier, but what happens when you enter the world and I'm with you?"

"For the first time I haven't tired of the same woman day after day. On the contrary, the more of you I have, the more I want. For heaven's sake, can't you see I'm content when you're with me?"

"You offer me a future, but do I have the right to take it? What happens if there's a man in my past, a husband, children?"

"We'll work it out. I don't intimidate easily."

She pushed away from him.

"I don't want to get paid for posing. I did it for you not for anything else."

"It's work," he said smiling.

"Well, suppose I did take that money. How far do you think it would take me?" There was an onerous tone in her voice.

"As far as ten thousand dollars will take anyone."

Natalie opened her mouth while she stared wide eyed. "You can afford to pay that much?"

Amused by her disbelief, he came closer, sure he wanted to help her. Such an amount was very little for him.

"If you don't want to live with me then get your own place in New York, but come. I'll help you any way I can, but obviously I would prefer . . . if you stayed with me, in my apartment."

"Sometimes I feel like I'm here to amuse you."

"You're much more than that." He smiled. "I could amuse myself with a new car or a good book, but you, you're a lot more than just a fling."

"Should I surrender to the likes of you?"

"I'm the one who has surrendered. Can't you see how I've changed?"

Was she restless over the future awaiting in New York, or had he succeeded after all, scaring her off with their clumsy beginning? Overwhelmed by the sad hue in the expression of her eyes, he moved away, trying to understand that she was slumping in the predicament of a life without a past and that trusting a man with her future was a scary thing to do, but he needed an answer. Whatever Natalie decided, it had to come without the knowledge of his fortune and perhaps he had said too much already.

"I don't know anything about you," she said, barely audible. Natalie sat at the table, waiting for his answers, because unlike her, he knew who he was. "I guess you're not going to tell me."

"What do you need to know? Is it about my bank account or about the man? "

"No more, no less than you know about me. Is that it?"

"We both take a chance on the other."

Claude came to the table and sat next to her. His hands swallowed her fingers.

"You're different from the rest of them. The innocence of the world lives in you — I must be selfish wanting to own a little bit of who you are, but you bring hope and the contentment I had forgotten. Up to now I came to these mountains to get away from the farce around me, to forget myself and forget the world from which I come. You think I'm careful, that I don't take chances, but I do, I take huge ones, but never with my feelings. If you're with me, I won't have to run away any more."

"You'll always go forward, whether you're with me or not," she noted.

"For the first time in my life I dare face myself. I always stood on the outside so nobody could enter," he said, clearing his throat. "When I thought of painting you, I did it so I could look at your picture and remember the way you made me feel in case you weren't around, but now I know I want more of an anchor, I want you."

"I'm not as strong as you think."

He took her hands.

"You have your own strength, different from mine. Once I helped you but you're a survivor just like me. Maybe that's why we get along so well."

After dinner they sat down in the den. He swirled the remnants of wine inside his goblet. The only light came from the fireplace, waves of orange radiance dancing on the walls of the room, warming to soothe a basic need.

"I'll go, Claude — " she said. "I'll follow you because I need to be with you even if I die of a broken heart."

Her eyes narrowed, her voice cracked, filled with emotion, forgetting pride and trusting her future to the likes of him.

"Nobody dies of a broken heart." His was a condescending smile.

"The thought of being without you leaves such misery that I'm afraid of staying in that state."

"Then be with me."

"But don't pay me for posing. Doing so would make me feel cheap."

They were lying in a pile of large pillows thrown over the floor. Claude came closer, taking her in his arms. Her words lingered in the air as he understood her plight.

"You're not a bought woman," he rebuked. "Never sell your soul to anyone, not to me nor anyone else. I admire the spirited person that you are, the brave soul who ventured with her thoughts into the likes of a man such as me. I love the fate which brought me to your arms — "

"I'm afraid," she said. Natalie threw her arms around his shoulders, letting out a sigh which filled him with her doubts.

"Of course, you are, Darling. I can only ask you to trust me as you have," he said, kissing her forehead.

"I don't know what our final destination will be, but I do know that I need you. Maybe you were right when you spoke about karma, about the destiny of our souls. I don't want to lose you, now that I've found you. Whoever you were, I know who you are now."

The music played, dusk drowned in the shadowed hours inviting them to their intimacy. He tousled through the softness of her hair, kissing down the sweep of her neck, careful not to hurt her sunburn.

"Make love to me, Claude."

He shut his eyes for an instant. When he reopened them, she was slipping off her jeans and then unbuttoning her blouse in the slow cadence of an offering, brushing softly against his open shirt. The nub of her nipples filled him with desire.

"I want you more than anything standing between us," she murmured in his ears. Her thighs shivered when his hand climbed over them, her breast cluttering in his mouth with nimble pleasure. He drank the nectar from her body a million times over, like the earth thirsty for water after a drought that has lasted for years. He unbuckled his belt, as she allowed for the ultimate possession.

Her soft moans filled him with the feelings of that night. He had waited for her sake, because she had to be sure the past could be conquered, and now being together seemed so right. She was the pieces of a puzzle, every part fitting.

The thrust of his body pushed in until she was driven to a climax, then he released into his own sea of delight.

After a while, she closed her eyes and fell asleep by his side under the red afghan. Her head nestled on his chest; one of her legs lay languid over both of his, reassuring him of reality because believing in such happiness was like a dream. She seemed like any other woman, but he knew about her incredible inner self, her passion, the truth inside her heart. He wanted her for longer than a short affair, and although it was too soon to talk about deeper commitments, he sensed they had something pure and genuine, unsoiled by the evils of the world. He could only hope that his money would not distort the future.

Before he fell asleep, wrapped in the stillness of that night, he remembered the unusual statement uttered during one of their philosophical duels. *Look at me with your feelings, not your senses, because time and the space we occupy is an illusion . . .* But she was real, very real, as was this time together.

11

"See you later." Claude retrieved a rifle from the rack where he kept the firearms.

Natalie remained behind, uninterested and embarrassed, he thought, to join a carnivore hunt. A few hours later, upon his return with four rabbits, he saw her watching from the window in the kitchen while he gutted the furry creatures. Promised a delicious meal, a casserole recipe learned from the days when he worked with his family at the restaurant in Vancouver, she crunched her nose unknowingly.

The serrated edge of the hunting knife severed what was dead, without thought dropping the body parts upon a bloodied pile inside a bucket. A curled string of molted purple — the intestines. A shiny olive-green body — the liver. Spongy tender pinks, crushed with a crackle between his fingers when he ripped them out — the lungs. He amputated the legs, exposing the quadriceps. The splash of organs as he scooped them out of the thorax left a hollow cavity. Evisceration.

For the first time since his arrival the phone rang, and he knew what it meant. He went in the direction of the house with giant leaps, opening the porch door with a swing as it made a loud snap when it hit the frame. He wiped his hands on his jeans, wet from the bloody carcass.

New York had reclaimed his life. He spoke to the man at the other end, and after the business was discussed, he disconnected.

"Your people called?" She asked with a flat voice at the instant he hung up.

"My lawyer," he said. "I spent more time than I meant to."

"When are we leaving?"

"In the morning, tomorrow."

*   *   *

The next day she made coffee while he stashed his belongings in the truck. He tied the canvases to the rack above, wrapped in blankets to keep them safe. Nostalgia filled his heart as he locked the door to the cabin, but he didn't say anything because she already looked dismal.

"We'll be back," he said. His fingers turned on the ignition, sure of his intent.

On the way down from the mountains, off the road was the town cemetery. As the tombstones grew larger, he noticed the restless movement of her legs, the squirming of her hands as though the car was a claustrophobic experience. The fog grew thicker, floating over the ground like a massive cloud that had forgotten its place in the sky.

"Claude, please stop. I need to go there."

A strange urgency took hold of her voice as she pointed a finger in the direction of holy ground.

"You want to go to the cemetery?" Claude asked, surprised by her morbid request.

Her eyes pleaded.

It was early, so he agreed to stop. Their flight left at six that evening, and they had plenty of time to spare. Turning ninety-degrees toward the tall iron gates, they crossed through the valley.

As soon as he stopped, she got down with one jump. She stared at the green under her feet as though she needed permission to go forward, and when she took off, her figure grew dim inside the haze faster than he expected. He realized it was better to go after her, otherwise she would disappear out of sight.

He ran, catching up to her.

"Do you know why we're here?" he asked, catching his breath.

In the silence of her empty gaze she was transposed by a strange mood. They were surrounded by monuments and crypts riising over the ground, crowding the early morning chill. They stopped in front of a granite stone.

"Do you know her?"

"1960-1989, Elizabeth Bates, beloved daughter, those who are loved, live on. " She read the epitaph with a voice that was hardly audible but enough to send a chill up his spine.

Natalie's face had grown pale, her breath shallow, while she coughed a few times.

"I'm scared."

"What's wrong? You look like you've seen a ghost."

"I feel like I want to leave this place — but without my body. Is that possible or just madness?" Her voice was just a trail with a strength that was failing. "Voices — none making sense. They're all around, they want to tell me, but I can't hear them, whatever it is they want to say."

"There's nobody here." Silence fell solid, the air was burdened with stillness.

"But they are here, with us."

Saying these words, she fell to her knees.

"What's going on?"

"I can't breathe."

Claude felt for her pulse, kneeling next to her, and he thought her heartbeat barely throbbed.

"Take me out of here or I'll . . . die."

She grew limp before his eyes as she fainted in his arms.

"Natalie, Natalie," he cried out. With the weight of her body in his arms, he walked out of the cemetery. This place had jolted her into an emotional vortex.

By the truck he laid her body over the grass, hoping she would come to. He thought about the name, Elizabeth Bates, his girlfriend from the past.

He never thought the name would resurrect, especially linked to the person he had named Natalie, and least of all to someone who was dead. Who was this woman? He refused to believe in the coincidence linking to the dead.

12

Natalie was a dismal sight when she opened her eyes. The weight of her head lifted gently from his arm.

"Claude — "

"You gave me an awful scare." She trembled in his arms so he took the initiative of closing the zipper on her jacket. "Let's get in the car. Can you get up?"

She shook her head in a silent response.

Claude helped her into the Jeep, then went in through the driver side, sitting in front of the wheel, still confused.

"What was that all about?" he asked.

"I heard them."

"Whom? We were alone in there."

"Them."

He slammed the door of the vehicle shut, leaving him with the thought they were sealed on the inside of a vault.

"Whose the woman in the grave?" he asked.

He saw her shiver and then hide her face with her hands.

An undefined assault struck his heart pressing with an ominous premonition. What horrible secrets burned in the mind of the woman he loved?

"Look at me, Natalie. Who are you?"

She didn't answer when she turned toward him consumed by a dream-lit-gaze. He understood that her spirit roamed through memories perhaps too painful to surface all at once, but significant enough to fill her with specters drifting through the haze of yesterday. Tears swept passed her cheeks, showing her broken, like something precious and dear that had been damaged. He put his arms around her, unable to understand any further, and when she stopped crying, he drove away as though the devil chased them.

The next twenty minutes into town were spent in the silence of their thoughts, but once they hit the streets of Everett, he stopped in front of UPS as planned. He had to ship the paintings ahead of their flight. She remained inside the vehicle, sunken in her misery.

When he came back, he saw how she startled when he opened the door of the Jeep. Invisible walls had grown between them, and he was worried they were too sturdy to tumble over.

"I'm stopping at the police station," he said. "I need to know about you."

"Don't, Claude." Her eyes begged him to be patient.

"I'm sorry, but this has gone far enough."

"Give me time. I have to put it together."

"Are you hiding?" His voice was a stern reproach. "Or could it be that you're running away from someone? You might be ill, in need of professional help. You told me you heard voices."

"I'm not crazy. I wish I could run away from the past, but now I know it's going to catch up and devour me in its jaws. I'm having flashbacks, scenes from the past that don't make any sense, and they fill me with terrible unrest."

"I need to know your intentions," he pushed.

"My intentions?"

"What do you know about me?"

"I'm sorry, I don't understand?"

"Don't play games with me. I couldn't stand it." .

"Why do you think I taunt you?"

"How could you know about Elizabeth?"

Paranoia sank into his head.

"About Elizabeth?" she asked.

He wanted to yell his *Elizabeth,* but he didn't know if they were one and the same person. Last time he saw Liz they had a fight in Snoqualmie Pass, here in Washington state. In seconds his mind leaped into the past. No, this woman in the grave couldn't be Liz and least of all, Natalie couldn't be linked to his old girlfriend.

Her eyes watered, but she wiped them off before they had a chance to spill.

"Was that your sister, maybe . . . a friend?"

"I don't know, I don't know."

"Then why don't you want me to ask around? I'll inquire about this woman, this Elizabeth Bates from the cemetery. We'll ask about you."

"It's going to come on its own. I'm sure it will, but don't push me. I'm not a criminal. Please, give me time."

By the way it started to pour, he thought God was backing her, because the rain was crashing over the windshield, more like buckets of water pouring over the hood.

"It's against my better judgement, but the only reason why I'll do it your way it that I don't want you to stay alone in town, and I have to go. I couldn't wait for you if you had to stay."

With anyone else he would have dropped a complicated relationship, but he couldn't do it to Natalie. The day became night, with the threatening weather, and the streets emptied when folks found refuge from the elements. Black clouds lurked above them like ghost riders in the sky, and he felt enslaved to the fate that linked them, knowing he too was imprisoned by her unspoken memories.

They drove through town, down Main Street to the parking lot of the general store.

"The owner is the caretaker of my cabin. I have to let him know I'm leaving for New York. I'll be right back."

"You don't trust me, do you?"

Claude looked for her eyes, and when he found them, he saw a pool of sadness, so great that her pain choked inside his throat. She looked tragic and at the same time beautiful, and he realized that their future depended upon trust. With a wave of the hand and a nod of the head she urged him to go ahead, and as he ran inside the building, he knew he was going to take a great chance with his feelings.

Inside, Tim McGuire, the owner, was unpacking cartons of produce behind the counter. Far from being friends, they had an understanding. He could have called from his cellular to acknowledge his departure, but temptation dared him to come inside.

"Do you need provisions?" The old man looked at him over gold spectacles sitting on the bridge of his wide nose. His high forehead and receding temples made him look wiser than a scholar, but Claude knew nothing about him because he had always considered him someone so unimportant.

"No, I'm leaving today, Tim."

Claude walked to the aisle where the bottles of water were stored inside a refrigerator and took two.

"I'll send Lee to close down this weekend," said Tim when Claude came back to the register.

"There's no rush. I won't be back for a while." He hesitated for a moment then went on. "I wondered if you know about a woman missing — anyone whose disappeared from these parts?"

"Nope, I can't say that I do."

"I found a woman who lost her memory, perhaps in an accident. She's been staying with me, but now I'm leaving and I don't know — "

"I'm sorry." The store owner scratched his head. "We're a dot on the map. With a population less than seven-thousand, we know everyone by face if not a name. When the tourists are in town, we know who they are because town people stay around. Nope, people don't get lost around here, nor forgotten if they leave. If anyone was looking for a woman, I'd know about it sooner than the cops."

"I'm going to drive into Seattle with her."

"That's a good idea." The ring of the cashier told Claude the man was ready to get paid. "Are you all right? Lost your balance there."

Claude felt woozy when he reached for his wallet in the pocket of his jeans and had to hold on to the counter. He gasped when he drowned the question in the pit of his heart, *Would you look inside my car? I have the woman with me.* Tim wasn't interested in his dilemma, but he paused for a breathless second when it dawned on him that those buried in the cemetery had to be from Everett. Elizabeth Bates must have lived among the town's people, and Tim had to know her. Natalie knew her, if not from here, from somewhere, but how did it all fit?

Claude took the money out of his wallet and paid for the water.

"If you hear about anyone looking for a woman, will you give me a call in New York?"

"Why sure," Tim said in an even tone. "If it means that much to you, of course, I will. I don't think we ever had anyone disappear. Ours is a quiet town. We have no crime, teenage pregnancy is low and child abuse is unheard of. Wives don't poison their husbands, either, and if we don't close our windows at night everyone will know about the fight at home."

"It means a lot to me," he said in a grave tone. "Reverse the charges but please, call me."

Back inside his vehicle, he jammed the keys in the ignition, tires screeching as he made his getaway, wondering about the name of Elizabeth Bates.

13

Foreign faces walked through the crowded airport on what had turned out to be one of the warmest days of June. Claude gathered the luggage from the terminal, and on the way out they met their limousine driver holding a cardboard sign reading "Aumont." They waited for a few minutes by the curb outside the terminal, and Claude made a few phone calls before driving off toward Manhattan.

In first class, the comfort of money was less tiring, even though Natalie looked weary-eyed and taciturn, so quiet that the turmoil of her thoughts was louder and more complex than the sounds of a philharmonic orchestra. The road into the city seemed short to them, nested inside the car with its air-conditioning. Natalie fixed intently on the road, avoiding his eyes, turning into the shadow of the woman she was once in Washington.

They pulled in by the early evening, into the stalk of sunset upon a dying day. Like the preamble of what was to come, angry hues of crimson-orange mixed in agony, while the sun set ablaze until it sunk into the western skyline. Mountains were replaced by skyscrapers, a distant world from Washington.

His watchful eyes searched for her mood as they took the elevator to the penthouse, but she didn't flinch when they walked into the luxury of his abode. White marble floors and titanium white walls opened to a modern space that was a display of wealth and power. A wall of windows allowed the view of the trees in Central Park and the small sign that lit into the limelight with the name Tavern On the Green. He surrounded himself with art, as a large Picasso of immeasurable price hung in the foyer entrance, followed by a row of impressionist paintings.

"They're exquisite," she said, sitting in on the arm of a chair.

"I told you I'm a collector."

"Yes, you did." Her voice lacked emotion. "You live here?"

"It's one of my homes. I have another in Paris and one in Hong Kong."

"Do you collect people, too?"

"Of course I don't."

Sinking his hands into the bottom of the pockets of his pants, he stood in front of her, dressed in a light beige, linen blend summer jacket and pants. A black tee shirt tucked inside his slacks contrasted against the light color of his suit. For all he saw in her reaction to his wealth, she could have lived in a mansion because she wasn't impressed by anything she saw, except perhaps the art work.

"You should have told me."

"I didn't want my money to get in the way of our relationship."

"Do you think I want any of this? Is it that simple for you?"

"It is," he said.

He saw her move to the edge of a chair.

"Your lifestyle has downfalls," she whispered.

"Being a business phenomenon isolates me. I didn't want money to confuse your choice to follow me."

"I couldn't care less about your wealth."

"I'm not saying you would, but it's the price I pay for success."

"I'm not a fortune hunter." Her demeanor was sure, her voice steady. "When I hesitated in Washington, I did it because of the hindrance in my memory, not because I lacked a feeling."

"Don't get upset. You were a stranger."

"Am I still a stranger?" The tilt of her chin was proud, her facial expression alive, like an exotic bird sitting on a perch, waiting to take flight.

"No, you're not," he said with regret.

"I can see why your world is difficult. Faces must confuse you, not every smile offers the truth, but I will never be a fake." She got up and walked toward the wall of windows, glancing at the park across the street. "The cemetery was an eery place. I'm not sure about what happened there, but if you have doubts, then I'll go."

"You ask me to trust you, but there's a lot you haven't told me."

"Don't you know why I'm here?"

He found her eyes and felt insignificant. Then without further words, he saw her walk toward the door. The suitcases were his, and there was nothing of hers. Moving swiftly, he cut her off.

"Don't go. I didn't mean to hurt you."

"Stop giving me the runaround. You think my memory is just a hoax, that I know who I am. You're implying that I want to swindle you and that I knew or figured out that you're a wealthy man and that I'm here chasing after . . .

whatever you're worth. That's insulting, don't you think?"

He couldn't tell her that the name in the grave brought disorder into his life. Elizabeth Bates was a closed chapter that had reopened. To imagine a connection between a dead woman and his old girlfriend filled him with a question. Ignorance made people vulnerable, and he didn't like the odds from under. It could be that if he looked into a phone book there would be a hundred Elizabeth Bates's but he had never stopped to look.

"Dammit! I want to believe you're an honest woman."

"Have faith in me or let me go."

He stood in front of her, knowing he didn't want to live without her. His instincts told him to trust her. She had trembled under his kisses, and she had forged in the pyre of his want. No, it couldn't be pretense.

"Where would you go?" he asked, taking her gently by the arm.

"There's a world outside your door."

"But it's not our world."

"I'm not sure if I fit into your life. You have too much and I own nothing, less than any other woman. Staying would be like walking over quick sand."

"I could unearth your past and the secret behind the grave in Washington with the money I have."

"I imagine you could."

"You're my last hope in the truth between two people."

"If that's what I'm supposed to be, then believe in me, because you're the reason for my presence. I followed you wanting the man, not his fortune," she said in a vibrant tone. "I came because you asked me, because you need me. Your assets have appeal, but I can do with much less."

"You want a lot, more than any other woman wanted out of me." He let go of her.

"I want you, but if that's a lot, then you're right. I do want everything."

He stood in front of her, knowing he could lose her forever.

"In all honesty, I have never met someone like you. What is it about you that drives me into your own madness, into the passion of wanting you against my better judgement?"

"I think you're used to getting what you want and that includes people. I'm saying 'no' to you because I don't want to be your object of art. I love you, Claude, and I need to feel the man I discovered in Washington, not the cold and distant you that has been lurking one step ahead of me. I couldn't stand to be with you like this."

"You're not a thing, but someone special. That's why I need to know about your past, about the woman who has changed the man I used to be." He touched her face. "Stay, stay with me."

She closed her eyes and he took her in his arms, crushing her into his body, knowing she had seeped too deep already. Her face warmed his cheek and then he noticed the wetness that touched his skin.

"You're crying," he said over her lips. "Please, don't."

Her nose was red, and she couldn't talk, trying to quiet her mood, but worse than anything else was the doleful look in her eyes.

"I don't want anything from you other than the feeling you have for me," she whispered, ". . . as little or as much as your heart can spare."

He brought her into the kitchen and made her sit by the counter. From the refrigerator door he filled a glass with water, then urged her to drink.

"I have to believe in you," he said. "I know it now."

"Hold me, Claude and don't ever let me go."

He did as she asked.

"I'm falling in love with you, despite the devils inside my head. Maybe you were right when you said I need you."

"I'm here for both of us," she said.

Forgetting Washington, the cemetery, and the questions left unanswered, he took her into his bedroom and closed the lights without unpacking.

14

Before he left the penthouse, Claude convinced Natalie to take money to buy clothing because she couldn't continue wearing his oversized clothes and her hiking boots. She swore to pay back the debt once she found work, but he knew it was unnecessary because to him it was a trivial amount. When he went out, angry heat paved the streets of Manhattan as though a furnace burned underneath the city. People were like insects, crowding every inch of space, crawling out of their burrows, unable to tolerate the warmth that spread in waves. He was grateful for the air conditioner inside the cab en route to the law offices of Shearson & Gaffney.

When Claude sat with his lawyer, he told him about the encounter in Washington that caused his delay, about the woman who had reached into his life, about her mysterious forgetfulness, but not about his doubts nor the alarm when the name of Elizabeth Bates emerged from his past.

"You have elicited my curiosity," said his attorney with a wolfish, carnal smile which swallowed his face. "Your innate characteristic has been to underutilize the pleasures of the opposite sex. It's about time, don't you think?"

"She's a lot more than a simple affair," said Claude.

"Hmm," he placed his hands behind the head, "You've gone head over heels?"

"Seems that way, doesn't it?"

"It's good to take a diversion from the rat race, but what's so special about this girl to make you change your modus operandum? You were away for a month. Most unlike you, don't you think?."

Brandon sat behind his desk, tilting back on the swivel chair. He was as close as Claude could call a friend.

"It must be time for a change."

"I never knew why you worked so hard. No kids, no wife. If I were you,

I would enjoy my money with a different woman every night." Brandon smiled. "I'm glad you found a spin from the routine."

"What about our deal in France? That's why I'm here," said Claude, getting down to business.

"Charles Villadas called me from Paris. The French want to sign in two weeks. I'm sure you'll fine tune the details, like whose going to be in charge of the set up, but I need to do my own review of contracts, building permits, leases."

"Seems straight forward. They want to fly commercial airlines by remote control and my software gives them the ability to do so with great ease. They'll pay me and we'll give them what they need. I've picked the staff for the project already and we have the perfect location to start operations. Way ahead of you buddy."

"I like the way you see things but I'm sure you want a quick in-and-out without glitches, and that's why I'm here. If they agree to our deal I want the landlord to give us tax exempt status as a foreign company doing commerce in France."

"Europe is a different beast, but I'm sure you'll do well for me."

Claude had worked for twelve months putting this deal together, and now it was panning out.

"Coffee?" Brandon buzzed and a young woman came in. "How do you want yours?"

"No sugar, dark," said Claude.

A redhead came in moments later with a cordial smile that went no further than Brandon. Something changed in the features of her face, imperceptible to others, but he knew people, and it was a brazen glow with a sultry greeting. The woman knew how her boss liked his brew, evident when she left with Claude's choice and no further directions for the other coffee. He noticed that the female staff at the law firm could have been hand picked for a harem, beautiful as they were, and he understood that Brandon was the sultan.

While they waited for the coffee, Claude said, "I have a favor to ask."

"What's up?"

"I want to take Natalie to the city opera tonight. I know you have a client who can get tickets at the last minute."

"Tickets for two? Tonight?" Brandon rolled back on his chair, rubbing his forehead with a hand.

"Orpheus — "

"Oh boy, you cut tough deals. I'll have to slice somebody's throat to get them."

"You're a miracle worker if you manage to oblige me on this short notice," he smiled. "You'll impress me."

"Dammit, it takes more than that to impress Claude Aumont," Brandon chuckled. "But let me see if I can impress myself." A sense of seriousness silenced the moment as Brandon arched an eyebrow. "You seem sincere about this woman. Should you allow yourself to get involved when you don't know anything about her past?"

The secretary came back with two glass mugs, handing each man his coffee and leaving.

"Trust me on this one,"said Claude. "I know enough to want her."

"Be smart about it." Brandon took a sip. "Never show your upper hand."

"Are you being protective?"

"Just cautious."

"What do I know about any of the women I meet? They tell me whatever concoction they choose to fabricate — most of it — to impress me."

"You're infatuated," said Brandon. "Her motives could be calculating. In a plot to access your billions, a woman could prepare a well-orchestrated scheme to hook you, especially if she's as beautiful as you say. This Natalie sounds like perfect bait. Conveniently, she has global amnesia, not partial but complete. Doesn't it seem odd that she would land out of nowhere?"

Claude thought about the night of the storm, the episode in the cemetery, and about the name that was revived from his past.

"I'll keep an eye open," he smiled.

"Well, enjoy her without surrendering. That's my favorite rule with women."

Leaving the Wall Street area, Claude took a cab uptown. At the firm he was inundated with meetings and telephone conferences as CEO of Transworld, but before long he asked his secretary to call Pilar Haydig to his office. Whenever he flew away from his post, she took charge with the zealousness that made her rise among the others. She was his most trusted employee and his lover.

"Is the system operational in D.C.?" He spoke from behind his desk as she walked in.

"It's running smoothly," said Pilar. "The ground beacons are set up on board ships, and our government has moved into the Middle East, Asia, and South America. Bill said the computers tested well from whatever strategic location they were placed. The President was grateful for your impromptu appearance at Camp David six weeks ago. They thought your personal touch was nice, but . . . can't you ask how I'm doing before the business?"

"So how are you?" He looked up and smiled as she sat in front of him.

"You're an interesting man, Claude."

Divorced twice, Pilar had an attitude about men. She rose in the corporate ladder of the firm because of persistence and because she never quit, something he thought was a great quality. She brought in good clients who made money for him. Her male counterparts found her sexy, but at the same time too smart as a woman. However, brains didn't intimidate Claude, they were just another asset and she was cunning enough to downplay her strong character not to antagonize his.

Their affair was convenient, as she was a master in discretion. Both of them knew that their relationship was more physical than anything else, and that gave them space.

"I hoped for a call from you during your absence."

"I knew you could handle the situation," he said. "Besides, you could have called yourself. You have my cell number."

"I was busy."

"Or maybe you didn't need to call me, right?" He cleared his throat.

"I missed you." Pilar stood up and came around his side of the desk, sitting on the edge. The skirt of her suit pulled up, showing off her legs high on the thigh. "Let's go out tonight. I'll treat us to dinner and then we can go to your apartment."

After three years of working together, love was never a part of her proposition. She was a businesswoman, even with their relationship and she had needs like him. From the first, she set the record straight: no children, no more marriages and no commitments, all of which suited him fine. But now that Natalie had come upon his life, everything was different.

"I can't," he said. "I have a lot of work today."

"Then I'll stay after the others have gone, and we'll use your private suite."

He looked toward the door at the far end of his office, and her gaze followed there. A studio adjacent to his office for those nights when it was too late to go home folded into a niche of pleasure many times. Pilar knew it, too.

She slipped off the jacket of her suit, revealing the lacy camisole that fell carelessly over her breasts. Through the light fabric he saw the bra grab the voluptuous mounds of flesh that were a pagan offering of joy. Before he could do anything, she was sitting on his lap, throwing her arms around him.

Like him, she was challenged by power and money, but until today, he never stopped to think about her feelings and for the first time, looking into the spark of her black pupils, he thought there was more than just a physical need. On second thought he was probably flattering himself because she was too clever to fall in love with him.

With Natalie in his life, it was too late to sort it out. He slipped from under her hold, but she insisted, and before he knew it, her hands were over his crotch.

"Stop it," he said, pushing her away.

"What's wrong?" She said the words so pointedly that he almost trembled. "You never stopped me before."

"You're beautiful and smart. Why don't you aspire for a normal relationship, not the casual sex I give you."

Her eyes narrowed. "Something's different in you."

"Nothing's different, but I need to talk about us. Our relationship has to stop. You deserve better."

"Cut the bullshit." She stood up and walked toward the far end of the room, putting on her clothing. "I've never asked you for a commitment. Why now the scruples?"

"Because I need it to stop. I don't want to feel like I owe you an explanation if I want to be with someone else."

"When have I asked you for them? You've never asked about other men, and I certainly haven't locked you in a jail." She lit a cigarette while waves of smoke came out of her mouth. He thought she smoked more than she should, but Pilar had told him nicotine diffused her nerves. "I thought you went alone to Washington, or did you take someone with you?"

"You know I don't take anyone out there."

"Yes, yes, it's a blasphemy if you do." She smacked her lips.

"I go out there to unwind, commune with nature."

"So why now this clean slate for us?"

"You said it, we have no commitments. We should have tried for greater depth, but we're too much alike, working, trying to get ahead." He lied when he said, "I meant to ask you before I left on my trip. I want the keys to my apartment."

"You want them back?"

"It shouldn't surprise you." Claude was toying with a pen between his fingers. "Things haven't been very good between us."

"Can I change that?" Her eyes taunted him. "Absence made me realize we are one of a kind. "

He cut her off. "It didn't work then, why should it work now?"

Pilar pushed back the blond strands of hair that fell to the side of her face. He sensed he was hurting her, but there was nothing he could do to change what had to be done. She put on her jacket.

"Uncommited sex is convenient and certainly more exiting than a constant partner. Keep it in mind, darling."

He could never betray Natalie.

"It's over."

"I'll drop off your keys before lunch time." Her voice snapped.

"I hope we can work as always."

"I'm not stupid."

She was practical, and he admired her for that. A valuable employee like her was difficult to replace. He stood up and walked toward her.

"It wasn't you, Pilar. This is my fault."

She didn't answer, but the tension in her face slipped off with a wave of smoke out of her nostrils. With a hand she held her cigarette, with the other she smoothed her suit. Then he saw her move closer and slump over the couch.

"You're a great lover, when you have the time," she said. "I hope when you get over this phase you'll look for me again. I'm not a complicated woman."

"Thank you. One last thing before you leave."

"What's that?"

"I need to get the phone number of the detectives who tracked down the corporate spies for us."

He pushed the ashtray close to her. He hated ashes on his desk.

"What for? Do we have a hacker?"

"It's personal this time. An old girlfriend of mine, I want to find her."

"Anyone I know?"

"We broke up ten years ago."

"Why now?"

"I need to know what's become of her."

"Sentimentality doesn't become you. There's something else."

Pilar knew him. He pulled on the cuffs of his shirt as gold cufflinks shone underneath the sleeves of his navy blue jacket. Made to fit by his tailor, his suit matched his corporate style, sober, cut to fit. She got up, putting out the cigarette in the ashtray and then came next to him, centering the knot of his tie. A blink, then a long stare, searching, curious, because she was a woman and perhaps a scorned lover.

"Why would you want to find someone from your past while you give me the pink slip? Humm, female intuition tells me it's all related." She was about to leave. "I'll call you with the number."

"There's more," he said raising his voice.

"Yes, yes, I know, the keys too."

"I need a neurologist. You're very good researching people." She took a harsh glare at him.

"You have uh, a headache?"

"Humor doesn't become you."

"Then?"

"He has to be knowledgeable treating amnesia. I need the very best in New York, not just any neurologist, do you understand?"

"Amnesia," she repeated, eyeing him from head to toe. Pilar took another cigarette from the pack in her jacket, lighting up through a cloud of smoke.

"You're full of surprises these days. You turn your vacation into a month retreat, then you need a detective to track down a girl you haven't seen in ten years, and now you want a doctor."

Claude broke eye contact. "It's too complicated to explain."

"I believe you," she said with an icy chill in her voice. She walked out of his office without saying anything else.

Work became the Himalayas, despite all that was pending because concentration failed him. Later on that day, after Brandon called him to let him know a messenger was on his way with the theater tickets for that evening, he called Natalie on the phone. The anticipation of meeting her reached a climax, as he walked out of his private office at five o'clock, carrying a portfolio of papers in a leather binder.

"You're leaving, Mr. Aumont?" his secretary asked.

Until that evening, he never left that early, but his new lifestyle was full of surprises, even for him.

"Yes, Betty. Seems unusual that I should leave before you, doesn't it?"

From the office to his apartment was a fifteen minute ride. Once at home, he loosened the tie around his neck and served himself a drink from the decanter of scotch, a single malt batch, from the bar. He went into his bedroom when he didn't see Natalie in the open space of the living area.

There, he found her dressed in a black cocktail dress, her breasts showing through the cleavage of her outfit, her hair up, her lips ruby red and her eyes forewarning of her mood. His heart stopped as the dazzle in her eyes took him by surprise. She came close, standing in high heels, showing off her legs under the nylon mesh. She took the drink from his hand and dabbed her lips with the scotch.

"Hmm, too strong for me." She left the glass over the night table. "Can you close the rest of my zipper?"

Claude walked behind her, pulling the zipper up, pausing afterward to kiss her bare shoulders.

"God, you look fabulous. I got so used to you in my oversized clothes. I never thought you'd — "

Out of his pants pocket he took a small box and opened it to show two karats of perfect diamond studs with a matching solitaire for her neck, twice the size of the earpieces.

"They're superb!"

"Much less than you."

"Why?" She looked at him in awe.

"We can say, I know you have no jewelry."

"I can't take them." Natalie sighed. "Your gift is too expensive."

"We won't talk about money tonight. Promise?"

She looked away. "Your money smolders me."

In the blink of an eye, during lunch time, he had bought the platinum ensemble that cost him seventy-five thousand dollars. He did it for the pleasure of having her glow that night, but now he realized that she was more glamorous than his gift.

"You didn't take the money for modeling. Please, keep my present." With a finger he raised her chin, forcing her to look at him. "Coming home has no equal because you're here. It's been a long time since I felt whole, and it's because of you."

"When two people love each other, they don't have to repay what's given freely."

"Then by the same token, you don't owe me anything," he said.

"Yesterday, doubt entered your mind and it ripped me apart that you could think I wanted — "

"You're the only woman who doesn't want to spend my money," he said smiling back at her, and then holding her at arms length. "I was a fool having doubts about your illness or you. I've lived distrusting people for so long that I can't recognize when someone pure of heart comes along."

"It's not altogether your fault. Everything about me is so strange."

"You can't help anything that's happened or the past that comes back to you."

"If you change your mind about having me around, I'll understand."

"Like a boy, I could hardly wait to come home knowing you were here. I don't want other women." he shook his head. "I hope you can put up with my type of man, because I'm not easy to tolerate."

"You're just a man with a past that has not healed."

She tilted on the tip of her toes and placed her arms around his neck leaving a kiss on his lips. Her touch was a soft caress, but sensuous enough to fill him with her want. Natalie slid his jacket off and unbuttoned his shirt, her fingers moved through the hairs on his chest, with baby kisses tickling his neck. She was on her knees, when he realized how easy it would be to lose himself in the moment, but he remembered Brandon's effort to get him the tickets.

For him, Natalie was the epitome of a woman who could vanish the waves of indifference from his life. She had spirituality, she could deliver him into the pinnacle of metaphysical discussions and then drive him into delirium with her femininity bottled like inebriating perfume.

"Let me wash up, Darling." He pulled away gently. "The opera is at eight. We must hurry if we're going to arrive on time."

"Then let me help you undress," she said, her eyes full of sultry.

With premeditated cadence she slipped off his shirt, then sat him on the edge of the bed, pushing with her body. She bent over, undoing the shoe laces of his Bally's, and he filled with the movements of her hands as they slid over his body, touching him with subtle premeditation. She rolled down his socks, tilting closer, allowing him a peek to the creamy white contour of her breast.

Undressed down to his slacks, he pressed against her body, kissing her hard on the mouth, then taking her by the hand, he brought her up. Any thing further would make him forget about the opera and the rest of his plans because lust and love mingled as her smile promised him a night of immeasurable delight.

"Don't go," he said in his deepest voice. "Stay in my life for a very long time. You're my gift of Incense and Mir, gold which can't be bought."

"Having met you, I could never leave unless you bid me away."

"Promise, no lies between us."

"No lies," she said.

He swallowed. "Don't change your mind no matter what you remember, even if you belong to someone else."

"I belong to you, Claude." She stared into his eyes. "There will never be room for anyone else."

"Then wear the diamonds I gave you and think of me every time you put them on."

"I'll do it because you want me to, but remember, all I need is you."

An hour later, they walked out of his apartments, a few blocks from Lincoln Center. They rushed toward the open plaza, past the fountain spraying water because they were going to be late if they didn't hurry. Yet nothing could dampen the magic of that evening because they were together. The warmth of that night invited romance as the lights of the city reflected in the glimmer of Natalie's eyes.

During the performance Claude watched how she submerged into the myth of Orpheus, the story about a man who journeyed through the underworld to rescue his beloved Euridice from the God of Death. After the opera, they ate at a dinner club. The evening had no end as the music entered into their mood, into the pleasure brought about when a man and a woman are right for each other.

The quiet of his bedroom was the final destination of a fantastic escapade. He grabbed the bottle of Moet chilling in the refrigerator and filled two glasses. Alone and at the end of the evening, he made a private toast.

"To us, Natalie."

"To the feeling of this night," she whispered.

In the privacy of their bedroom, he helped her with the dress again, only this time to take it off. Her dress fell to the floor, leaving her in stockings and a garter belt which filled him with playfulness. How naive of him to bring home the papers inside his briefcase because the gentle giving of her love had dismantled all his plans to work. The secret of her beauty belonged to him, feeling swollen with the most devastating hunger for a woman.

Moonlight beams entered through the windows, bathing with its bewitching light. Love had transcended beyond life for Orpheus, and like the man in the Greek myth, Claude was captive to the fate of a woman. He would follow into the depths of the underworld, just as Orpheus did for Euridice, empowered by his needs for Natalie if it came that he should challenge death for her. Only she could tame the longing in his soul as they fused into the same breath.

"I love you," he whispered, looking into her face.

She gasped under his body, caught by the fever of the moment when her body filled with his. Theirs was the frenzy of a powerful feeling, spawned from the dawn of time.

Touched by the truth between them, he would fight to retain her against any mortal who came between them, against life and even death if it crossed their path. He also knew that he would wait until she was ready to tell him, as her memory came back.

15

Pilar barged into Claude's office, holding an envelope while Betty took dictation in front of his desk. Betty raised her eyes from the pad, but the rest of her didn't move a millimeter, like a pole stuck in cement and it bothered him twice as much that she took the intrusion so non-chalantly.

"Claude, I received an invitation to the mayor's fund raiser, two thousand dollars per couple." Pilar stood in front of him, flapping the cream-colored envelope against the palm of her hands. "It's a black tie affair at the Waldorf. Did you get one too?"

"I'll continue later, Betty." His voice sounded as flat as he could make it.

The middle aged secretary stood up and disappeared.

"I know about the ball," he said with a curt voice.

"It's darn flattering that they would place me into their VIP list."

"When my door is closed, knock before you enter, especially if Betty's not at her desk to tell you who's in here. Don't barge into my office again."

Pilar swiped the smile off her face. "And what's the matter with you today?"

"Nothing's the matter. It's my office, and you have no right coming in here like you owned part of it."

"All right, all right, don't get huffy with me. I'll try to knock next time." She dropped onto a couch. "A hefty amount of money, isn't it?"

Claude raised an eyebrow.

"The money is for charity, Pilar. If you want to be a player, then you have to roll the dice."

"Sweetie, you're so profound these days." She lit a cigarette.

"Aren't you afraid of lung cancer?" he asked.

"Nope." She shrugged her shoulders while she inhaled even deeper. "I know, the game is about people schmoozing and these folks are good aces in our pocket. Hmm, use it as a tax deduction while we have a blast. Is that it?"

"I'm certain the list of guests will be a splendid one."

"You can pick me up at seven."

He smiled.

"Not this time. I told you it's *fini*."

"Don't tell me you would rather go alone?" She sat up, stretching her neck.

"I'm taking someone else."

Her crossed legs bounced with restless staccato.

"Is she my replacement?" Her voice betrayed her disappointment. "Is that why you wanted my keys to your place?"

"Theatrics don't become you, and you're too suave for this."

Pilar gave him a devouring look.

"Don't worry Claude. This will be my last."

"You're excellent with business, and if I allowed for your temptation it's because I was convinced you could handle it. If I miscalculated, I stand to lose double."

"And if I told you that you mean something to me?"

The sunlight hit the corner of his desk as it came through a wall of windows. The waves of smoke from her cigarette were swirls of gray defusing into space.

"Tell me you're kidding, right?"

"I got married twice, only the first time for love." She dropped the envelope on his desk. "It's just hard to let you go."

He could see that her heart sank.

"Be my friend, Pilar."

"People like us don't have friends. We don't have the time to culture relationships, and as we climb the ladder we're envied and hated. My marriages fell apart because the men in my life expected a housewife, mother and lover. Disappointment comes when others realize we feed on the monster inside us — ambition and success. What's going to happen when your girlfriend starts to miss you because you're not the type to settle down?"

What he didn't tell Pilar was that he was thinking of stepping down as CEO of Transworld. He thought it was important to slow down for the sake of his relationship with Natalie. Frequent trips, long days, and new markets to acquire — an emotional continuum would be in the way — and she would linger into a secondary role.

Pilar would make a good replacement for him. She deserved to be one of the candidates because she was smart and worked hard, but he had to be careful because she was a rejected woman, and scorn could make her dangerous.

"Who is she?"

He was caught off guard by her question. "Who's who?"

"The woman you're bringing to the ball?"

"Are you sure you want to know?"

He saw her nod, while she stamped out the cigarette and uncrossed her legs.

"It might be more serious than you think," he said. "She's the one. I'm thinking about getting married, about taking her for my wife."

"Where did you meet?" Pilar had her mouth open.

"I met her in Washington, and we came back together."

"You scare me, Claude. You just met her."

"Natalie feels as though she has been there forever. How long do you I have to be with someone to know they're the perfect mate?"

"Is she someone I know, or maybe heard about?" Pilar lit another cigarette.

"No. You don't know her, and she's a *nobody,* not a penny to her name."

"How the hell did this woman gain so much access into your life?" Pilar ground her teeth so hard her jaw could have snapped.

Claude sat back in his executive chair, crossing his hands behind his neck. He thought of Natalie most of his waking hours. The continuum of Seattle had followed him to New York, and he was happier than ever before.

"When you think of me, count her in," he said with absolute resolve. "She's different from all the women I have met, including you."

"I won't take that as an insult."

"She wants me for the man inside the shell, not for my money."

"How can you be so sure? You said yourself, she's pennyless."

"You're shrewd, Pilar, and that's why you're an asset to Transworld.. You're as ambitious as I, and that's not bad, but trust me when I tell you that I found someone different. She's made me change with her passion about life, taking every second for what it's worth, looking not for the grand moments that arrive rare and few, but for the common ordinary happenings that come every day."

"Men are such fools, especially when they think they are in love." She smashed the butt of her cigarette in the ashtray because she'd smoked it too fast. "We're a lot alike. We like money and power, but I'm not a hypocrite about it. I'm not ashamed to tell you that there was nothing more delectable than spending your money when we were an item. Pay me well, and I'll continue to be as efficient as always."

"You'll get a bonus for the deal in France, but remember, I put in longer hours than anyone else at the firm."

She looked up as her voice filled with mocking. "Suddenly, there's a vulnerable quality in the impenetrable Aumont."

"I don't like your tone. Your rights to me are over."

"Sorry," she said between teeth. "Just think, your girlfriend could be smarter than I, playing the ingenue while all along your money is her appealing substrate."

Claude got up from his chair, feeling the flow of blood through his temples.

"You're a viper. Don't trample over Natalie because I'll forget every thing that's been between us." He didn't raise his voice but his words were charged by the adrenaline that pumped through him.

A silence between them served as a moment to calm down.

"I'm not sure if this new Claude Aumont becomes you but here," she said, giving him a card taken out of the pocket in her slacks. "It's the neurologist you asked me for. I did my homework, and he's very good."

"Thanks," he said.

"Then I'll see you at the Waldorf."

He pulled his glasses from under a stack of paper to read the name in the card, Moises Tananbaum, MD.

"Yes, sure," he mumbled, distracted by his thoughts. Pilar had written the date of the appointment on the back: Friday, August thirtieth, a month away.

Natalie had not regained her memory, and he wondered if she ever would. He realized the date fell on the Labor Day weekend, something which was fine, because it would give him a chance to start the weekend early. He typed his agenda into his computer and as he did, he knew Pilar was right. He was a changed man. Work had taken second stage.

Pilar left him alone but they would meet in an hour to review the production agenda with the board of trustees. He looked for the remote control which opened a panel on the far wall in front of him. He sat back, listening to the stock market channel on a wall of plasma screens. Earlier that day CNN had recorded an interview of him reflecting on the report issued earlier that week where his company topped quarter expectations.

From the drawer on the side of his desk, Claude pulled out a folder. A letter from the President of the United States thanking him for availing his technology to safeguard national defense. He looked at it once more, savoring a smile.

Right before his meeting, he dialed home and heard Natalie's familiar voice.

"It's me," he said. "Are you busy?"

"I spent half a day looking for a job."

"Did you find one?"

"Without a social security number, I'm not alive."

"I've told you it doesn't matter," he said.

"It does for me. I want to have something, even if it's minuscule compared to what you have." There was a silence at her end. "I miss Washington, and I miss you."

He knew what she meant, because he also missed the intensity of their days together. Long hours at the office were the impediment that kept them apart.

"How about dinner?"

"Sure."

"There's a place near home, Ramiro's. Take a cab and meet me there at six thirty. I'm going to try to leave here earlier tonight."

"I'll see you then."

"Natalie?" he wasn't sure if she were still there.

"Yes?"

"I made an appointment for you with a Dr. Tananbaum from Mt. Sinai." There was another silence. "Think about it, darling. It's time to do something about your illness. I need to find out about you."

He could never imagine wanting to be free of her.

"I'll see you later, okay?"

"Yes "

The click at the other end signaled she hung up. Aware that members of his staff were waiting for him at a meeting, he had to go.

16

The mental anguish of being late stressed him out of proportion. It was one of many difficult days, and tomorrow he was leaving for France. Mirrors along a long wall made gave the restaurant a greater depth, but in reality it was much smaller. The illusion in perception made him look at tables and people that weren't there, but when he saw Natalie, he made it to the table without the maitre-de who was busy with a couple. He felt responsible for the bored look on her face as she sat toying with the rim of a water goblet.

"I got caught up at the office, forgive me." His voice was deep and warm, lamenting being an hour late.

The bus boy brought a basket of buns, bread sticks and butter on a small dish. He went to retrieve the place setting for Natalie but Claude told him his friend would be eating too. Then the boy filled both goblets with water and left him a wine list.

"You're a busy man." She shook off his tardiness, forgiving in generous acceptance.

"I don't like to make you wait." For a few seconds he studied the face in front of him. "You're too impressive to sit alone, waiting for me or any other man. Remember it always." He interlocked their fingers over the table. "Have you ordered?"

"No, I was waiting for you."

"I hope you're hungry, because I'm starved." Taking back his hands, he spread butter on a warm piece of bread. Instead of eating it himself, he passed it to her and then went on to prepare another one for himself. "They make a great Paella, two can eat out of a single serving: lobster, scallops, shrimp, chicken, chorizo, mixed in a saffron rice."

"Sounds delicious, I'll have some of it."

"Did you pack?"

"I did your luggage and mine."

He smiled back, noticing the diamond studs he had given her two weeks ago.

The waiter came and he ordered. After a while the man came back with the food and a bottle of wine.

"I'll serve myself," Claude said, looking at the steaming clay pot between himself and Natalie.

"Why are you smiling?" she asked.

"I can't help it," he replied amused. "Being with you makes me want to smile, but if you must know, it's common knowledge that people eat the way they make love. I would never marry a skimpy eater."

"You're teasing me." Her face turned red as she looked at the plate she had served in front of her, it was a mound of food.

They talked while they ate.

"Where did you go, looking for this job of yours?"

"Hmm, I walked most of the city, took a bus, and at random made some stops. If nothing else, it was a good way to discover Manhattan. I visited a lot of coffee shops, some of the restaurants."

"Why don't you work for me? I could use a smart woman by my side."

"And owe you more?"

"Silly — " he said. "It'd be easier to let everything fall into place."

Natalie looked up and found his eyes.

"Something unusual happened today."

"And what was that?"

"I found myself in front of a brownstone, in Washington Square."

"Washington Square? God, I haven't been there in ages."

He rubbed his chin with a hand, making a connection and a mental count. Liz lived there. At that moment he remembered he never got the number to the detective agency because Pilar never gave it to him.

"I knew I had lived there before." Apprehension flared in the tone of her voice. "I remembered the apartment on the inside. I'm so sure, it's the way I recall it, small, not too much furniture but full of books — bookshelves made of white pine boards covering the entire living room walls."

"You were a student in New York?"

"Yes." She returned a melancholic glance. "And I lived there."

"Alone?"

"Elizabeth, Elizabeth was there."

"The dead woman in Washington?" His hands dropped over the table.

"Yes."

He stopped eating because he thought he was going to choke on his next bite. His Liz couldn't be dead, buried in the outskirts of Everett.

"The cemetery — will you tell me about what happened there?"

Natalie looked away. Her eyelids blinked as the expression of her face lost all apprehension. Her voice became steady, organized as though she read lines off a paper.

"Elizabeth lived in the town near your cabin, and her parents buried her there, an untimely accident because she was young." Natalie found his eyes. "She was pregnant, but she never told her boyfriend about the little girl who was born, beautiful and sweet."

"Go on, Natalie."

"She wanted to hide for a few months, until the birth of her child. Afterwards, she meant to go back to him. As her pregnancy progressed, she understood more and more that sharing the news with him would have been the right thing to do, but she made a mistake and thus changed the future. The secret of the child belonged to two people rather than just one, but she died before she could ever tell him."

"Died? How?"

"At childbirth. She bled from a complication."

"Does he know she's dead or that he has a kid?"

"No. The wrong choices worked against them."

"You knew him?"

"I guess I must have known him too. Yes, he was a good man, only he was lost, confused by the choices in front of him."

Mesmerized by her tale, he looked in awe. He felt saddened by the death of a woman he did not know, or did he? Intrigued by the fact that his old girlfriend had the same name, he wanted to know more.

"Do you know the man's name, the one she left behind?"

"No." She shook her head looking into his eyes.

A horrible thought moved him to a restless flutter, forcing him to look away.

"How is Elizabeth related to you? Were you her girlfriend, a room mate?"

"She must have been someone very close, because I feel the plight of her ordeal as if it was my own. I wish I could find him and tell him how much she loved him, how much she misses the future they never had."

"What do you mean she *misses?* She's dead so she can't miss anyone."

"Of course, it's funny the way it came out."

"Natalie?"

"Yes?"

"Are you sure you don't know his name? That you don't know who he is?"

Her eyes clouded with the water of her tears, but blinking them dry, she kept a steady tone of voice.

"No, I can't remember him."

"Why did I find you?"

Natalie drank water from her glass, and held her breath so long that he wondered if she really needed the air for her lungs until she let it out.

"It's confusing. Pieces are missing."

"And the child?"

"She lives with her grandparents — they're humble people who love her."

"I need to know more about this Elizabeth Bates," he said, irritated because she couldn't clarify the mystery in the unmentionable.

"Did fate put you in my way as an incredible coincidence?"

"Coincidence?"

"I don't know," he replied. "I'm not sure anymore."

"Tell me, Claude," she begged. "What's bothering you?"

He couldn't tell her about Liz, about their discussions over getting married before she left. Was he so blind not to notice that she was going to have his child? She left and he had never heard from her again.

"Are you sure you never saw me before I found you?"

"You were a stranger, Claude."

In all the time he knew Liz it never occurred him to ask about her friends, family, or origin, so when she left, it was impossible to look for her. Certainly, he had paid the price, being self centered and detached.

"I want you to show me where you lived. Let's go there after we finish eating."

"I don't want to remember the past," she said, her voice trembling. "I'm happy with you."

"I have to know."

"My memories will drive us apart."

"I hate anything which threatens our happiness, as much as you do," he spoke with a grave tone, "but I've lived wanting to know about you, and now — I wish I could let it die, but I can't."

Natalie's voice was a hush. "I'm afraid that just like her I will lose the man I love and I don't want to forfeit our happiness in exchange of discovering anyone else."

"Oh, Natalie, Natalie. Can't you see it's impossible to lose me? Even when I want to run away from you, I end up chasing you again." He kissed her hand.

"New York is not a good place for me. He's here, yes, the man who broke Elizabeth's heart lives here." Her body quivered with the recollections of a past.

"I'm going to pray that you'll be forgiving when you find him."

Feeling that his heart was aching from the same pain as hers, he couldn't run away. Instead, like all unpleasantries in his life, he would confront the future.

When they left Ramiro's, he hailed a cab, and she told the driver where to go. He made small talk, but he couldn't stop his heart from racing as they drove closer to Washington Square. As they passed 14th Street he knew he was minutes away from finding out, and his legs grew numb before the car stopped because this was the way to Liz's place.

"There," she said. "I lived there, on the ground floor."

The taxi stopped in front of the building he knew so well. Without a flinch he told the cab driver the address back to their apartment. He was responsible for a woman's death, but what he feared more than anything else was that Natalie knew it already, or worse, that she could have known it always. For now, Paris was just a few hours away.

17

Claude read through his papers during much of the flight, knowing he had to present a perfect product to the French, while Natalie sat next to him, reading a book. His meeting was at three o'clock that same day, and it left a few hours to go home at the Champs Elysees and rest before going out again. Although the Concord made a long trip much shorter, discovering that Elizabeth was dead kept him up all night.

Sooner or later he would have to confront Natalie with the real possibility that he was the man who made Elizabeth pregnant, and that a child belonged to him. He remembered that Elizabeth's disappearance left a feeling of something unresolved, and now he understood.

The company envoy met them outside of customs. Píerre was a quiet man, speaking only when spoken to, addressing only Aumont. Claude conversed in perfect French, while Natalie couldn't grasp any of the exchange. Unlike him, she seemed renewed, leaving behind the concerns that had come up the day before.

Home was at the Avenue De Marigny. Píerre took them through an iron gate that opened to a small garden in a courtyard. Their footsteps cupped over the cinder blocks paving the floor, while the rolling sound of water came from a fountain in the middle of the garden, big enough to hold fish and aquatic plants. Foliage grew out of many terra cotta containers, adding a touch of green to the portico of the house, while a long staircase made of squared marble blocks brought them upstairs.

Unlike New York, an old world flair dated the building to three hundred years ago, now it was renewed with the amenities of modern living. The only similarity to New York was the expensive art hanging on the walls because the mood of its owner reflected a serious tone of textures and patterns interconnecting throughout the house, different from the contemporary style of the apartment in New York.

The kitchen was drenched in sunlight coming from French doors that opened to a terrace overlooking the garden. Ten-foot ceilings and long casement windows made the rest of his home and someone had taken care to fill the refrigerator and stock the cabinets with food.

"It's beautiful, Claude," she exclaimed, taking off her shoes to walk barefoot. "It's warm, provincial and maybe . . . a home to ghosts."

Claude unclenched his teeth and formed a smile, because he didn't believe in such possibilities, but the fantasy of her mind was full of abstract thoughts.

"There's no such thing as ghosts," he replied with a smirk.

"How do you know?"

"Uh . . . I'm just a clever guy."

He heard her giggle.

"I love this place because it speaks of the past. There's living history within these walls. Had I died here, I certainly would come back to visit the living," she said softly.

"You're such a child, allowing your imagination to run away." Saying that, he pulled open the drapes and sunlight bathed the living room.

"Hmm, spirits are all around us," she whispered in a mystic voice. "Their matter is spread out, but they have a nucleus that on command allows them to be seen when they organize. They can move our physical world if they become solid enough, but it takes a great effort. When they are less solid they can move through the pores of other substances like walls, furniture. Limitations are few, but they seek embodiment for the intensity of the flesh.

Was she just trying to psych him out? "I'm not in the mood, Babe."

"Why can't you accept that maybe one or more people who lived here and died here would return in spirit, just like we have arrived from a long journey?"

"I'm not even going to answer that."

"Man's imagination has taken him into the future. The fantasy of yesterday has become the reality of today. Faith is our greatest tool. Do you believe I have come with you to Paris?"

"Of course, I do."

"Someone who hasn't seen me might not be willing to believe you."

"For Heaven's sake, Natalie, it's not the same at all but we'll get together with Brandon later tonight, and we'll ask him if you're real."

"As a man of vision, you should live above the expectations of what seems impossible."

She walked through the room with light steps, her voice filtering through the air like a symphony of words. It was as though she knew better and her sentences tempted with morsels of wisdom originating from the secrets of a different parallel.

"Darling, you're as beautiful as you are fleeing in your thoughts. It amazes me when you try to make sense of what has none." He cornered her against the chalk-blue frescoed wall.

"Ah, time will show mankind that there is an immortal soul." Saying that, she pressed against his body and threw her arms over his shoulders.

"You are a delightful visionary," he said over her lips.

Her thoughts were amusing, but he couldn't go beyond them. He let go of her and started lifting the white sheets covering the furniture.

"Pierre should have made this place more livable." He sneezed twice. "Remind me to ask him to get a cleaning woman before we get here next time. By the way, how do you like Juana?"

"Oh, I never got a chance to meet her. She comes to clean your apartment in New York when I'm out of the house."

"Then I encourage you to do so. You're the woman of the house, and she should get to know how you like things done. I've noticed the fresh flowers, the subtle changes like the towels folded differently over the bars in the bathroom, and I know it's you. Even the holes in the wall where you chose to hang my paintings tells me that you're with me."

"You must be in love, Mr. Aumont."

She smiled and came to help him with the covers. The mood was serious until she slipped under one of the white sheets. In fun, she stretched out her arms letting out a boo that led Claude into a chase until she tripped on the sofa and toppled over it. His larger body landed over her and he uncovered her face.

"So you're the ghost?" he laughed.

"I am, if you say so. Did you notice how Pierre ignored me? That's because he couldn't see me. Nobody sees me. I'm only for you, only for you."

"You're so silly. He didn't talk to you because you don't speak French, not because he didn't see you."

"Do I scare you a little?" She was coy.

"Sorry, not in the least bit. Maybe tonight, when the lights are off, you'll have better luck."

"Hmm, Paris at night."

"It's a wonderful place." Claude got up, collecting a bunch of clumped-up sheets under his arms. "I promise, despite our brief stay, you'll want to come back."

"Why don't you rest for a while before your meeting?" she asked. "I'll wake you in about two hours. Ghosts don't get tired."

"Stop that kidding around. If you don't mind, I'll take you up on the offer to rest."

"Here, let me take those sheets from you." She started to fold them. "Go lie down. I'll unpack later, because I'm too wound up to rest."

"Thanks."

"I like your place," she said, smiling. "Much better than your home in New York."

A feeling of lived-in surrounded them, despite the fact that he did not use this residence as often. If his business deal went through, the company would need a man in France to direct operations, and this could be just the transition he had longed for. It would mean less responsibility and much more time to spend with Natalie.

Before he disappeared into the long hallway of the second floor, he saw her sweep with the palm of her hand over the tapestry on one of the dining room chairs. The table sat twelve. Rich ochre and cobalt blue predominated in the palate of color which had been selected and he imagined sitting at one end, she on the other, and a room full of guests to entertain.

Later, half asleep, half awake in the twilight of consciousness he heard her in the walk-in closet adjacent to the master suite. That was the last he remembered, surrendering into deep sleep.

When he discovered her again, Natalie cuddled like a kitten, smooching against him, now in her jeans and a cotton top. She kissed his face with tiny touches of her lips until she reached his mouth. Aware of her intent, he surrounded her waist with the embrace of his arms and opened his eyes into the slits of a squint.

"Is it time?"

He yawned, stretching out his arms in the air.

"Sleepy head."

"Hmm, too bad I have to leave. I could stay in bed the rest of the afternoon."

He enjoyed the closeness of her body, her head over his chest, her arm carelessly abandoned over his torso, compelling him to take care of business as soon as possible.

"Don't eat dinner. There's a wonderful restaurant at *George the Fifth*. Maybe I'll ask Brandon to join us tonight. It's one of the most exclusive places to dine."

Their plans agreed upon, he regretfully let her go and went to take a shower. Dressed in his business attire, he fixed the knot of his tie in front of the mirror.

"Don't let the girls grab hold of you, because you're taken," she said.

The squared off angles of his jaw gave way to a smile, amused by her possessive outburst. Although his hair was still combed to one side, it was wet, but he had no time to waste drying it off.

"Don't worry, it's all over my face that I'm yours."

"You thrive on the kill," she said from the bed, drawing a shallow smile as her eyes followed him around the room. She lay there, one arm pressed under her head.

"What do you mean?" he asked.

"Just remembering your words back at the cabin and the animals hanging from the walls. You're dressed for success, and everything about you says you're a winner. When it comes to business, you are an expert hunter. It'll be difficult to give up the thrill of such a hunt."

"You're more important than anything else," he said.

"Finance comes easy for you, but for that other life you propose, you'll have to learn new steps."

"Then I will learn those steps. I'm like the granite stone back at the cliffs, and you're the ocean, chipping away."

She gave him the gift of her smile.

"What time will you be back?"

He sat at the edge of the bed, wishing he didn't have to leave her lying there, stretched out on his bed.

"Not soon enough, Darling," he said, filled with desire. "I hate the obligation that calls, so I hope to be back in two or three hours. I'll try to wrap up between today and Monday so the weekend can be ours." Claude walked toward the doors. "You'll be exhausted tonight unless you rest. Don't be a stubborn girl, try to sleep."

"How can I stay indoors on a gorgeous day like today? Paris is too tempting, and time runs away."

The bell at the front gate rang. That was Pierre coming to pick him up.

"Don't get lost," he said.

He walked out, carrying a briefcase in one hand and anticipating the evening ahead.

18

When Claude arrived from his meeting, Natalie was about to take a shower. Hidden underneath a terry cloth bathrobe, her nudity filled him with temptation, since even without make-up she had the natural beauty to corner any man's attention. She tied a ribbon behind her head, collecting her hair into a pony tail.

"Your hair is my favorite like that." His hands kneaded over the round of her shoulders as the tie around her waist loosened and the robe spread open. His hands rubbed lower over the softness of her back.

"God, that feels good!" The mirror gave back a face full of pleasure.

"Do you have oil? I'll give you a rub down."

"Aren't you tired?" she asked.

"Not at all. I took my cat nap."

"Instead of sleeping like you suggested, I walked too much and now I'm paying for it."

"Then let me relax you."

"I was going to dunk in a warm bath."

"You can do it afterwards, but I think you'll like this too."

He went to change his street clothing, and after a moment, he was back wearing his jogging pants and a bare torso. She lay on her stomach with arms crossed under her chin.

"How did it go?"

"Great. These guys are going to use my program to fly and land their airplanes. Most of Europe has integrated my software for air controllers, and France finally realized that my competition is more complicated to operate. My technology translates into easier language the computer program they have without changing the whole kit-and-caboodle. They have updated at a more reasonable price. Brandon has to change a few clauses in the contracts, but it's just a matter of signing on Monday."

"Will he be joining us tonight?"

"He won't. He made other plans but I'll introduce the two of you sooner or later."

His lawyer had suggested an escapade through the red light district but Claude had no need for such levities. There was nothing more pleasurable than his intimacy with Natalie.

"This deal is worth a lot to you, isn't it?"

"Millions," he said.

As she lay over the bed, his hands dug, dissecting out muscle groups while her knots released. He came to the curve of her buttock.

"Claude? I wish I had been the only woman for you."

The muscles on his face pulled up one corners of his lips.

"Sex is not love. Sometimes I feel as though you have been the only woman in my life."

Destiny was double dealing them, making Natalie an acquaintance of Elizabeth. He wanted to tell her his suspicions, about the bleak forewarning growing stronger every passing day. His Liz was her Elizabeth Bates.

As though she guessed the restless wandering of his mind, she rolled over in bed, her glance searching into his eyes. Then she sat, cuddling against his chest, teasing with the brush of her lips over his chest.

"Don't worry." He took her face with his hands. "I don't need anyone else but you."

"I'll try not to," she said. "For now I'm going to wash up before dinner, so you can't complain I made us late." Wrapped in the bed sheets, she lost herself in the bathroom. "How much time do I have before our dinner date?" The sound of the water filling the tub came with her voice.

When he walked into the bathroom, the scent of peach bubble bath filled the room with its sweetness.

"We have to leave in about an hour." She was soaking inside the tub. "Can I wash your hair?"

He noticed that her eyes were curious. Kneeling on one knee, he pulled off the ribbon holding her hair and with the utmost care, not to get soap in her eyes, he wet her hair and massaged the shampoo into her scalp.

"I wasn't going to wash my hair," she confessed.

"You weren't?"

"Nope, that's why I had it up."

"Then why didn't you tell me?"

"If I stopped you, I would have spoiled your fantasy."

There was a small silence between them.

"What would you do if you found your friend's boyfriend, the one who made her pregnant?"

She thought a moment.

"What does it matter?"

"I want to know."

"I don't know," she said looking past him

"Would you seek vengeance?"

"Nothing could bring back Elizabeth, not revenge, and not hate."

He couldn't bring himself to talk about Liz, but sooner or later the truth would find him; better that he told her soon.

Holding on to the prelude of that evening, they walked into the warm Parisian night. Dinner turned into a luxurious culinary experience. Later, they enjoyed the entertainment with the choreography of the Lido. Done with a long day, back in his apartment they left a trail of clothing over the floor that led into the master bedroom. Night covered them in a blanket of pleasure.

The next morning, while Natalie still slept, Claude slipped out to the *patisserie* a few houses away from where they lived. He brought back fresh bread and fruit tarts for breakfast. By the time she got up, coffee brewed in a French percolator and frothy warm milk filled a small pitcher on the bistro table of the kitchen. The nook was intimate, full of light exuding through the windows, and when she found him setting the table, her smile was like the sunlight that came from outside. The secret of how to make happiness was theirs.

Together they made plans for the day ahead, because Paris was a city for lovers, and they were in love. Montmartre found them at the church of Sacre Coeur, where they started their rendezvous from the highest hill in the city. Claude knew all these places, since he had been to of them, but everything seemed like a new experience in her company. Natalie was intent on carrying out their expedition without the company chauffeur, like typical American tourists.

He liked her adventurous mood. In their jeans and sneakers, they used the Metro to venture through town. When he suggested Cartier's, she whisked him off saying she wouldn't know what to choose from the many beautiful pieces. She was content to window shop instead. When he wanted to take her for the fashion show at Channel, she was not enticed by the frivolity of expensive outfits, but instead settled for a straw hat from a boutique.

He discovered that she lived with neither vanity nor self indulgence, and that her simple likes were highlighted by the richness in her heart.

At the Eiffel Tower, the opposite end of town from where they started in the morning, daylight was still out at seven. The long lines of tourists kept them waiting more than expected, and they missed their reservation at Victor Hugo, the restaurant at the base of the tower. She urged him to a simpler meal so they got French Baguette, cold cuts, cheese and half a kilo of red grapes for a picnic by the Eiffel Tower.

And so they did, at the Emplanade Des Invalids, on a bench across the playground, in the park which was a stretch of blocks across from the monument built by Gustave Eiffel. A group of young children crowded the play yard while they ate.

"Do you like children, Claude?"

For a moment he thought about them.

"I wouldn't know what to do with them," he said. "They seem to entertain themselves, but I'm sure they're difficult to raise."

The young ones playing before them, jumping and screaming at random, seemingly without much aim were a handful. They yelled and ran around, with no purpose to the fun they had. One after another, children went down a slide, others played in a maze made of plastic bubbled compartments. To get in, they had to climb a pirate's net made of a weathered thick rope, like the one aboard ships. Their small feet tackled the obstacles in a clumsy sort of way, but it was obvious their challenge was a favorite.

"I imagine you were a brainy kid, the sort that sits in front of his computer most of the day. Is that what you were like?"

"More like the quiet type, but for sure, not a nerd. I didn't have the time to play with friends. Time was a commodity and I had my school work plus the job at the restaurant in the evenings. My mother couldn't afford a VCR, let alone a computer.

She watched the children for a moment and then caught his eyes.

"I like kids. I would like to have two or three."

"It's easy to be a woman, hard to be a mother," Claude said, reflecting out loud. "You could do both and manage fine."

"I can see you riding your bike to school."

"The only bicycle I owned almost cost me my life." He thought about his own childhood and realized no one should ever face such terrors.

"Why? Did you have an accident?"

"Birth can be our worst accident. Nothing about my childhood has fond memories. I was a serious kid, but only because other alternatives were absent."

His voice sounded flat, dug out from his guts. "As the offspring of an alcoholic, my childhood was cut short by my father. He couldn't keep a steady job, so Mom and I worked to pay the bills. I never saw a playground, but that was the least of my problems."

"Don't, Claude. I didn't think my asking would lead to your unpleasant memories."

He placed an arm behind her, over the back of the park bench, while she placed the leftovers of their meal inside a brown paper bag.

"The past can't hurt me anymore." He paused to look toward the teeter totters in front of them. "Two weeks after my tenth birthday my father came home and discovered my new bicycle on the front porch. I sold newspapers for a year, saving half the money from every pay period to buy it. It was great, with it I did my route twice as fast. I was doing my homework when Marcel barged into my room. When he staggered in, he smelled of alcohol like all the other days. Blood shot eyes looked at me through a grotesque physique. I knew the frightening stare too well."

His voice became intense rekindling the fear of the child he had been.

"My heart stopped," he said. "I wished I had been invisible because I knew he was going to hurt me like other times when he was drunk. Nothing had to incite him. All I had to do was to be there. It was my bad luck to be home alone."

"For God's sake, Claude."

"I knew I was in trouble when he cornered me — rage without mercy nor love. His mouth uttered distorted words because his mind was bottled with the substance he had abused while I stood there, holding my breath, very still, hoping he would go away. I prayed for my mother but there was no God because Mom never came. When he learned that I held out on the route money, he nearly broke every bone in my body. This was the man I called my father."

Claude's eyes narrowed. He swallowed saliva and then went on after a moment.

"My mother walked in when he was beating me. Otherwise, he would have killed me. His punches cracked my ribs. I tasted something pungent when he split my lip, and blood streaked into my mouth. Later he kicked me on the floor, so many times that my blood splattered the walls. I lost consciousness because at one point everything became numb, and the next thing I remember was my mother holding me in her arms. Until I came to, she thought the brute had killed me, but I held onto life, surviving him because it was my will to do so."

"Oh, Claude, how could he do that to his son?"

She took his face into her hands, mingling her fingers into the hair of his temples and kissed over the small scar that marked the corner of his upper lip.

"I hated him for the abuse, for being my father only in name. He broke the wings of my spirit again and again, but I grew new ones every time he snapped them."

"I'm so sorry," she whispered with pain in her voice.

"When I came back from the hospital, I slept in my mother's bed until she realized he would never come back. I'm sure he thought they would give him the death sentence if they caught him. I knew Mom was afraid, afraid that like other times he would force his way back into our lives, but this time he though he'd killed his son, so he never came back."

"You learned too young."

"When a child discovers that there's no God, no mercy nor justice, solitude is his best friend. Not much can hurt you there but even the unsightly seems more tolerable with you. Do you realize how much you mean to me?"

"I do, Claude." She made a pause, and then went on to say, "You have opened your heart but don't let me hurt you either."

"Your love is the home I never had."

"The return of my memory will bring us heartache." Her mood had grown profound. She closed her eyes an instant as though she sensed disaster. "I've had the feeling meeting you was never coincidence, that there's a higher purpose to the relationship we have developed, but that inevitably, I will hurt you against my will. But I don't want to leave you, and yet something tells me, I will."

"You won't," he said, "because I would miss you all my life."

"Be strong for both of us. Send me away, while you still have a chance.".

"It's too late," he smiled. "You and I are made of the same essence, sharing the same strength, the same risks, no matter what." He looked at her face and absorbed the sadness in it. "I'm beginning to accept that you're part of my destiny, the destiny of which you spoke when we first met."

"Never forget that I love you, Claude."

The power of that love could heal them both.

They turned toward the playground. The little ones were so oblivious to the saga in their hearts. Some of the parents were leaving with their children because the evening is growing late. The sun was a large ball of orange, low in the sky, tinting with hues of purple and red. A streak of white clouds filtered near the horizon, and Claude understood that God was the artist painting this canvas.

"I'm afraid of being a father one day," he said. "I carry the devil in my genes."

"You will be a wonderful father, Claude." She squeezed his hand. "I know it."

Perhaps she knew better, as though the future had been revealed to her. He understood the solemn promise in her words, and as though she could foresee, he believed her.

He was distracted from his thoughts by a young girl, not older than four or five who came up to them. The child was smiling at Natalie who smiled right back, and then she said something in French after which she ran back to her mother, not before returning a shy look toward them,. lost in the titter of her daring actions.

"What did she say?"

"She wanted to know if you were really an angel."

"Oh, come on, Claude. She didn't say that. You're just teasing." Natalie nudged him over the ribs with an elbow, laughing quietly.

"Then don't believe me, but that's what the child asked."

"If I was an angel," Natalie giggled as her face colored in blush. "I would force you to stay with me forever."

"Then the child might be quite correct, because I don't want to let go of you, and that's a very possessive thought for a man like me."

19

Disaster seemed far away as they spent the weekend roaming Paris, holding hands, and every once in a while stopping for a stolen kiss. The inexpensive straw hat purchased in one of the French boutiques gave Natalie a girlish look. She bought bread to feed the pigeons at the park, surrounding herself with hundreds of them, tame enough to feed from her hands. She became childlike, playing and laughing while birds stood on her shoulders and hugging her Mary Jane shoes.

By noon of that Sunday they were at the Grand Palais, the sophisticated home to the kings of France, known in modern days as The Louvre. They walked the long corridors of the museum, finding magnificent art pieces but unable to visit all the pavilions because they lacked the time. They decided to see the paintings out of mutual agreement, and Claude admired the masterstrokes of artists from Rembrandt to Velazques.

The Mona Lisa cornered their attention as they moved closer through the crowd of people. Leonardo Da Vinci's obvious fascination for energy and motion fell upon his paintings, be it the windstorm or the charged moment in a woman's smile.

"Your temperament reminds me of Da Vinci's." She turned to look at him with a smile. "He often left his work unfinished because he was impatient with himself. Like you, he was a practical man, a man of science, but then inside him lived the fervor of an artist. "

"You flatter me."

"I mean to bring out the similarities in two men."

"You could have been the Mona Lisa and I, Da Vinci." He taunted her. "If it's true that our souls are reborn many times then, I want to find you again in the future."

Her smile invoked secrets, promises of immortality and love never ending but above all, he was bemused by the riddle of her universe. Natalie was so sure of her ideology.

"Da Vinci was an unconventional man in every sense of the word. He was the scientist looking to express his art. He lived during the Renaissance, but he didn't follow the teachings of the Christian Church. Instead, he formed his own dogma acquired from observations and conclusions about life and death. Who brought these thoughts into his mind, what moved him to be the man he became?"

"A woman, perhaps like yourself. Historians have been seeking the answers to his genius for five hundred years, and here I have figured it out," he said. "It's the whim of my imagination that he met the wife of a Florentine merchant, the Mona Lisa, and he fell in love with her. She was an impossibility and his only recourse was to paint the enigmatic face of the woman he loved."

"Her smile is alive because he fell in love with her?" she asked mockingly.

"Why not?"

He laughed. Then the silence of his own thoughts took over. Could his spirit be immortal? Could the energy in Natalie's life-force seek him out eternally? He laughed, but this time inwardly. Natalie had compared him with the vision of a man who was brilliant, and he felt giddy with his thoughts. How little he knew about Natalie, and yet she had become as precious as his own life.

"She's pretty ugly, isn't she?" said Claude.

"Beauty is subjective to the eyes that watch." They were walking to another corridor of paintings.

"Not everyone has your luck. You're beautiful to everyone who looks at you," he said, lacing her around the waist.

"Stop teasing." She giggled while her arm went behind his back, allowing him to pull her closer.

"Should I ask him?" Claude was looking at the man standing next to them.

"Don't you dare," she screeched in a low, intimate voice.

"I have found my *Mona Lisa* and I'm lost in her smile." Claude whispered into her ear. "You were brought to me by the earth, by the thunder of a storm. Heaven broke open and you became an angel stolen by a man, she who gave away her memories of Heaven to live on earth with me for the purpose of guiding me to love. Life can never be the same having learned to live from you."

She stopped walking. He wasn't sure if it was her heartbeat or his own, when her breasts pressed against his side. The noise from the room disappeared, and the people melted out of focus when her lips opened and pressed against his mouth.

"You're an uncontrollable romantic."

"I want to be with you longer than forever," he said.

"You shall."

If Paradise could be earth, that's where he lived for the rest of the day, marveling at her cognizance of the artist's backgrounds, their techniques and style. He grew even more intrigued about the mysterious absence of her memory, and how she linked with the study of art.

"Darling, you could work in a museum. Where is it that you've been looking for a job?"

Natalie smiled at him as they walked on.

"Promise me that you will work on your style, and never lose the passion that you found," she said.

"So long as I have you, I will paint."

"No, you must continue even if I'm not with you. To create is a gift."

"You are devastatingly in love with me."

A giggle endeared her face.

Upon leaving the museum, he remembered his friend, Paul Plaçhet. Paul's father had known van Gogh during the last century, owning rare pieces of the artist's work as well as other French contemporaries. On the outskirts of Paris, Plaçhet and his wife lived in a chateau that had been inherited from his ancestors, dating to the sixteenth century.

"Would you like to meet a friend of mine? He lives in the countryside, we can drive there in a rental," he said. They had left the museum and walked aimlessly through the streets. "The man owns a private collection of art."

"I'm grateful for your thoughtfulness, offering something out of the ordinary, however, I'm not in the mood to socialize. If you don't mind, we'll leave it for next time."

"Hmm, you're possessive of our privacy."

They chose some of the galleries where he had purchased good art work, this time browsing by, but promising to return on their next trip impressed by some of the magnificent pieces they saw. At the end of their day they took a seat in a sidewalk café for coffee and a crepe.

The Parisian tempo had cast its spell.

"What is it?"

She had discovered his silence.

"I too knew an Elizabeth Bates." He broached it without preambles.

"She was my girlfriend."

Natalie put down the fork and looked up at him. "Why didn't you tell me at the cemetery?"

"I wasn't sure if she was the same woman I knew."

"Why tell me now?"

"Now I'm sure it's her. There are two apartments in the brownstone in lower Manhattan, the rental occupied by Elizabeth and the landlady's who lives there. I know, because I went in there many times."

Natalie didn't reply, and he talked some more. Telling her about Liz was like expiating a deep, dark secret. Strange that his heart could ache for the absence of someone gone ten years ago and even more unusual that he could have regrets about past actions, now that he loved Natalie.

"Liz was gentle, beautiful, but more than that, I might have married her if she hadn't left."

"What happened?"

"We had a disagreement because I couldn't marry her when she wanted. She got angry and left me."

"If you loved her, why couldn't you marry her?"

"It was stupid," he replied too quickly.

"What was it?"

"I'm not even sure what it was. She got so pushy." He squinted, focusing on the light fixture above him as though he searched for something. Mortified and restless, he couldn't look at her.

"Elizabeth left you," she said.

"I let her go."

"Are you apologizing or telling me a fact?"

"I'm not sure." Silence rose between them. "It's not easy to imagine a kid of mine somewhere out there. None of this is easy. Once I thought I could live without a conscience. Today I know different."

He stopped talking, wanting to laugh and to cry. at the same time, but doing neither. Glad he had found the courage to tell her, he wasn't sure if he had the guts to search out the offspring of a woman who was dead. He didn't want the responsibility of raising a child unless they were his children with Natalie, and for that matter, certainly still not for a few years.

"Are you absolutely sure I took you to the same building where she lived?"

"Of course I am."

"I could have learned about Elizabeth from the landlady, after she left. I'm sure I'm not the only person who lived in that apartment."

"I have a feeling you were room mates, close friends. I don't know — " He shook his head as though that could straighten out his thoughts. "After you told me her story, I knew I had compelled a woman to her death. I killed her."

"You didn't murder anyone," she said.

He took her hand into his own. "I destroyed the life of a woman misguided by my greed." His breathing grew unsteady. "How could I go forward in our relationship without speaking up about the thoughts that haunt me?"

"Your truth is that I love you," she said, leaning closer as they sat. "Destiny has been cast and nothing will change what is. I don't care about what happened. You didn't know that she was pregnant. How could you know if she didn't tell you?"

"But I knew she loved me and her love scared me away just as it has frightened me away from people most of my life. If only I could forgive my mistakes as readily as you have done, if indeed I'm the culprit of her demise."

"Poor Elizabeth . . . but poor of us too."

"We won't know why you were in Washington until you remember some more, but revenge and hate are powerful emotions that can push people into horrible deeds. You might find these motives in the content of the pieces that are missing."

"Why did you find me, Claude? Why did it have to be you and not someone else? Trauma, hypothermia, they could have taken my recollections but I feel like there's more, something greater than both of us."

"Coincidence doesn't exist, does it?"

"I have touched you with my concepts."

"You have touched me with your past." He made a pause aware that he had to ask. "Are you here to break my heart the way I destroyed hers?"

"Would the carnage of your soul bring her back? There is no justice in vengeance. If I were here to destroy you, I would have come much earlier into your life. No, it doesn't make sense to wait so long."

"You could destroy me if you chose to."

"No, I'm not here to avenge her nor to hurt you." She let out a deep sigh.

"My ambition has unfolded. Here I am, thinking about giving it all up, relinquishing my place at the firm to spend a lifetime in your pursuit and I'm afraid, fearful of losing you, of your feelings toward me when you figure it all out. You said you preferred Paris to New York, and immediately I contemplate taking over the efforts of my company in Europe to live where you want to be. Your wants have become my needs. I would do anything for you. Bid me to live and I will live; bid me death and I shall die. Can't you see the control you have over me?"

"It's not anything but the experience of loving someone."

"It's crazy."

She took in a deep breath and her face smiled back at him. The moment charged with spiritual intensity, and he understood Natalie wanted to quiet the hammer bashing inside his mind. He envied her innocence and the steadiness of her gaze. Her words had the effect of calming, his mental struggle sinking into an abyss, like the deadly fall in his dream.

"I'm here to love you," she said.

Claude brought her face closer, not caring who watched. Her mouth parted as he fell into a sweet plateau when her tongue played upon his.

"Can we go home now?" she asked softly.

Yes, he wanted to go home, every day to one woman, to the one who had taught him how to tame his nightmares, to the one who had opened life like a miracle. His heart ached for a wonderful continuum, and he could only hope that the past would not stand between them.

20

Upon their return to New York, nothing was foreign about Natalie, like a bud revealing more and more of her petals, maturing into a rose but roses have thorns. The key to their happiness was sharing as many moments as they could, and he had figured out after years of living only for himself that giving back happiness was as good as taking it for himself. With her acceptance of his actions against Liz, his mind was at ease, thinking nothing she remembered could tear them apart. Natalie was part of his whole, and above all, she had become the reality of every day.

However, New York also brought growing unrest because the days had become full of work in the race to deliver new products and meet expectations. Business obligations took over their idyll, and he knew too well the monster he had created, a major corporation, devouring most of his time. Feeding it for so long made it difficult to relinquish its grip, and tonight was just one of many where he returned from work feeling tired and upset by the lack of progress in his goals to find someone to replace him. Yes, he had considered Pilar for the job, but he wasn't sure if she was the one.

He had been coming home so late that most of the times Natalie was well asleep, but tonight he made an effort to leave earlier than most other times. Yet at nine, he was still on his way and not home. In the drag of the routine, Natalie had lost the euphoria surrounding them in Paris. She kept to herself, sometimes unable to look him in the eyes, and he thought it was just as well, because if she didn't look too deep, she would avoid his frustration.

The search for employment had been unsuccessful because employers saw an empty résumé, leaving a suspicious background. To him this was a minor dilemma, but not for her.

Resurrecting the name of Elizabeth Bates made him think more often about his old girlfriend, and he became obsessed about the link between two women. Two days ago, he had called the detective agency demanding answers because he needed concrete proof of his suspicions.

But most of all, he realized how wrong it had been to live secluded from the world, because friends would have been welcomed to distract Natalie. There were days where he was sure his was the only voice she heard, but he had never been a social man, and he couldn't offer her these friends. The people he knew were his business acquaintances, nobody getting too close now that he wanted them there.

The honking of cars drove his nerves to final madness, the traffic being just like the city — a rat race. In the back seat of a yellow cab, with the cars staggered one behind the other, it was inevitable to count every bump on the road. His day was busy, but it was more than that. He didn't have the time for Natalie, and Pilar was the silent reminder that love and relationships were not part of the equation. What woman would endure his abandonment?

He told the cabby to leave him off at the nearest corner and when he got out he slammed the door, and the car shook. He walked the remainder of the distance to his apartment feeling stifled by the sweat under his suit. The breeze was hot, the smog thick in his lungs because the buildings kept the car exhaust close to street level, and his eyes burned with the acid in the air

At home, he welcomed the arctic cool of the central air-conditioning. A demi-lune console in the foyer served as a place to put away the keys, then he walked toward the inside of the apartment. The rattle of pots in the kitchen told him Natalie was there. He went there and found her cleaning up the mess in the kitchen, exchanging the rancid smell of streets for fresh baked chocolate chip cookies. He couldn't resist taking a few.

She poured him a glass of cold milk. In white hip huggers and a pink top which left her navel exposed she looked as delicious as the food in his mouth, and he thought how her casual style suited him well.

"God, it's good to be home," he said.

"I ate, but I can warm up a plate for you. I wasn't sure what time you'd be home tonight."

"No, don't bother. This is all I want." He heard his words, realizing he had forsaken her for days. "I'm sorry, but there's been an awful lot of work. I've been putting together the entourage of people for my business abroad. God, I'm busy."

"I was going to call you, but I didn't want to bother you," she let out a sigh.

Dressed in a gray suit, he was all business. At that instant he felt sorry for the two of them, because drifting away seemed so easy.

"You should have called." He frowned and then nearly ripped off the tie around his neck.

"What's wrong?"

"Walk with me," he said, unbuttoning his shirt to mid chest. I feel claustrophobic."

"In this heat wave?"

"Yes, I need to burn out my mood. Let me change." He walked away, not before saying, "I've had a rotten week."

Back in no time, soon they were downstairs on the streets.

"Where are we going?"

"Wherever our feet take us." Burdened by his own problems he missed the troubled look in her eyes. "You and I alone for a while, we haven't had much time together."

They took off through a well-lit path inside Central Park, with no set course about their wandering. A jogger passed them by as the full moon gave perfect clarity to its sister, the night, while fairies could have danced in flight over the pearlescent reflection of the lake.

"I gave my written statement at our board of director's meeting today," he said. "It's official that I'm stepping down."

"How did they take it?"

"As you might expect, it was a bomb shell. I'm not just the CEO but founder of Transworld. I told them I would choose my replacement carefully and offered the names of some of the candidates within our organization. There was concern about the stock market shares, but I explained I was resolved to do it."

"Are you sure you won't regret it?"

"A dozen people asked me the same question today. You were the one who told me living is a poor experience without taking chances. Interesting, I have assimilated every statement of yours." His voice sounded certain of himself. "I've made a lot of money and I will continue to make it, but now from a different perspective, more in the background than the forefront. This way I'll be closer to you."

She took his hand and made him stop along the way.

"I need you, Claude. Hold me so I have to stay with you."

He took her by the waist, not realizing something was very wrong.

"I want to see a doctor, " she told him flatly.

"Are you ill?"

"Since we came back from France, I have dwelled with the thought of a frightful end."

"What do you mean?"

"I'm frightened of myself."

"I'm here for you."

"You'll think I'm crazy, but my mind and body are undergoing a transformation."

He chuckled, ready to make fun of her. "What are you talking about?"

"I'm not kidding."

"For crying out laud, Natalie, how am I to think you're serious when you say something like this?"

"I'm convinced I'm going to die soon."

Indeed she had concerned him with these thoughts. By the tone of her voice she wasn't kidding.

"You're depressed because I've been too busy, or maybe frustrated about the job you haven't gotten, but your life is far from dismal. You have me to help, and I've made arrangements for a neurologist to see you — I would have liked sooner — but he's got a long waiting list. It's in two weeks."

Silence ensued as he noticed she was fidgeting with the beaded bracelet around her wrist, as though it were a shackle enslaving her.

"I don't want to kill myself," she clarified. "On the contrary, I want to live for you. I want us to grow old together, to spend a lifetime by your side, but it's the same feeling I had in Washington, at the cemetery. I feel as though my time is ending. Have I done my job well? The closer I come to completing my mission, the sooner I'll go."

Afraid that her mind had snapped, he took hold of the hand that moved erratically.

"What mission are you talking about?" he asked.

"Don't tell me that you love me." Natalie covered her ears, shaking her head, speaking out in a screech. "Can't you see? I'll leave and you'll want me, and it'll hurt me to do what I must do when I break your heart."

"Slow down and take a deep breath, will you? Why are you going to break my heart? Why would you want to leave me?"

Her eyes bulged out so much that he saw all white.

"This is not about me, it's all about you." She looked frightened. "You had to fall in love. You had to fall so deeply that none of your common sense would bail you out. Without blind love you couldn't accept what is to pass."

"Stop it, or we'll both go crazy." He spoke in a low and intimate voice.

"I toss and turn at night plagued with nightmares," she shouted. "Nightmares about specters resurrecting from putrid bodies, full of maggots and rot. I can't stop the rummage of my thoughts."

"Natalie."

"Fragmented pieces of memory shove inside my head, scaring me to death." Her voice was the sound of a desperate cry in the night.

Without warning and before he could stop her, she ran toward the lake, a fleeting shadow of unrest. He caught up to her, as she broke down into the tremble of her sobs.

"I didn't realize your state of mind was this bad," he said. When he went to touch her, wanting to comfort her, she tore away from his arms. "Don't run away from me."

"I couldn't do it even if I wanted to, at least not before the end," she sobbed. "You should have let me be, while you had a chance, while you didn't care about me."

"That's impossible. I cared from the moment I found you."

"I forbid you to love me." She turned to look at him.

"You scare me, Natalie."

"I scare myself, too."

"Why don't we go back home?"

She raised her eyes and looked at the moon as though her answers were there, written with invisible ink, hieroglyphics that only she could read. Her face looked so miserable, so desperate that he couldn't venture to decipher the message from the heavens. He wiped the flood over her face when he swept his hands over damp cheeks.

"Why do I feel the agony of Elizabeth growing stronger, as though it were my own, crawling into my flesh, ripping open every pore of my skin?" Her voice was a ghastly moan. "Why do I remember the plight of someone else with vivid lucidness when I can't remember mine? Why do I rummage about an illegitimate child?" Natalie turned toward him. "Who am I?"

Claude had no answers. He couldn't bear to look her in the eyes because there was a lot he didn't understand and so much more unknown about her. Memories were like phantoms in the shadows, scaring her because they were distorted. This was the end of a less than perfect week. Tired and confused about her actions, his apartment seemed like a refuge. There was nothing more important than their love, and yet, at the vortex of all these thoughts, he knew there had to be more.

21

Sunshine thrust the world alive with light. In the view from the windows of his apartment, the streets of New York were an invitation to the outdoors, perfect for Natalie's doctor appointment, in prelude of the Labor Day weekend. Without definite plans, other than the ball on Saturday night, Claude felt free to explore the next four days and he was determined to give her his full attention. Their romantic interludes had disappeared over the last two weeks as Natalie's unrest cornered her inside the house, apprehensive to venture for a walk or go out to dinner. She was nervous and introverted, as though a haunting secret preyed on her, something menacing but at the same time essential. Until she figured it out, repression burdened her with suffering.

The brick structure of the hospital pavilion loomed before them. He gave her a nudge after paying the driver because she wouldn't come out, glued to the vinyl of the back seat. His patience had grown in leaps and bounds, coping with her abrupt mood swings.

"Leave me alone." She shoved away from him, stepping out onto the curb.

"We have to get going or we'll be late for our appointment. A few days ago you seemed to realize there was something very wrong. Why do you hesitate this morning?"

"I changed my mind, that's all. You don't understand."

"You're right, I don't." He raised his voice. "Humor me by going inside."

Her eyes kept dodging his as she squirmed to loosen the grip that kept her hand. He was holding on to her afraid she would run away.

"You're antsy. What's wrong?"

"Don't you know what's bothering me?" She laughed out of cue and some of the people walking by stared at them. "It's too late now. They're here."

"Who, who's here?"

"There are shadows behind me, moving faster than my eyes can grasp. Voices . . . I hear them all the time. At first . . . they were far away. Now they're closer. They whisper. They talk to me. I can hear them as they tell me why I came."

"Why you came where?" he asked, trying to make sense of her delusions. "For Christ sake, let me bring you inside."

"They tell me who I am, they tell me everything there is to know but I don't want to believe them."

Their future seemed like wandering waters, a current driving forward in a river, at vertiginous speed, unsure if they would find an ocean, but knowing they were being pushed forward by what was inevitable. Destiny.

He humored her for the sake of getting to the final destination.

"Then tell me what they say to you."

She looked from side to side, hiding from something or someone he couldn't see.

"They tell me about the threshold of life, but I won't surrender. I'm not going back. I'm going to stay with you."

He stopped. A knot formed in his throat, wanting to hug her, to reassure her there was nothing to fear, but he could only lead her forward.

Natalie covered her lips with a shaking hand, like the hands of Marcel when he missed a drink and was starving for the substance.

"A week ago when I was getting dressed I looked in the mirror and I saw the face of another woman — old — older than I. Deep lines carved into her skin and she wore a handkerchief over her hair. I knew she lived near a coast, perhaps near Tierra del Fuego, an Indian woman in Chile. I saw the beach, I felt the wind on my face, I heard the sea wash ashore. She was a peasant woman, a villager from another time. It was me in another life. You see, I have lived many lives.

"The night before last, I woke up from a nightmare, but you weren't home yet. I thought I was covered in my own blood, the sheets were red, blood dripped onto the floor, and it was coming from inside me, between my legs. I was scared, alone and laden with thoughts of loss, of death. Do you still want to know what's wrong?"

She had crossed the thin line separating sanity from madness, and he couldn't believe it could happen to her. With the look of a wild animal trapped inside a cage, he kept hold of her arm, afraid that if he let her go, she would run away. His only hope was Dr. Tananbaum.

"My God, Natalie, you know yourself there's something wrong with you," he pleaded, dragging her through the double doors of the entrance.

"Leave me, run away while you're still able."

"For whatever lucid thoughts remain, follow me inside. I beg you."

Sunk into the deepest silence, he filled out forms at the registrar while she sat, her legs bouncing up and down as though they were powered by a separate nervous system. He became the guarantor for the medical expenses, and his signature went all over the papers. After that brief interlude they went to the seventh floor, where they stopped in front of the counter by the elevators.

A black woman dressed in white instructed them to be seated, until the doctor was ready for them. Comfortable cushioned seats were pins and needles, fidgety as she was. As she picked at the polish on her finger nails, Claude thought he had never seen her so distraught.

"I don't want to see anyone," she cried out. "My ability to perceive has evolved. I extend beyond the ability of my senses." Her pupils were dilated as her eyes swung without a definite focus, as though she watched people moving past her but there was nobody.

When the nurse called, he got up first, extending a hand to fingers that were cold and wet. Natalie clutched to his arm so hard, he grew numb at mid arm. He had heard about the strength in people who are crazy, and feeling her grip, he was sure if she took a swing at him right now, she could loosen a few teeth. Halfway down the corridor she bent forward with dry heaves, and before he could say anything, she ran toward the door of the restroom to the right of them.

He crossed his arms over his chest, cornered by frustration. Then, when she didn't come out, he went up to the nurse who had called for Natalie and asked her if he could speak to Dr. Tananbaum before the patient went in. He explained she was sick. At first she looked at him with misgiving but the sincere plead of his voice made her accept his proposal. After leaving him inside the consultation room, she reassured him she'd wait for Natalie, right outside the door to the ladies' room. The doctor was on a time schedule.

The attentiveness of the woman made him feel Natalie was in good hands. Soon the figure of a tall man with a graying beard came into the consultation room where he was seated. Bald, with dark eyes that contrasted under white bushy eye brows, the man introduced himself as he shook hands.

"My nurse informs me the patient is a little nervous about coming in."

"I'm sorry. She got sick. Could be the anticipation of meeting you."

Claude sat in a chair in front of the doctor's desk.

"Maybe it's White Coat syndrome," he said with a condescending smile. "Some people are very intimidated by the idea of coming to the doctor but tell me what can I do for you?"

"Natalie lost her memory but it's returning in distorted fragments. She seems terrified of the thoughts that are awakening inside her mind."

"How much has she forgotten?"

"Everything, everything about herself and the past."

"I see. How long ago did this happen?"

"Early May, I found her in Washington, hypothermic, unconscious. I don't know what brought her into the middle of nowhere, alone and at the mercy of a terrible storm."

"The loss of body heat induced shock and that's enough to produce amnesia. Where is she now?" asked the doctor with audible concern.

"Your nurse is with her because she got sick. I think it's a case of jitters, she was nervous about seeing a doctor."

"You're her husband?"

Mentally Claude answered with a yes. He couldn't love her more if they were married.

"We live together," Claude explained. "Natalie means everything to me but she has changed so much. She says she hears voices and sees people who are not there. I'm worried."

"So am I." The older man's voice was neutral. "Hallucinations can be the product of a psychotic mind or the difficulty interpreting memories that are coming back. She *hears* what her mind is recalling, not really voices hovering around her. She might project visions of a past which is difficult for the cognitive mind to grasp. All this might be quite normal or on the other hand, extremely dangerous. I need to do tests, ascertain the pathology in her case."

"I'm going to hope for the best."

"Has she been vomiting or complained of dizziness before today?"

"I don't think so but I've been working a lot and most of the day I'm away from her."

"As far as you know, what seems to bother her most about the things she has remembered?"

"Part of her agony is fighting off what she thinks is inevitable to come. Natalie seems to feel that the return of her memory will separate us."

"I see . . . It's reasonable to fear something like that." The doctor cleared his throat. "Patients can become erratic and confused, forcing a difficult dilemma for both you and her. Her unrest is understandable and common. The mind shifts, trying to decipher the messages asleep inside of it. Her memory will come in its complete spectrum. Try to cope with her reactions, be patient."

"Lately it's been difficult." His semblance hardened.

"If you love her, she will need your support, more than ever. I understand your concern, but most of the time patients have no metabolic or neurologic malfunction. If she needs to see a psychiatrist, I will refer you to one of our best. But I warn you, I might find that she needs immediate hospitalization."

"Your words alarm me, Doctor. Please, let me see why she's taking so long."

When Claude stepped out, the nurse was not by the restroom and Natalie was not in the waiting area. He found the nurse who had assisted him before, on the other side of the main desk. He asked for Natalie.

"There was no one in the bathroom," said the woman. "I thought I missed her and that she was with the doctor. I thought she was . . . with you, Mr. Aumont."

"With me?"

"The door was unlocked when I went to get her."

"You're a nurse, I thought you would make sure — "

"It's crowded in here," said the woman, looking away. "Believe it or not I have a lot of work to do."

Natalie had deceived him with the distraction of her illness. He had been stupidly naive. Disconcerted at first, he stood planted in the middle of the floor but he regained his composure about what had to be done.

"Tell Dr. Tananbaum what happened. He'll understand my problem much better now." Saying this, he ran to the elevator and pushed the button repeatedly until the doors opened. The ride down took forever, but once in the lobby, he looked for the familiar face in the people who stood around.

Natalie wasn't inside the coffee shop, and the security guard by the door couldn't recall someone fitting her description. He ran out, hoping to catch a glimpse of her but the sidewalks were full of people and none of them were Natalie. He kicked the garbage bin at the corner of Fifth Avenue so hard he had to grab it to keep it from bouncing off the side walk.

When he thought all was lost, from a distance he saw someone who could be she, sitting on a bench in the park under a huge tree. The sounds of honking cars chased him across the avenue as he rushed through oncoming traffic. Then he got a closer look: it was she, frozen, her hair wild and disheveled blowing with the breeze.

"Natalie! What are you doing here?" he demanded, trying to catch his breath, livid with anger. "Why did you leave me behind?"

"I had to get out of there."

"I have never run after a woman the way I chase you." Silent tears streaming down her face stopped the avalanche of his words; it was a silent and painful downfall. "Do you realize we came seeking a solution for the problem, and you left me up there by myself? You're going nuts on me, and I can't help you by myself. For crying out loud! What are we going to do?"

"Forgive me, Claude. I should have stayed."

"Why do you rebuke me and the doctor?"

The tears streamed down her face

"I'm . . . sorry, so . . . sorry."

"I want you to feel well again."Claude sat next to her and put his arm around her, drawing her closer.

The only thing holding on to reason was the love between them and he understood that she was fighting to retain coherence. He stopped pushing for what was so against her will, remembering what the doctor had said. *Her memory will come.*

"Maybe we should go to the emergency room."

"Please, take me home, Claude."

Natalie closed her eyes, and he took her into his arms, consumed by the sight of the woman who had given him so much. She brought him to a pinnacle of pain, so steep that looking down scared him. Against his better judgment, he took her home, to the other side of the park. Once there, he tucked her in bed and went to search for a bottle of tranquilizers which had been dispensed for him a while back. This seemed like the moment to grab one.

He met her with a glass of water and one of his pills. As she drank, he noticed the circles under her eyes.

"Sleep a while," he whispered. "You'll feel better when you wake up."

He drew the shades.

"Lie with me, please," she asked.

He did as she asked and when he felt the weight of her head rest upon his outstretched arm, his eyes burned with the salt of his tears, but he thought, *men don't cry.*

"I've been thinking, thinking that you're right," she said.

"About what?"

"Nothing remains after death, there's nothing left after we die."

Her words came to him like a thorny bramble of lost faith. He wanted to tell her it was okay to believe in God, to believe that death was not an end. That it was fine to have her abstract thoughts, that at times he envied her faith, her clear challenge of his skepticism, but he couldn't bring himself to say anything. Instead he bit down until his jaw hurt. His lack of sensitivity had driven Elizabeth to her doom. In a different way, but just as effective, he couldn't do the same with Natalie. He had to believe that their love was stronger than their wounds and that it had to heal them both.

"Don't think darling, just relax," he said.

"Promise me that no matter what happens you will always remember me," she said with a string of voice.

"Your name will be on my lips on my dying day. "

For a while neither of them spoke, lying in bed, holding each other until he realized she had fallen asleep when she breathed through pursed lips. The tranquilizer had managed to release the stiffness of her body.

A cool, end-of-summer breeze touched through the tangled drapes of the open doors leading to the balcony as the shadows of nightfall bled through darkness. Eyes closed, he lay on the living room couch seeking rest, but unable to fall sleep at one o'clock in the morning. Then, through the silence that invaded darkness, a snap inside the floor, muffled though the yarn of the rug, made him think that someone had come near and that these were footsteps.

He opened his eyes, but saw no one there. Then smell of lilacs made him think he was in a garden not his apartment. Alive with the overwhelming strength of something taking over, the memory of his dead mother assaulted his consciousness. A second step, this time louder and closer. He straightened up in the sofa to take a better look, but either he was blind or dumb because he couldn't catch anyone as though some process had cut the nerves and paralyzed his eyeballs, disabling vision.

The thought of his mother came as unexpectedly as the crackles on the floor. He spoke to his mother in his mind, not with words, as though she could hear him through a fine veil of space, and like a child when he asks for a favor, believing she could help from an invisible place — but ever so much real.

A sharper noise came from the ceiling as he looked up, convinced that the place was coming apart. Then he looked up with the thought of being surrounded by the flight of invisible spirits arriving through the metal girders of his apartment.

Above the petty faults of people, in a place without hunger, sadness, or pain, his mother was alive. She was the immortal spirit, enlightened by the wisdom of ages before the present, of many lives before. Now she came to him, bound by the love that had united them. She chose birth and death, gender and consequence, solitude and companionship, and the vehicle through which to live, the human form he remembered with fondness.

Into his mind came an image, a small box made of steel, with nothing else around it but a sea of black. The box was polished and sealed impermeable, made to be unbreakable. As perfect as it looked, it was inadequate to hold a man's soul. Beautiful but ineffectual, imperfect because entering into such a cavity

-133-

would imprison our eternal spirit forever. Then Claude realized the flaws of the flesh were not imperfections at all. God was masterful, wiser than all. He had created the unblemished vial, the faultless little box — but the one that could break down.

The reason why people got sick, the reason why people grew old was to detach, to let go. Bodies must deteriorate because the spirits living inside grow attached to the process of living, not just to the flesh but to its relationships, anchored by friends and family. The physical pain of illness and the unmerciful sags of aging were tools to pass on, to break out of the box, to release an imprisoned soul. God had given people a perfect body — one that was mortal.

The gallop of his own heart stirred wild and unstoppable, knowing the building wasn't coming apart, but that his mind was receiving a message, and he closed his eyes with the thought of his mother's gift.

The wail of an ambulance came from the city streets. The drone of traffic seemed otherwise dead. He got up and went to his bedroom where Natalie lay on her side and he, next to her, cuddled underneath the bed sheets, finding the calm yearned for. As though his mother had covered them in the magic of her love, silence came on the wings of a wish, and then, he fell asleep.

22

Modern European cabinets lined the walls of the kitchen, and stainless steal cookware hung over the island in the middle of the room where a bed tray held Natalie's breakfast, almost ready to go. Claude absorbed the cold from the surface of the granite counter top as he stood there, waiting for the percolator to finish, lost as he was in his thoughts. Today he had to deal with her again and after the horror of the day before he was afraid to start. A month ago, when he planned out the weekend, he never expected such a complicated disaster. Now he rode the roller coaster, and making breakfast was a comforting attempt to start the ride. The gurgling stopped and the coffee was ready.

By the bedside, as though she had perceived his presence and his hesitance to disturb her, Natalie turned toward him and opened her eyes. From the side of her nightgown her breasts sloped, crowned by the small mounds of her nipples as her arms outstretched in the air. Playful and suffused with her delicious sight, he threw himself in bed, still in his pajamas wishing to splatter her with a taste of his earlier plans.

She soothed his hesitancy by coiling next to him, throwing her hair ruffled by the pillows over his arm.

"How do you feel?"

"Better," she said. "I'm surprised you're here after yesterday's spell of lunacy. Anyone else would have run away for good."

"I'm here."

"Yes, you are." They lay in silence a few minutes and then she climbed over him, taking the tray on the night table with the food and placing it over her lap. "And you made breakfast for me?"

"Why not? You look better this morning."

"I am," she replied.

There was butter in a small plate, coffee, toast, two strips of bacon. A rose, the color of blood adorned a small vase, the petals splattered of yellow pollen fallen from the pistil at its center. He'd taken it from the bouquet in the dining room, but he knew she didn't mind this flaw. He took one of the black figs in a bowl, and ate it under one of her smiles.

"I wanted to do something nice for you," he said chewing. "Yesterday was a day right out of hell. I was curt when I should have been sensitive about your fears meeting the doctor. I push too hard."

"I scared you, didn't I?"

Yes, she had scared him, but this morning her face was the epitome of equanimity and she was eating with enthusiasm while they spoke. He got up and sat across the room in an armchair, resting his bare feet over a stool.

"I like you better like this," he said, matter-of-factly. "If you want, I'll take you shopping today." His eyes were fixed on her.

"You will?"

"Yes, I want to dress you in a beautiful gown for tonight. Do you think you'll be up to partying?"

"Ah, the mayor's birthday party. I had forgotten."

"Natalie?"

"Yes?"

"I want you to stay with me a long, long time. The day we met I was afraid of getting close to someone. Don't you do the same now that we have found each other. Please, don't shut me out." He noticed that she was staring at him. "I'm going to love you all my life, despite yourself and no matter what."

"I wish I had a lifetime to give you," she said with a husky voice.

"But you do," he said laughing. "You're wonderfully alive."

Her face grew quiet, her eyes filled with something he couldn't make out but it made him sad to look in them. He could have sworn they got brighter, and full of tears but there was no reason to cry. She was sick, but he hoped his resolution to pull her out of her gloom and a shopping spree in his company could mend some of it. He knew that with patience he would conquer the dilemma of her memory.

She stared at him some more, taking a sip of coffee.

"Why are you looking at me like that?" he asked. "Can't be the shaving cream on my nose because I haven't shaved yet."

"You're very handsome, Mr. Aumont."

"You're the princess and I'm the frog." He hid behind a smile.

Saying that he blinked twice and then rubbed his eyes because his vision blurred with the tumultuous feeling that invaded him. He looked at Natalie, her face, her body. He heard her voice. All his senses gave him her, but something was wrong.

If human eyes could see a person's aura, he was sure she had one when a radiant wash of sunlight coming through the window to his left enveloped her in its brightness. Bathed in this gleam she looked spiritual, enlightened by her own grace. The particles of dust bounced off each other, floating in the air around her, as though time had made its own warp, enabling her to be part of every particle. If a white dove had perched on her hands, he would have conceded the Holy Spirit had descended upon her.

"Lord, for a moment I looked at you and I thought you were — " He rubbed over his eyelids. "I wish Liz was alive, that her death was a mistake and that no harm had come to pass as a consequence of my actions."

Her eyes gazed into his. "I wish I had it in my power to grant your wishes but all I can say is that I love you."

"Too little." He teased, forgetting his crazy thoughts.

"More than you imagine."

"You're going to give me a swelled head," he said with a smile. Then his tone got as heavy as hers. "Sometimes I think about life, about why things have to be a certain way, and it bothers me to be ignorant about so much."

"Being human has limitations, but in the plight of living, ignoring the outcome gives us the guts to walk forward. If we were aware of how it was all going to end I'm not sure we'd have the courage to take the chance. And now I have come to understand there's nothing to fear."

"One life is very brief. You and I should live at least two hundred years together because one life is much too short."

"Think of the oceans, of the planets that have been here millenniums, that's how long we have, the here and beyond."

"I wish I could."

"Your soul has been forever and so has our love."

"Tell me that you need me as much as I need you."

"There is nothing between heaven and earth that could stop me from loving you," she whispered.

"I felt as though you had betrayed me yesterday but I was the one who abandoned you. I hated when you ran away from what I thought was for your benefit, but maybe I've been searching for my own selfish reasons. I met you at the park and I realized it was me, I hated myself, because I didn't understand your needs, your desperation, the fear that pushed you to run away in order to survive the moment."

"Oh, Claude. Who owns the strings that hold us?" she asked with melancholy in her voice. "Who cuts them loose?"

"We do — " he said, meaning to comfort her mind. "Don't stop being who you are for the sake of conforming to what I need. Believe in everything you've told me and don't worry, because if you're mad, then so am I."

"It's so hard, so very hard."

He sensed her turmoil once again.

"We're together."

"Promise me that no matter where life takes you, you'll listen to your heart above all else, to guide you through the hardships of life, toward the reality of truth." Saying this, she left the tray on the side and came to his side. She braised against his chest, and he took her in his arms searching for her lips which parted in a kiss. "You deserve everything which is good because you're the most generous man in the world."

"Silly girl, I'm the greediest!" he said playfully. "I want the biggest treasure which is you, and I won't let anything come between us."

"My God, Claude. I could talk to you about the universe, about life, about the end of the world or the beginning of time, but all I want to tell you is that I love you!" Saying this, she closed her eyes and pressed against him like a castaway in the waters of life, clinging to the saving piece of shipwreck that kept her afloat.

"You feel so different, Natalie. It's as though higher knowledge had given you peace, delivering the inevitable of a future which is to come."

"You can say I live with the resignation imposed by my quest."

"A quest?"

"A quest of love and faith."

"If your riddle involves me falling in love with you and accepting all the consequences of my actions, then your quest is complete."

23

The hours of that Saturday went too fast. They shopped along a strip of expensive boutiques in Soho where she modeled various gowns until she chose a black organza dress with a slit that was more daring than most. The store owner promised to deliver it later in the afternoon. Lunch was a light apres midi at Balthazar's. Uptown, a sweep of Tiffany's got her a spectacular diamond and emerald necklace with earrings to match. She seemed to accept his excitement for life and the lavish affair that was forthcoming, and he could only hope that the party would do her well as she mingled with influential people and the very select of society.

That evening the limousines came, one after another, while the police barricaded the street. Security was at its best with the guests attending the gathering. In a black tie, he walked into the Starlight Roof of the Waldorf for the cocktail hour with Natalie by his side, and it pleased him to know that she was his. They would be one of the '*in*' couples because of his status and her beauty.

"Brandon should be here," he said, scanning the ballroom. "His law firm deals with many of these people."

He wasn't worried about meeting Brandon but introducing Pilar to Natalie could be trouble. Pilar could be swift like a snake, poisoning her prey with words chosen to attain a lethal end. Natalie was no match for a woman like her.

"Is it important for you to have these people know me?"

"Yes, I want them to envy my luck," he said.

"Our appearance is a superficial diversion." The tone of her voice was flat, pulling on the stole over her bare shoulders as though the coldness inside these people had touched her soul.

"Good looks might be ephemeral, but it's a great introduction."

"These are your friends?"

"They're acquaintances. In my circles there are no real friends, but these people are a segment of the crowd that surrounds me and you're part of my life, so they should get to know you. Maybe we'll find someone to befriend a little deeper."

He moved through the crowd, smiling here and there, but not stopping to talk to anyone.

"Forgive me for not being impressed by gatherings full of important people. They don't do too much for me. I would detest if you dressed me up for them." She looked at herself and then up at him. "I had hoped it was for you."

"Of course it's for me, but I like showing you off. You're a gorgeous woman and you're with me," he said, trying to defend himself.

"They'll look at me and see my designer gown. Who cares if it's Escada or Donna Karan. They will judge me by my hairstyle, by whether my teeth align perfectly and be impressed by the fact that I'm the woman who came to the party with Claude Aumont, one of the richest men in the world. Don't you realize I'm a nobody to them? I have no name, no money, and that's the only valued treasure in this room."

"I know there are more meaningful aspects of life, but for tonight please try to relax and pretend like you belong."

"I'm . . . invisible to them."

"This is life."

"I don't like these people," she said plainly. "They are fake and empty. One day you will find that real friends won't care if you're rich or poor. They will have a good time with you, no matter where you are or what you are. When I met you, you told me you didn't believe in much, that's because what surrounds us isn't much at all."

"Let's not debate the better principles of life. We'll end up disagreeing, and I'm not in the mood to fight. I'll get us a drink and while I do that, why don't you get something to eat?"

Saying that, he walked in the direction of the bar, leaving her in line by the food table. Near the bar he ran into Brandon, secluded by a group of men, talking and smoking in a crowded corner. An effusive handshake with an exchange of greetings and brief introductions drew him into an interlude that left the two of them alone at the bar.

"Where's Natalie?" asked Brandon.

"She's over there." Claude pointed toward a table where a few women were seated. "The woman with the black sequined dress."

"You'll have to introduce me," said the attorney, shaking his head as he took a puff from a Havana.

"Let me get her a drink and then we'll come over." He addressed the bartender, "Two White Goose Martinis." Claude took out his wallet and placed a ten-dollar tip inside a glass for the man serving them.

"I'm anxious to meet your mystery woman," said Brandon, smiling. "In Paris you kept her to yourself, but not tonight, my friend. Hopefully, she'll be a breath of fresh air among all these snobs."

"Funny, that's what she thinks about these people."

"I socialize with them because it's profitable, but they are a bunch of stiffs. Too stuck up for my taste," cleared up Brandon. Then, turning to the bartender he asked, "You want to freshen up my drink? Gin and tonic."

"Want one?" offered Brandon, taking out a Cuban cigar from the pocket of his tux. "I picked them up in France. I can hardly wait until they're legal in the states. I guess it's just a matter of time."

Claude shook his head because he didn't smoke nor was he a political man, although the room was saturated with politicians.

"Our friends from *Caterpillar* are over there. I heard their company moved five billion dollars of equipment into Cuba last year. They're building hotels. It's not just the European investors in the island, Americans too," said the attorney in a cunning tone of voice. "I can see Transworld Communications landing in there. All you need are the right people on your side."

"I guess you also heard that I'm simplifying my life."

"Kind of hard keeping something like that under the sheets. It's a loud secret in Wall Street that you're leaving the firm. I'm sure you've been thinking about your replacement. Do I know any of the candidates?"

"Andrew Zaria."

"Hmm, his name comes with a good track record. Any one else?"

"Pilar Haydig."

"Pilar? Watch your back. She's a woman chasing power, and that makes her more dangerous than a wolf on the prowl."

Claude looked at Brandon.

"And what got you pissed off at her? Is this about the copyright infringement deal six months ago?" He thought it was about business, nothing personal, but maybe he was wrong.

"We've had our differences here and there but this is about you," retorted Brandon. "I always thought she was after your job. At first I thought your bed was the touchdown, but now I discovered a more underhanded scheme. She gets what she wants."

"What are you talking about?"

"I thought it would have taken an earthquake to uproot you out of Transworld. Instead a woman did it. It's Natalie, isn't it?"

"You're a paranoid son of a bitch."

"Yeah, I'm a lawyer and we're a different species altogether, but open up your eyes. Natalie shows up and Pilar moves in, check mate. You and she were getting nowhere, but now the strategic placement of a pawn in chess can win the game for her. Did Natalie come upon your life without premeditated purpose or is she a hired player to haul you aside? Both women benefit from your love affair."

"You piss me off, Brandon. Whoever I choose will capitalize equally."

"Be honest with me, whose got the edge? Zaria or Haydig?"

"If it's Pilar, it's based on merit. She has a firm grip on the competition, and I like her because she's like a chameleon that camouflages Transworld to better deal with predators. I work hard, but so does she, and her record is pretty straight with me. Last year she convinced me to branch out into the government. She brought the executives together and sold us on her ideas. Now that we have accomplished this, all we have to do is show the facts to our stock holders and the share prices will sky rocket. Yes, she's cunning and smart, but she couldn't scam me out of my firm, not because she's a decent person, but because I'm me. You must have a bone to pick with her, and I suggest you do it now while I'm still on board, because if she feels about you the way you feel about her, you're right, she'll pull Transworld from under you."

"Sorry buddy, didn't know she was so high in your esteem."

"You're wrong. It's not personal. I'm a business man."

From across the room he felt Pilar's eyes land on the back of his neck. He turned around and found her talking to a group of women and men, but it was obvious she was about to come their way. He was surprised when she laced an arm around him and kissed him on both cheeks in front of Brandon.

"It's good to see you, boss." She acknowledged Brandon with a cold smile and he returned a brief exchange. "Were you talking about me, or is it my imagination?"

"We were waiting for our drinks," said Claude.

He wasn't sure how Brandon knew that Pilar and he were once an item because he had never told him. But he was certain that the smile on his lips was counterfeit pleasant.

"And where is your forgetful muse?" she asked.

He got free from her hold to take a sip from the rim of his martini glass.

"Well, I think it's time I went to Natalie but why don't you take this opportunity to explain to our friend and valuable attorney that the five billion you coached into research and development has produced twice as much."

The tone of his voice made it clear he wasn't in the mood for stupid comments or the paranoia of conspiracy.

With drinks in hand, he tried to made a break for it, but the guest of honor was walking toward them. The group of lawyers accompanying the mayor cornered Brandon into their circle of conversation, and it was obvious Pilar was tickled to be left alone with the mayor. Making the acquaintance of a powerful man in politics had captivating appeal and the potential for profit. She made sure the mayor caught her name as well as her charm. Brandon became unimportant as Pilar became the hunter. As for Claude, he exchanged only a brief interlude with the mayor, on his way to meeting Natalie.

"I saw Brandon. He'll find us later, I'm sure," he explained, standing over Natalie, now by the cocktail table. "He got nabbed by the group over there."

"I'm sorry if I spoiled your mood before."

"Forget it. Maybe you're right about this place. Let's go outside a little bit."

They walked toward the balcony, her arm locked onto his. A soft breeze touched his face on the other side of a long wall of glass that opened to the Manhattan skyline.

"Everyone uses everyone, and one of the reasons why I fell in love with you is that my money didn't seduce you. You were interested in me, instead of the outer layers of *green,* so don't apologize for being the way you are. I don't mind you speaking up, even if we don't agree on a point of view. I would hate to see you fitting a convenient mold for my sake."

"I don't want to fight with you," she said careful.

"A little disagreement is not bad for me." He made a brief silence, hating the thought of Brandon's conspiracy.

"What's wrong?"

"Nothing, nothing at all."

"I saw the woman who came up to you. She's very attractive. Who is she?"

"Pilar Haydig. We work together and . . . we had something before I met you."

"Something?"

"We were lovers."

"And now?"

They were secluded from the main ballroom out in the terrace. He couldn't see the stars in the skies but her eyes were enough to light his night.

"I told you once before. Sex is not love. There's nothing left between her and me other than our business arrangement and the fact that she would make a good CEO for my firm."

"Then there is nothing to explain," she said. "I can handle the situation."

"She's a shrewd woman, Natalie. I would hate to have her make you uncomfortable."

"Don't worry so much about me." Natalie smiled.

The impulse to hold her grew stronger as his thoughts were assaulted by the possibility of her absence.

"I would hate it if anything broke us up."

A silence mounted between them.

"What you're feeling is the truth of life," she whispered, looking at his face. "Everything else is an illusion of happiness, a deceptive camouflage which will leave you empty."

"What makes you look at life the way you do? Your thoughts are basic, primordial if you will, but never deceived by the superficial gleam of artifice. It's your provocative nature that forces me to stop and think about life, about myself and about what has to be between us."

"I have remembered, Claude." Her voice was a lull.

He stood facing her, but not sure of what to say. His heart beat quickened while his respirations increased, forced by the rush of blood. He wanted to ignore Brandon's warning about Pilar, about corporate intrigue and about Natalie.

"When did it come to you?"

"This morning," she said, hesitating just a moment. "I woke up and the past was there."

"My God, Natalie, why didn't you tell me right away?" He held his breath a moment, swallowing the entire content of his glass from one gulp. This was that *something* that was different in the expression of her face, because even the tone of her voice told him she had changed inside.

"I had to reconcile within myself first and now I've told you." She paused. "What I have to tell you is not easy, and what I have to do is even harder."

He despised the forewarning of her words. Claude took a deep breath and then closed his eyes.

"You have your memories," he mumbled, looking at her once again.

"Shall I tell you what I have to say?"

Not there, not now that they were surrounded by so many people. Brandon and Pilar would be on their trail soon.

"We need a more private place, because I don't want to be interrupted," he said, reflecting on his thoughts.

"Then where?"

"Let's get out of here." He took her by the hand.

"Are you sure?"

"I'm certain of it, Darling." He smiled reassuringly.

"But the banquet, your friends?"

"They belong with each other, not with us." Claude chuckled as he took her by the hand. "Let them think you continue to be an evasive woman."

She left the martini on a table and rushed behind him as he dashed away. Leaving the Waldorf in such haste, they were like thieves, running away with all the secrets of life, and strangely, he felt free, pure of heart when he breathed the air out on the streets. Despite the burden of the past which was going to overwhelm with its presence, he chose to believe nothing could come between them. His mood was euphoric filling his heart with a wonderful joy, as though nothing really mattered other than the choices they had made. He hailed a cab to go to Windows on the World.

"One World Trade Center," he instructed the cabby.

In no time they made it to their destination and through a line of people waiting to go up, Claude addressed the young man dressed in a white tuxedo and slipped him a fifty in exchange of a cut in front of the other visitors.

Natalie held onto his hand as they took a private ride in the golden elevator, one hundred seven floors. Their ears popped, pulled by gravity as they climbed.

"Is this what you do to impress women?"

"I aim to impress only you."

When the door opened, he led her toward the entrance of the restaurant. The maitre d' greeted them onto the rotating floor. A table by the windows, quiet and removed from the noise of the band gave them a panoramic view of the bay as he pulled back the seat for Natalie. He asked the waiter for a bottle of their best champagne.

Free from all social restraints, they talked. The city below was a ball of small lights. The Hudson Bay, as it opened to the Atlantic, was a wide mouth of black with minuscule lights coming from the water like the sparks of a match. The moon, round and full, shone above the statue of Liberty, immutable, vigilant, facing out to sea.

"It's beautiful in here," she said. "What made you chose this place?"

"This was as close to Heaven as I could get while still touching the ground."

"It's breathtaking!"

"You're the one who is breathtaking." He took her hand, anxious to know the truth behind her. "Will you tell me what you''ve remembered?"

"I'm not whom I seem."

Her voice quivered as she touched him with her eyes, and he remembered Brandon's words.

"Who are you, Natalie?"

"I'm the woman who will love you always. Don't ask me why inner growth has to be tempered like steel with the fire and the blows of pain. If I hurt you, it's unwilling."

"Don't prepare me," he stood up to her glance. "I can take it."

"I must go back to Washington."

"Why?" Without realizing it, he squeezed her fingers in the grasp of his hand and she pulled out.

"Do you think love can redeem the mistakes of a life?"

"Dear God, Natalie. You are not only the most dazzling woman in my life but the most mysterious," he said with a weak smile. "I've told you, nothing could stop me from loving you. If you've made mistakes, so have I. When I met you, I told you I was no saint."

"I have a daughter."

"I thought Elizabeth was the one with a kid?"

"The child is mine."

"What's going on, Natalie?" he asked, his heart racing.

"Elizabeth died during childbirth."

"She has a child, and you have one too? Did you adopt her kid?"

"No, she's my own, born out of wedlock. It was impossible to kill the life growing in me, so . . . I kept the baby. She's everything," she said, looking right past him. "She's sweet, all goodness. The very best of me lives in her, but I miss her, and now she's with my parents."

"I don't understand."

"Our stories are too similar. Aren't they?"

"But one woman's dead," he said with a chill in his voice.

"I'm here with a chance to make it right."

"And the father? Do you still love him?" he asked with heartache.

"I love you. You're the love of my life, and I will love you forever." She paused a moment, looking into his eyes. "Can you accept my sin?"

Claude didn't answer right away. Then he said, "A sin of life. Abortion would have been easier."

"It crossed my mind, but I couldn't end her life, not for my selfish reasons. Instead, I left her father."

"He was the fool who let you go."

"I never told him about the baby."

"You didn't?"

"He was too busy with his life. I didn't want him to marry me just because I was pregnant."

"Why are two stories so similar?"

"Because they are."

"What am I to think?" The similarities between the circumstances of the past were like an echo of himself. He blinked, looking into the face of the woman in front of him, then rubbed his eyes, as though doing so could clear the unmentionable. "I can't believe that you and she lived such parallels."

"Then what should I say, that I'm Elizabeth?"

"Jesus Natalie . . . I know that's not the answer."

"I lived in the brownstone."

"Then you were room mates and you saw me. You saw me with her."

"The baby is yours."

For a moment he wasn't sure whose baby she was talking about, hers, or Elizabeth's. He shook his head.

"How can you be so sure it's mine? Liz never told me."

Natalie gave him a look that drew a pain like a knife going through the pit of his stomach, but the silence that followed was worse.

"Look, she's dead and it's going to be impossible to clear her facts, but there's you and I'm here. If you have a kid, I can accept the circumstances that got you pregnant, but why were you in Seattle when I found you?"

"I'm from Everett, you were right about that. I went to the plot where Elizabeth's mortal remains rest to pray for a miracle, for a chance to help my child. Next thing there's a radiance, a deafening blast that left the ground sparking with fire and me on the floor a few feet away. I didn't know who I was, or why I was there, and then I was lost in the storm, disoriented, frightened, cold with nowhere to go. I ran, and I ran and— "

"And I found you."

He didn't want to think, but his thoughts were inevitable.

"Is this some kind of scam?"

Her eyes filled with tears while her cheeks flushed. The words had come too easily, and after he said them, he was sorry.

"Do I have to be Lazarus for you to find the truth?" There was a moment of silence between them.

"I want to believe that you love me."

"If you don't know that already, then you will never find my love."

He couldn't hate her even if she trampled on his mind, and at this point in life it was impossible to let her go, even if she didn't add up with the facts. She sat in front of him, head high, shoulders straight, full of the poise which made her look wiser than anyone he'd ever met. Then he saw it, in the shine of her tears: the anguish of two women.

"I don't know if I could cast you away, even for my own self defense."

"Oh Claude, my daughter needs me," she told him with an urgent voice. "I have to go back to Washington."

"Then we will go together. I'll make arrangements, and in a few days we'll leave. She can come back with us."

"When you see her, will she remind you of my past?"

A silence came between them and he wasn't sure of the feeling Natalie's child would foster, but the thought of her absence and his future without her was unbearable. He didn't want to know anything else about the past.

"Don't say any more," he commanded. "I'm scared of the things you might say, I'm afraid of the thoughts that fill me with an odd feeling. I don't even want to know the name you left behind if you don't mind the way I call you. Marry me, " he said in a deep voice, knowing that he wanted her for the rest of his life. "I need to hold on to you the only way I know. I sense that I can love a child of yours as if it were my own and maybe I can redeem my mistakes in being a father for her. "

"Are you so sure you can live with me like this, knowing what I've told and fearing what I haven't said to you?" Natalie's chin trembled. Her hand wiped the tear that streaked down the hollow of her cheek.

His eyes fell upon the table, then he looked at her again.

"You'll let me know whatever I need to know about you but if memories can take you away from me, then I don't want to know anything else."

"I don't know what to say."

"Say *yes* and you'll make me the luckiest man alive. You don't have commitments to another man. You're free. I don't care what turns you had to take to get wherever you are now. All I know is that I know the woman you are, and I won't let you get away."

"I would love to be your wife."

"Then you shall be," he smiled. "What's your daughter's name?"

"Katherine," she said taking a deep breath. "She's ill — dying."

"For heaven sakes, what are you saying?" He raised his voice, concerned.

"The doctors found that she has a condition blocking the outflow of fluid from the brain. It's called congenital hydrocephalus. The specialist tried medications, but after many years the pills don't work anymore. Katherine needs surgery, a shunt to unload the fluid into the intestines, but we don't have the money to pay for her surgery. My parents tried mortgaging their business, but we're a poor risk. In a few months she will be dead unless—

"Unless — " He held his breath a second."Unless you get the money."

"Yes."

"There is no shame in asking for help. I'll pay for anything she needs." His voice was sure. "I want to help her because I love you. My money must be good for something other than the frivolities of life."

"You didn't have the money to help your mother, but you have it to save . . . Katherine."

"Yes . . . Life is strange, but you were right about what's important; it's not the way we dress, but who we are and what we do with what we've got."

Claude raised a glass of champagne for a toast and she raised hers shyly. In the worst of cases, if Natalie had fallen prey to Pilar's scam, as Brandon had claimed, to save her daughter's life, he could forgive her. He could even thank Pilar for putting Natalie in his way. When his mother was ill, he would have done anything for a handful of money. Who was he to judge desperation? He loved her more than ever for her pain and suffering as a mother, for the man she had redeemed, and for the happiness that had touched him with her by his side. The melody from the band reached them from a distance.

"You're not afraid that others will whisper about my intentions?"

"The only opinion that matters is what I think about you," he said.

"They'll say I came looking for your money."

Claude made a silence as he looked at her.

"Does it matter? I know you love me, and that's all I need."

"It doesn't bother you?"

"Tonight, here and for all eternity, I swear my love to you," he said filled with emotion. "You and I will grow old together, and through the loving eyes which gaze at you, you will never age beyond this day. All that I am, everything I own belongs to you. I have changed, haven't I?"

"Claude . . ."

"I'm yours, to do as you please. You can make me immensely happy or destroy me completely."

"Can you love me that much?" she broke through with a string of voice. "Money has guided your life. If I'm an adventuress, I can clean you out."

"I'll bargain that my intuition about you is correct."

"That's a huge change from the man I met."

"Marry me, and be the love of my life. Love is our prenuptial agreement. Simply swear that you love me."

"I will love you always, Claude." There was an ache in her voice and a beautiful softness in the reckoning of her promise.

24

Natalie frolicked around him, rising on the tip of her ballerina shoes as the skirt of her peasant dress tapered off in veils of silk crepe. Like a black and white movie, there was no color in what he saw except the ripe ruby of her lips, parting to say his name, the invitation to come closer, but more like a sound reaching from the grave, while she leaped, a muse hypnotizing with the rhythmic gyrations of her dance. Then, growing larger with proximity like a rider getting closer, the figure of a young child coming from the distance, getting closer every time Natalie completed a swirl.

This was a place removed from civilization, a valley made of earth, without foliage or grass of any kind. The view of the girl remained crystal clear despite the taps of an arduous rhythm over the soil that was packed into solid cracked blocks, drained of any moisture. The child came forth, closer and closer from afar, while Claude remained steadfast with a sense of knowing that they were here for him.

Waves of blond hair fell over the sides of her face, reminding him of wheat spikes, moving with the wind. Natalie took her by the hand, and with graceful synchrony they played in a swirl, singing something he couldn't make out, a melody as mesmerizing as the music from a cobra tamer. When he tried to come closer, barren oak trees sprang from under the earth, guardians with skeleton arms that connected, grotesque figures that broke the harmony of this place. Huge, heavy roots sunk in the ground forming a closed gate around the woman and child while immutable, the two kept dancing, unconcerned.

When the music stopped, the two seemed to notice he was there. Curious to discover him, the child broke away from Natalie and came closer, staring into his eyes with the yearning of a wish that was unspeakable. He would have sworn it was his own wish, the wish awakened to be part of their circle. More than anything else in life, he wanted to join them, but the trees kept him out.

He knew this was Katherine. He heard her voice come in a song, a song for him, a song giving hope to the sadness of his isolation.

> *"Awaken,*
> *for the sake of someone else,*
> *unafraid of the past,*
> *un afraid to look back.*
> *Go,*
> *where you should've been,*
> *because I've come,*
> *to set you free."*

The chant repeated over and over again until he memorized it well. For a second he rubbed his eyes, stricken by a fleck of dirt and when he looked up again, the girl had vanished. Music came from invisible speakers as he paced, searching, longing, wanting. Then the music stopped.

The earth opened with a great roar. An earthquake threw him on the ground, and the trees were swallowed into whence they came. Natalie, who had remained inside the circle, was free to come closer, free to take his hand. He heard her voice inside his head.

> *"More than spirit, less than matter, I'm enough for you to feel me. I'm suspended between two worlds, not for here nor there, just for you."*

He wasn't sure if her words were part of the girl's song, but they flowed smoothly through the space between them.

> *"I couldn't pass the chance to bring you where you should have been when I retained the secret that had to be shared between us. It was my free will, the small curve ball to the destiny chosen by our spirits! And now, it is done . . . I have come . . . And I must go because you have found the truth between us and the goodness in our love."*

In the sky he heard the shriek of an eagle, circling as gracefully as Natalie had dance. At that instance he knew she would leave him, like a bird who is set free.

> *"Find Katherine. For you it's not too late."*

In front of his eyes, Natalie turned into a beautiful bird of plumage, the mystical phoenix. Her arms grew wings, with rays of sunlight blazing through violet feathers, tinted by streaks of yellow. Three tears from her eyes touched the ground, and like a miracle of life, grass grew where there was none. Trees sprang out of nowhere, growing tender green leaves of early spring and water filled a lake when it erupted out of the rock, forming a waterfall. She took flight, ashe stayed behind.

And right before the end of his dream Claude heard one last message.

"*Remember* . . ." commanded the voice of the child.

25

Claude's body turned, and one arm fell over Natalie's waist. He discovered an indulgent smile upon her lips. Idly, wanting nothing other than the friction of her cool skin against his own, still half asleep, he brought her against his larger mass with the embrace of his arm. The night before had ended when they made love; their bodies fused as one. In his mouth, the taste of her body lingered.

"Hmm, what a great awakening," he said, notching her ear with his nose.

"Slept well?"

"Like a log." He moved his head so they were face on face. Her breath was his, and so was her soul.

"How long were you spying on my sleep?"

"Oh, I don't know."

There was a moment of silence between them as he closed his eyes and lay there, wrapped around her.

"God, I had a wild dream."

"Did you?"

"You were dancing with this girl, must have been all the stuff about your daughter last night."

"I'm sorry if I gave you a nightmare."

"It wasn't a nightmare, just weird."

Her lips spread in a soft smile. "I've prayed for you and for Katherine."

"I have become part of your answers."

"What would you say if I told you I had a few hours to live?" she asked.

"Don't play with such thoughts, Darling." He thought about his dream, and a shiver slid down his spine.

"But what would you do with me if I told you I had until the end of this weekend to be with you?" Her voice trembled with the refrain of a feeling he could not understand.

"You're so melodramatic."

"But tell me. What would you do?" she insisted.

"Hmm, if I must answer . . . then I guess I'd ask you to let me paint you one last time, not for posterity, but for me. I would steal your spirit and imprison you in the image on my canvas. Like Da Vinci and his Mona Lisa or maybe . . . ," he corrected. "I should spend the last thirty-six hours seeking your pleasures. Ah, but whatever we did, you would be the last memory my immortal soul would know, because then I would ask you to take me with you," he said, kissing her fingers. "You see, without you my life would have no purpose."

"And if I couldn't take you because your time to die had not come?"

"God, you make this difficult," he said, smiling, playing with what could only be a game of words. "Who are you supposed to be, death or the goddess of love sentencing a man to his doom?"

"Do you think I'm playing with you?" she asked extremely serious.

"Aren't you?" He smiled again.

"I'm not death nor a goddess." Her words had an icy undertone.

"Then who are you supposed to be?"

"I'm your soul mate." Her voice turned profound. "I'm the spirit which was meant to live out this life with you, as we have done so many other times and as we will do again."

"Not bad," he said, frowning under a half smile.

"Will you paint me one last time?" she asked.

"Sure . . ."

"Now, Claude, I want you to start now," she said, sitting up in bed. "I won't go until you fuse my soul into a painting, until you carve me so deep inside your eyes that not time, nor other lives will darken the truth between us."

"Jesus, Natalie. What madness has come over you?" He stopped smiling, watching her leave the bed, going to the closet where his paints were. Charged with sudden energy, she dug out the easel from the closet and a blank canvas.

Last time he had painted was in Washington. This was his Sunday morning and he was in the mood to catch the news, read the New York Times, and rest in bed for a couple of hours. At this very moment he was not in the surroundings nor the frame of mind to start any kind of project. Besides, his bedroom was not the paint studio in Washington and it would be an inevitable mess. Yet she was so enthusiastic.

"Slow down, Babes. I'm not in the mood." He stood in front of her, trying to detour her determination as he took the easel from her hands because it was too clumsy for her to log around.

"You said you wanted to catch the woman that I was," she said, daring him. "This is who I am. Look at me with the reality of the woman inside your heart, not the person that you see. My flesh is a delusion brought about by your senses but if you feel me alive, inside of you, then you can find me anywhere. Remember the essence of my spirit, even when you look at a different face, even if it's another life, another place. We come back so many times, but my energy will be the same, no matter what I look like."

Her eyes burned into his soul. Her words charged with her life force.

As though he took nourishment from the same blood flowing through her veins, using one will instead of two, he felt more and more compelled to take her challenge because she summoned his spirit.

"No deceits, no contempt, only our truth," she whispered.

"I hear you, Darling," he said, getting closer to her zenith. "You inspire me with your beauty, with the drama in the woman. You have become the obsession which drives my life." He was opening the case of paints. "My white rug is going to get ruined. Painting here will only make a mess but I'm going to let your impetus be my master." The charcoal was between his fingers to trace over the cloth.

"Will you find me each and every time?" she asked.

"I will find you always. Go there, on the bed, lie down on your back and let your hair dangle over the side." His voice turned into a deep command. "Take your clothes off and cover your torso halfway with the sheets."

Her negligee dropped on the floor, followed by his eyes. He positioned the easel and the canvas. She lay on his bed.

"I'll leave you my soul," her voice broke. "I'll be your Mona Lisa, and our love will be immortal."

He smiled, taunted by her words. Common sense had disappeared and life had no rules.

"Imagine that you're reaching for your last breath of life," he said. "Furthermore, knowing that you don't want to go, you must do so. Forfeiting your life is possible only with the knowledge that we will meet again, because this life is just a moment for our immortal souls."

"Paint me, Claude, and then I will take you there, where our daughter waits for us," she said, looking at him before acquiring her pose. Her voice was soft, almost peaceful.

"She will anchor you to life. Katherine will soothe the ache inside your heart, and you will realize what a great father you are. She will give you all her love and you will give her yours, and when you see her smile you will feel the love between us."

Natalie's eyes searched above her, as though she could pierce through the ceiling, looking at perhaps a glimpse of Heaven. Her arm reaching upward grabbed onto the invisible cord of energy giving life to her, just as he bid.

Breathtaking could have been this moment as silence became time's companion. Her dark brown hair touched the floor at the foot of the bed as she lay motionless. He filled with the desire to suckle over her breasts, to climb over the mounds of firm, voluptuous curves, thrusting between hips, ripe in the round of their shape, but he gave into the abstinence of the artist and painted.

Claude wasn't sure if he could create better than he had done already, but it was clear she aimed to make him try. Nonetheless, filled with the frenzy which had invaded his soul, he spent most of the day painting like a man possessed. The brush strokes flowed better than ever as he accepted that his hands obeyed the spiritual awareness within. Sunday became Monday on that Labor Day weekend, and the hours passed too fast. Food and rest were unimportant comforts, because on Tuesday his routine would resume, keeping him from finishing what he meant to complete.

Finally, almost thirty-six hours later, an hour before midnight, he concluded. Never did he imagine that his love to paint would come with such intensity, so distinct, more like a frantic need.

"I could paint you with my eyes closed," he said, dropping the brush into the paint thinner. "I know your body better than I know my own."

She had grabbed his robe to dress her nudity. Then he noticed the pallid color on her face and the small tremble in her hands.

"Are you tired, maybe weakened from the lack of food? Tell me it's my imagination, but you look sad." He too was slumping with a strange melancholy, not knowing why. He thought the feeling came from the end of an unforgettable weekend and because Tuesday would take him back to work.

"No, I'm not hungry, nor am I tired. My weakness is that I love you," she said.

"No, our love can only be a strength," he said, lifting her face by the chin.

"Maybe you're right, a dichotomy of parts. My love will give me the power to go on." She shook her head and took a deep breath. "Don't give up painting, because it would be a waste of wonderful talent."

"I would starve, darling — surviving on my skills as a painter."

"It's good," she whispered, moving closer. "I'm in there, in the essence of your feeling upon an image. No, don't sell this one. Keep it . . . because with it, you have conquered the future."

When her voice broke, he sensed she was fighting her emotions.

"You're so silly," he said laughing. "I'm not selling this one nor any of the other paintings. The only one who would buy them is you, and for that, they're already yours."

"The human form brings forth strong feelings and deep attachment," she looked down, "sometimes — so difficult to control. My soul is vulnerable embodied in the flesh."

"You say such things. How am I to take them?"

Natalie took her hand and placed it over his chest, searching for his heartbeat. Her head pressed against him, and he knew she was listening to the beats of his heart.

"I'm glad I came to you."

"My present and my future," he placed a kiss over her forehead, bringing her into his arms, standing tall and sure of himself. Natalie had enveloped him into her madness or maybe he had brought her into his. Filled with a strange despair, he looked at her and whispered, "Our house will become the home in which to raise a family. Katherine will be the first of our children and then we'll move to France, where you want to live. I'll work and come home every day to you, the only woman I will ever need. The heartbreak of disillusionment is behind us."

"Please, don't say any more." She broke away so he couldn't look into her face. "My feelings move me beyond the reason of my wisdom. I want to rebel against the higher knowledge of the universe. What I say doesn't make sense to you, does it?"

"I like your eccentric moods. I couldn't live without any facet of you."

"Close your ears and don't listen to my gibberish. Forget it and make love to me." She turned and her face was alive with the need to be his. "Take me like you've never done before, hold me to keep me from the hands of death," she demanded urgently. "Let me fuse into the memory of a kiss."

"What's come over you, Natalie?" he asked.

"Don't talk, my sweet." She lead him to the altar of their bed as her robe fell on the floor. "Take me one more time and savor this love of ours. It's better not to figure me out tonight."

To resist the plight of something as delightful as her proposition was impossible. Claude tapped into the secret place behind her eyes and found eternity in the look she gave him. The sadness in their past, the mistakes of youth and selfishness had ceased, but for an inexplicable moment he was overtaken with the incredible sensation that she was going to leave. A tear pierced through the flashing pain of solitude with the thought of her loss. In equanimity, he dismissed the thoughts that made his breath falter and his heart skip a beat in the microsecond of its existence.

Then he forgot about everything but the reality of the present and the pleasure in her touch. Natalie was there, for him with all her splendor. And then he felt her gently over his body, forcing him to give way under her soft caress. Her passion was his. She was his perfect counterpart, and he loved her with the past, with the child she loved so much, and with anything he would discover.

"You never told me your real name, Darling."

"Does it matter at this moment? Many names, many lifetimes, but you knew me always."

"You are my mysterious goddess. You'll have to tell me," he placed a kiss on her lips, "but you're right, it doesn't matter at this moment." He was a man and she, his woman, and he was going to please her with each stroke of his hand. Her body was the vessel of his want as Heaven and earth were going to split open with the surrender of their love. Destiny would unfold, but never again with the two of them apart.

"Take my life, my soul, the woman in your arms, and brand her into your heart," she whispered between his kisses. "I'm yours, only yours. Remember that I love you with all my might."

He did as she ordered, taking her body like never before, fusing into the torch which exhumed two bodies. Sweat wet his body and mixed in her own. Then she mounted his body, moving to synchronous thrusts. The gates of the impossible had surrendered and they belonged to each other for the eternity of time. Drained, consumed by the intensity of his passion, he fell asleep by her side.

"*Remember . . .*" she said. Natalie had said goodbye.

26

The new day found Claude in bed alone on Tuesday morning, so he got up and went straight for the shower. He figured Natalie was making breakfast, as she often did for him. Full of the ecstasy of the night before, he still felt her burning and the want for more, so he was glad she fled his side. Otherwise, he would have been late for work, detained by her touch. He walked past the canvas where her image was painted in oils, smiling inward, remembering their frenzy and the giving in her passion.

The drops of water felt warm over his back, wetting his hair, sliding down to his toes, making a flat noise as they smashed on the gray marble. With eyes closed, he stood in the shower, allowing the strokes to renew him.

When he stepped out, the mirrors had fogged with the water vapor. He pulled out the blow dryer from the closet, using it to wave hot air on the mirror surface and with the view of himself, he went ahead to dry his hair. Soon he was shaved, groomed and dressed, ready to go to work.

He came out of his room, thick silence dwelt in the shadows of the new day. The lights were off and in the kitchen, the percolator was off. Nothing had been disturbed. He rushed back to the bedroom, as though it was possible to miss her in his bed, knowing she wasn't there. He lifted the sheets off the bed, as though she could be lost in the volume of blankets. He stared at the empty bed.

His heart drummed with an omen when he opened her closet only to find that all her personal effects were as always and the suitcases were untouched. He tried desperately to rationalize her disappearance. He thought that she could have gone for milk, but when he took a second look, the refrigerator had plenty.

"Natalie? Where the heck are you?" His voice was a whisper when he stood in the middle of the dinning room in his black suit.

Then he saw the folded note on the table and he knew.

My dearest Claude:

All my memories live inside and the realization of who I am weighs heavily. There are facts that will be difficult to understand for you, especially in the next few days, but know that leaving you is the hardest thing I do. I must go, carrying with me the seed of our love. Trust me that if there were any other way, I would have waited for you, but my time with you has kept me from the responsibility to my daughter, to her who is our child now.

In the love that has grown between us, I am sure you will forgive my haste and understand why I will hurt you. When you get to Washington, I am certain you will find us and then everything will be so obvious. There are things which are, because it's the only way they could have come to be. You and I are the recipients of a special chance, and love is not our burden but our gift.

Don't doubt for an instant that I love you. Neither you nor I have it in our power to change the destiny which calls, but know that I will always be yours. Nothing is impossible if the human mind can envision its possibility. Faith accepts the inconceivable. Remember this above all else.

Neither time nor the space between us can change the bond between you and me. You will find me over and over again. We are bound through all eternity! Follow your instincts, for this is your spirit speaking to you, and accept that which seems so unacceptable.

Love you more than life itself,
Elizabeth.

The heartbeat of his life stopped and he realized he had allowed himself to be vulnerable. Like a madman he slammed out of his apartment.

*　　　*　　　*

Unlike his usual mode, he took the subterranean route to work, getting lost in the tumult of people crowding the subway, wanting to get lost, lost out of sight into the deepest crevice of the earth and away from his thoughts and the feeling that tore him. He had forged a concept, a way of living which Natalie had crumbled, and the ache inside his body was nothing new, only it cut deeper and more shrewdly than anything had ever done before.

To make a logical explanation of her unexpected departure was difficult, but most of all he couldn't understand why she had signed the letter, *Elizabeth*.

When he entered the forty-sixth floor, familiar faces at the firm looked like alien substitutes. People smiled at him and gave their 'good morning.' Irritable as he was, it was impossible to return their kindness. He meant to follow Natalie in her trip to Washington, and he had told her this two nights before when she told him about Katherine, but now it seemed obvious he had been a fool tolerating the eccentricities of her illness.

He asked Betty to call Pilar Haydig into his office. Minutes later she walked in, impervious to his dilemma and sat in the black leather armchair in front of him.

"I need your help." There was a grave sense of urgency in his voice.

"What's the matter?"

"I need to leave for Washington, today, this afternoon."

"You have to go where?"

"Seattle, get me on a plane this afternoon. Show me whatever is most urgent out of the business which is at hand, and then I'm going to ask you to oversee this place for me. Make an excuse for my absence, attend my meetings, and do some of your magic for the next few days."

"What's going on?"

"She's gone."

"Natalie?" Pilar raised an eyebrow.

"She went back to Washington." Claude swiped back the hair, which disheveled, fell over his forehead. "I have to go."

"Lovers' quarrel?"

"Don't be stupid," Claude said sharply.

"So then what happened? You stood me up at the party on Saturday night for her and then you leave me with that womanizer, Brandon. I looked for you and so did he. Where did you hide from us?"

"It's unimportant now," he said with a heavy heart.

"I was looking forward to meeting her"

"Drop it," Claude said bluntly.

At that moment he was struck by the realization that for some reason or another, neither Pilar nor Brandon met Natalie because something always came up. More than that, no one other than himself had ever remarked upon her. He held his breath, overwhelmed by the sensation of being peeled out of his skin.

When they left Washington, Natalie had remained in the car every time he encountered people, Tim, the UPS depot. In New York, Dr. Tananbaum had not met her, and the nurse acted as though she had never seen her face. Pierre in

France never addressed Natalie because she didn't speak French. No one at the mayor's ball seemed to even notice that he was with a woman and he thought it was because they were such snobs. And at the restaurants, if they remembered him because he left a generous tip, his female companion would be less than a pretty memory of nobody.

Natalie had been passive, like a shadow in his presence. For all intents and purpose, she could have been invisible or not there at all. He had been exhausted, sleep deprived, more wasted than any human could tolerate on the day when he arrived in the storm at Washington. Was she someone conjured out of his fatigue?

"This came in on Friday." She dropped a manila envelope on his desk. "You took the day off, and I was going through the mail, . . . you know, the way I've always done when you're out. I didn't realize it was private."

He glanced at the information written on the report from the detective agency. The report on Elizabeth. He read, hungry for the knowledge in the bold type. She had been an only child, born to Alfred and Lee Bates of Oregon. No sisters, no mention of any friends or roommates while in New York. A death certificate read the cause of death: Myocardial Infarction secondary to internal bleeding and exanguination during childbirth, due to a ruptured uterus. Date of death, September 8, 1988, buried in Everett, Washington. The medical examiner had performed an autopsy because the death was at home, the victim a young woman in good health, and no doctor had been in attendance of the delivery, just a midwife.

A statement from Agnes Morella, the landlady at the brownstone in New York, said her tenant had a boyfriend who came to inquire about Elizabeth's whereabouts a few times, until he himself disappeared.

That had been Claude, asking for six months until he gave up hope of ever seeing her again.

There was a list of relatives with addresses, but the names meant nothing to him. The final report would come in another week as their investigator was on the way to Washington.

"You found her grave, the dead woman in Washington, your girlfriend." Pilar inched forward on her chair." You suspected she was dead all along, but you had to put your finger into the wounds like St. Thomas, didn't you? That's why you asked me for the detective agency when you came back from your last trip."

"Don't ask me anything, Pilar."

"She died nine years ago giving birth to a girl. Was it yours?"

"Help me out," he begged. He could have asked Pilar to push him out of a window, but he didn't. "Get me tickets, a car, just like last time. I'll wrap up at the office, and you let me know about the arrangements later on at my house."

"You're acting erratically, too impulsively and it's going to lead you into a crash. Don't you understand you can't walk out and leave everything up in the air like this? There are two executives sitting out there, waiting to interview with you for the position which is being relinquished because of Natalie. You can't do this."

"If you don't want to help me, that's fine too. I'm leaving with or without your help. It's my company, and I can do whatever I fuckin' please."

Her silence was a wall of stone.

"How long are you going to hang around here?" she asked. "I realize your mind is set."

"You have two hours to wrap up my day at work," he said, looking at his watch. "These two men outside, you talk to them. My mind is too screwed up to think straight. I don't want to deal with anyone."

"Look, Claude, you know I do more than my job description for you but don't patronize me like this. I'll be interviewing these men for a job that should be mine."

"But it's not, it's still mine and I'm your boss."

"I'll try to help you because looking at you, you're a sorry sight. I realize that you're terribly upset, and I know that if you're going to Washington, Natalie must be the cause of your dilemma. Do you want to tell me what's happening?"

"I'm not sure I even know what's going on," he answered with gloom in the tone of voice. "Don't ask me any more."

"Very well, I'll let you be and may God help you out of this."

"Leave God out of it," Claude answered harshly. "He's got nothing to do with it."

A few hours later, he left his office, one hour later than anticipated. His anguish was marked by deep lines over his forehead. Natalie was gone because her child was dying, Elizabeth was dead and it was very probable he had a daughter somewhere in Washington. He didn't want to think any more.

*   *   *

While he packed, the doorbell rang and with giant steps he strode toward the foyer. For a split second, he hoped it was Natalie with tickets from a travel agency telling him she had run out to get them, but it was his heart hoping for something that was not. It was Pilar with his itinerary for the flight. The walls of his apartment trembled with the slam of the door behind him.

"Hey, I'm sorry I'm not her."

"I'm not in the mood to joke," he huffed, walking back toward his room to finish packing.

"I told you, falling in love is a fool's game. Once you do, you've lost the upper hand. Women know how to take advantage." Pilar followed into the house at a much slower pace. She was talking almost to herself because Claude was way ahead of her.

"No, that's why I know better. I'll never fall in love."

His apartment was familiar and she had been in his bedroom. Against the walls of the hallway, about twenty paintings were leaning on the floor, all of the same woman, but unframed.

"What are those?" She mumbled standing by the doorway of the bedroom. "Did you acquired a small private collection?"

"I painted them," he replied.

"Not bad. It's her, isn't it?"

"Yes, it's Natalie," his voice sounded flat.

"Well, one thing I'll give you. She's not ugly. As a matter of fact, you've painted a most erotic vision of a woman. I'm impressed."

"Thanks, but I don't have the time for your flattery." His tone was ornery. "Do you have my itinerary?"

"You leave at three."

She had purchased an electronic ticket for him and she gave him the printout from the fax machine.

"Then I'd better hurry."

As Claude finished in his frantic pace, Pilar stopped at the easel standing in one corner of the room. The carpet was stained with fresh oil paint, ruined. Her eyes skimmed the contents of the bedroom until she found the painting that was drying, hidden in the disarray, propped up against a corner and cast out of the way.

"Good God! This stuff is good, very good." She walked closer to the picture, lifting it with both hands and placing it on the easel to glance from a distance.

He stopped, looked at her in front of him, and burned with the sight of his painting.

"I didn't know you painted, Claude. You're full of surprises these days."

"Please, put it back," he asked with a dull ache in his voice, hesitating a fraction of a moment. "Pilar . . . ?"

"Yes?"

"Tell me that in the scheme of things you have nothing to do with Natalie's disappearance or for that matter, for her presence in my life."

She looked at him, eyes cold.

"You're the first man who treated me like an equal, and I think you're a fair sort of guy. We've had our disagreements, but I would never stab you in the back, not for a job or to help anyone else. I'll never say this again, so hear it well and keep it to yourself. If I was going to have a weakness for a man, that someone would be you." She made a silence and then went on. "There's a heart buried somewhere inside of me, and because of it, I could never strike against you."

"I'm sorry if I hurt you with Natalie."

"You didn't."

"Thank you."

She looked away, as though embarrassed by the debility inside her soul.

"Listen, I have a friend with a gallery in Soho," she said. "Do you mind if I show him some of your work?"

"I don't care about anything that happens but don't touch this one," he said, pointing at the painting on the easel.

"But it might be the best one."

"Don't touch it, okay?"

"All right, all right. Boy, you're uptight today."

Pilar sat on the bed, her eyes stopping on the dirty plates over the small bistro table in one corner. Clothing was scattered all over the room, and the bed was unmade, the comforter and sheets on the floor.

"What happened between you and Natalie?"

"You wouldn't understand." A bitter smirk drew on Claude's face. "I'm not sure myself of very much."

"I guess men would envy you for having such an impressive woman in your life."

"There's nothing to envy in the way I feel right now."

"It might do you a heap of good to talk about it."

"I'm all packed, so I'm leaving." He turned around to look at her. "Just know that I'm going after the woman I love and that I don't know why she left me in such haste. We were going to Washington together, in a few days, but I guess she couldn't wait. She must have thought it would take me longer than I wanted to settle business in the office, and now she has her memory back. It makes her less dependent upon me."

"She got her memory back?"

"She did. I asked her to marry me Saturday night."

He was walking out with his suitcase.

"Wait a second, Claude!" Pilar stood up, mouth open. "You're not going to leave me like this, are you? What kind of a woman would leave you so unexpectedly without an explanation after you've asked her to marry you?"

"Someone like her, but now I have a plane to catch." With that, he walked out, leaving Pilar alone to draw her own conclusions. Nothing mattered except to find one woman, the one who had betrayed his trust.

27

Like the motion of continental plates, the future was a cataclysmic experience, and it all had started with the subtle smile of a woman's face. More than chance, more than mere coincidence, meeting Natalie had been an act that had altered life forever and the passion born was more than hormones and neurotransmitters promoting a natural attraction, because the feeling went beyond the physical plan in the survival of the species.

Washington was cold and rainy, and breathing left a soggy feeling in the airways. Claude drove south through the coastline, sighing more often than usual, and when he realized it, he forced himself to stop. Nothing but the will to find her moved him, as he had no idea of where to start looking. The names and addresses on the report were certainly a possibility, but he was traveling toward his cabin, hoping she would be there.

From the moment when she acknowledged her memory, the hours had passed in the vertigo of the two days that followed. He could have dwelt on many questions, all of which seemed important now but instead he barely deepened on the details of her past. With the thought that they had a lifetime together, he cursed himself for being so generous.

His journey was a familiar one, not requiring a map at all, now that for so many years he had come upon the same roads. Long ago — on an impulse — he drove up through this underdeveloped coast line, from Northern California to the town of Everett, when an inner feeling took root, pushing with tumultuous clamor, saying this was where he belonged. *Was all of it part of the same karma leading him to find the name in a grave?*

Never rationalizing his choices to more than a manifestation of a whim, he had returned every opportunity he got, but now these woods were linked to the woman he loved, and the countryside took more of an enigmatic grasp on his mood.

The familiar fork in the road leading to town caught him by surprise, almost missing the turn. His foot sank on the accelerator, realizing his anger would vanish with a reasonable explanation from Natalie. He would forgive almost anything, knowing it impossible to live without her.

Past the cemetery, he dug inside the pocket of his jacket and crushed between his fingers the letter she had left behind, and when the shy thunder from the storm approaching broke through silence, he expected her to cross the path in front of him, like once before. Why had Natalie signed *Elizabeth* on the letter?

Twenty minutes through a winding road ended in his cabin. The lights were off and the place was vacant, the way they had left it in June. Natalie knew about the spare key hidden over the ledge of the door but when he felt for it, it was still there. He walked inside the house, her absence making it feel wrong and strained nostalgia ran *au par,* caught in the cradle of his memories.

He looked around but emptiness desecrated his tortured feelings. Everything was the same, the stone and mortar fireplace, the red Indian rug with geometric weaving, lying on the lacquered pine boards of the floor. Large colorful pillows on the sofa, the afghan that covered her once, everything was as it had always been, but something was missing. His *senses* couldn't pick up that she was there.

Suddenly he heard a noise upstairs. His heart jumped out and his legs carried him upstairs faster than a cycle of blood through his veins. Opening the door to his bedroom, he found it empty. Less hopeful, he went into his painting studio, and as he stood there, a cold chill forced him to shiver while his breath glazed in the air. He looked at the windows and then realized one of them was open. The latch had come loose and the noise was the banging of a shutter.

He turned around in a full circle, scanning the four corners of the room, listening to the noise of his Western boots over the plank floor. He would have sworn she was looking over his shoulder, that Natalie was humored by his inefficiency to discover her presence beside him. The phantoms of absent paintings crowded the barren room, feeding on his loneliness. Then he remembered the sketches in his drawing pad, tucked away inside the top drawer of his desk. He had no pictures of her, but his drawings would serve well. They were good enough to help his search.

On his way back to town, he resolved to stop at the police station, but to get there he had to shoot across town. He figured that would be as good a place as any other to start his investigation. He had the envelope from the detective agency in his briefcase.

Driving through the narrow streets, he came by the general market, and right away he thought of Tim, the caretaker of his property. Tim McGuire knew everyone in Everett and could be a source of valuable lead. Without further pondering, he turned into the familiar parking lot, convinced Natalie was somewhere in that town together with Katherine.

After the Labor Day weekend, all the tourists had left these parts. When Claude walked in, sketch pad under his arm, the old man was stocking cans on a back shelf of the store, while Mrs. McGuire placed a row of homemade pies inside the shelves of a refrigerated counter. Breads and jars of raspberry and blueberry jam, all homemade added a warm country feeling.

"Hello, Tim," he said, reaching the man, as composed as he could be under the circumstances. Tim turned at the call of his name.

"Mr. Aumont! You've returned."

"I have," he said, mumbling to himself. Then he spoke up an octave. "I'm looking for someone, that woman I told you about before I left."

"Why yes, I remember but I told you I didn't know her."

"I need to find her. Please look at the picture I drew of her. It's a rough sketch, but maybe you'll recognize someone you know."

Claude opened the pad, showing Natalie's face. Silence slumped between the two men. Then Tim's face grew red like a pomegranate, making it obvious that he knew who she was. He thought there was a disturbing glint in the man's eyes.

"Are you mocking me?" asked Tim, speaking with an unexpected hostile tone.

"Of course not, Tim. Do you know her?"

"Why do you wanna know?"

"I'm in love with this woman. She's my fiancé."

"This is my daughter." Tim took a step back.

"You must be mistaken." Claude stopped to look at the man next to him.

"Of course it's my daughter." There was a break in the steadiness of his voice. "Do you think I'm a fool?"

"Maybe I'm the fool if this is true. I don't mean to insult you but you'll have to admit this is peculiar. Here I thought I would have to search forever and instead you're telling me she's here? Has she told you about me, about us?"

"My daughter is dead."

The hollow words dissected through Claude's mind. For a moment he stood there, not knowing what to say. If this man's daughter was dead, obviously she couldn't be Natalie.

"My girlfriend is alive," he explained, clutching back the sketch pad. "She was with me a few days ago. I'm sorry about your daughter but it's obvious we're not talking about the same person."

Full of suspicious disbelief, Claude turned around and rushed toward Tim's wife, Lee McGuire, who was oblivious to their exchange, as she was in the front of the store. The possibility that an accident could have taken Natalie's life drove him wild.

"Have you seen this woman, Lee?" Claude asked in a loud voice. Tim was following at a much slower pace because of the limp from his arthritis but in a few moments he would be by their side. The sketch pad was open once more, and Natalie's face was vivid within the image on the paper.

Lee grew pale and the whites of her eyes pushed out, leaving her speechless. Could the similarity between two women be so great that two people could confuse them?

"Where is she?" he asked in a voice that was more like a cry. Tim was upon them and Lee looked at her husband and then back at Claude with a beatific tolerance for the intrusion of their past. This was Natalie, not their daughter, and they were wrong confusing her with someone dead.

Always calm, today he was a mess, making an unusual sight. The metal surface on the door of a freezer in front of him made a mirror for his reflection, the tired and pale grimace, as though an accident had crushed the muscles of his mouth, leaving his eyes sunken, the cheeks hollowed by the tight clench of his jaw.

"I told him, Lee," Tim turned toward his wife, "but he paid me no mind."

"I told you she's alive," Claude said, losing control. "How long ago did your daughter pass away?"

"Elizabeth has been dead for almost ten years," Lee whispered.

"Please, don't tell me your daughter's name is Elizabeth Bates." A cramp slashed his body in two. His knees buckled as he waited for an answer from Lee.

"Tim, please . . . close the front door. Let's go to the back," Lee pointed toward the back of the locale, showing him the way. There were no customers inside the store so to escape into the small rustic nook drenched in an ashen light was a reasonable pursuit. The room was packed with boxes, at least ten feet high, like unsteady pillars ready to topple if he brushed against them. A staircase made of two-by- fours and sheets of plywood lead to the second floor apartment. The old woman took Claude by the arm like she would have done with her son if she had one, guiding him to sit at the table in the middle of the room, but despite her kindness, a different sense of grief was creeping in with the thought of death.

"This woman on your notebook looks like our child," said Lee as she sat in front of Claude. "Tim is her stepfather. My first husband and I got divorced when my daughter was five. This is why she doesn't carry the same last name,

McGuire. How do you know her name, Elizabeth Bates?"

"The cemetery outside of town, it has a grave, there's a name — " mumbled Claude.

"Yes, our daughter is buried there," said Lee. "You look ill, Mr. Aumont."

"I don't think I can ever be well again." His voice trembled. "Hear me out, but at your own risk, because once you enter my maze, you will never come out."

"Please," said Lee with a quiver in her voice.

"Liz vanished ten years ago. The Elizabeth I knew was an art student and she lived in New York. My love of money was greater than the commitment to our relationship. Money and triumph weighed heavily in those days. She wanted to get married, I didn't. For all I know she could have been pregnant with my child — because come to think of it — she left in a very *bizarre* way. When I looked for her, there was no trace to follow, and she dropped out in the middle of a semester. Her apartment was vacant, her phone disconnected, and I always thought she would call me after a while, but she didn't. I never heard her name again until a few months ago, outside this town, at the cemetery.

"I went there with Natalie, the woman I found during the storm that greeted my arrival during my last trip to Washington. Natalie had no memory of the past, but she brought me there, to that plot of land, compelled by the cry inside her lost mind."

His eyes landed on Lee. She sat petrified, listening to what he had to say.

"I fell in love with the stranger in my life, despite her illness, regardless of everything that made no sense." Claude went on. "We left for New York, and after a few months of living together, I asked her to marry me. People who know me speculated about her presence, so obscure, mysterious in so many ways, but I chose to believe that her intentions were genuine and that she loved me as much as I did her. However, Natalie warned me, there are no such things as coincidences, and there were too many of them.

"She left me twenty-four hours ago, leaving me a crazy letter that led to Washington. I come here looking for her, and you tell me you have a daughter who died about the same time as my girlfriend, and whose name is Elizabeth Bates. Not only that, but the two of you seem to think the deceased looks identical to the woman on my pad."

Claude slammed his hand over the notebook, which was unfolded to a picture of Natalie.

"The name of Elizabeth Bates follows me like a ghost, only I'm not a superstitious man and I will never concede that I've been living with the spirit of a dead woman. A detective agency confirmed that the woman at the cemetery is my girlfriend, but she can't be Natalie."

"Your tale is incredible," Tim said breathless. "When our Elizabeth left us she was full of dreams about making it big. We never thought she would come back with a broken heart and . . . pregnant."

"There was mention of Alfred and Lee . . . Bates."

"Alfred was my first husband."

"And you are Lee Bates," said Claude. " . . . but I would have recognized Liz, even after all this time. She looked nothing like Natalie."

"Elizabeth never told us about the father of her child, being the private person that she was. I'm of the belief it's easier to share a burden between two."

Lee's head dropped down, the tears filled her eyes and she shook with uncontrollable sobs. Tim grabbed for a roll of paper towels over a box.

"She died giving birth to our grandchild," said the old man while he comforted his wife.

"That evening she went into labor, and because of the weather it was impossible to drive out to the hospital," said Lee between sobs. "Seattle is far away, so instead we called the midwife. The birth went well, but after the baby was born, Elizabeth bled. She hemorrhaged to death."

"Natalie told me she saw herself bathed in blood. She was horrified of the visions that were coming," he said almost to himself.

"There was nothing anyone could do," continued Lee. "Tim wanted to go in the midst of the storm, but it would have been suicide. We thought she was too weak to travel and that the long trip would make the bleeding worse. You know the roads around here. They're treacherous: many are unpaved and mud slides are all over the place. We prayed for a miracle, but it didn't come. Since then, we have lived with the memory of our choices."

"She wasn't meant to die," he said. "I'm sure she would have returned with our child."

Lee opened the notebook and looked through the pad. Her fingers turned the pages slowly, caressing the paper as they moved forward. Claude thought the old woman had to be in her mid-sixties, maybe a little less. Tim had to be older. Her eyes were warm, profound, just like other eyes he knew, Natalie's. He understood that love and pain lived closely intertwined. He also realized he had to trust someone because madness was just a step away, but he couldn't bring himself to believe that one woman could return from the Beyond.

"Why have you mistaken Natalie for Elizabeth?" His voice begged them to reconsider.

"There's an incredible resemblance between this woman and Elizabeth," added Tim. "Wait here. I'll show you some of her photos."

Saying that, the old man walked up the stairs and into the apartment. The McGuire's lived on the second floor of the building, but Claude had never been up there. Lee sat in front of him, her facial expression stricken by the memories awakened, and he felt ashamed to disturb the heartache of these people.

When Tim came back with a photograph album, Claude's hands opened the book. Instantly he recognized Liz. There was no mistake about it. Then he looked at the sketches and as though he had regained sight after being blind for months, he stared at the same face. His eyes widened; his pulse raced when his heart hammered out of his chest.

"No . . .   No . . . it can't be. It can't be." The photographs and his sketches were of the same woman. Like a revelation, two faces had become one. "How could I fail to recognize her? Am I blind or just out of my mind?   She hasn't aged, she looks as young as she ever did. Stop it, I don't believe in hocus-pocus. Don't ask me to believe in something which my senses can't explain," he said.

"We don't want to make you believe anything," Lee cleared up with a tremulous voice. "I would find it difficult to believe that my daughter would be a physical presence once dead. *Wonders* like that don't happen except in the lively imagination of someone playing a prank."

"Believing in such a possibility is impossible," said Tim.

Nonetheless, a haunting thought had emerged with the reality of the pictures. "The child, there's a girl." Claude said, as he looked into Lee's face. "She's sick, you need help to pay for her operation."

"How do you know?" Lee stood up, assaulted by Claude's knowledge of their secret.

"Natalie spoke about Katherine, before she left. The child is dying, isn't she? You don't have the health insurance or the money to pay for the medical bills."

"Oh my God!" Lee gasped as she covered her mouth with a hand. She wasn't crying any more but the veins over her neck bulged out, and he thought she was going to have a stroke right there.

"We're trying to get a loan to pay for the surgery," Tim mumbled, "Our collateral is not enough. The bank thinks we're a poor risk. Could it be that your Natalie is truly our Elizabeth?"

"No, it can't be," said Lee.

He could understand why Lee refused to accept anything of what was being said.

"Katherine is our grandchild," Tim spoke up, as he looked at Claude once more.

Claude swept the room with his eyes as though expecting Natalie to make her presence and clear up the entire mess, but a difficult reality was setting in; Elizabeth Bates and Natalie were blending into the same person. Claude's senses were fighting to sustain an unreal possibility because the universe had rules, but all his logic was tumbling in front of the facts. He was not a man of faith. He needed to grasp at something real to believe in the violation of metaphysical rules playing out before him.

"Where's the child?" he asked.

"She's upstairs," Lee managed to say.

"Our grandchild began to complain of headaches . . . about six months ago. We took her to the doctor when she started to say a lady was visiting her room at night, a kind . . . and beautiful lady who told her stories . . . about the man who would come to take her into the big city. The headaches, her fantastic and vivid stories, we weren't sure what was happening. After many tests they found she has a narrowing in the drainage system of the brain, congenital hydrocephalus."

"The doctors said her visions were produced by the intermittent compression of brain tissues. That's why she has the headaches, the hallucinations, or what we at least thought were such. Eventually, she will go into a coma, it's a matter of months," Lee whispered.

Claude smoothed back his hair, thinking they were all going crazy. The possibility that Katherine was his child knocked all the sense out of his head, but not only that, he had made love to a dead woman, someone from his past. He started to laugh under the silent watch of the two other people in the room.

"What madness is in all of this?" he asked, demanding an answer. "She came looking for me, so that the money which initially tore us apart would help save the life of our daughter? Is this supposed to make it all okay? Am I to believe such things?"

"I don't know," Lee shook her head. Her eyes were red, her face looked ill with the realization of such a contingency.

"Natalie was as real as you and I," Claude ended his sentence with a bang of his closed fist over the table. The physical pain reassured him of reality, but he needed more. "I want to see the child."

28

The universe was rearranged when Elizabeth Bates was allowed to come back from the other side of life. With the upheaval of these changes the rules had been altered, modified to allow for the impossible. Answers that held no questions made him realize that the journey of life would never be the same. Minute after minute, Claude came closer to the face-to-face encounter with Katherine, his thoughts reaching into regions deep in the murky waters of possibility, full of abysmal impact linking death to life. When he came out from these depths, he looked at himself, at the people around him, at the empty cavity the world had become, only to feel like he himself was as unreal as everything else around him.

With a clumsy step, Tim followed behind his wife with Claude timidly further back. A mouthful of bitter acid from his stomach reached his mouth forcing Claude to spit out yellow liquid.

"Are you going to be ill?" asked Tim.

"No, no, I'll be alright." Nothing could be further from the truth because the pain in his stomach was caused by the twisting and turning of his guts. Maybe the next time instead of bile, red blood would stain the floor.

For an awkward moment, he expected to hear trumpets and horns blowing in his ears, announcing the end of the world or maybe his own demise because the dead had arisen, and this had to be his judgement day. Each step brought him closer to his destiny, and there was nothing more frightening than to meet the child upstairs, the apocalyptic child waiting in the house.

The McGuires led him through a short hallway where a homemade quilt hung against the wall. As he passed the living room, he saw family photographs resting on a table. He was too far away to distinguish the people in the pictures, but Liz had to be somewhere in there. The house was clean, spotless, and although their furniture was modest, the place had the warmth of these people.

He could smell the leftover scent of the pies that were downstairs, baked to be sold. At any other time he would have bought one of them because he knew how good they were, but now the thought of food filled him with a repugnant crawl in his mouth.

He hesitated on the other side of the door before walking into the bedroom that belonged to Katherine. He saw her right away. When he looked into her eyes, he saw the hope of an early morning sky, and in the color of her hair he found the sun over a field of light. This was the girl in his dream. Could this really be his child, and of Natalie, the Elizabeth Bates from his past? Katherine sat on the floor playing, surrounded by inanimate dogs, pigs and cows, two horses, and wobbly peg-like figures that made the people of her farm house. Other toys were scattered around the area, all part of her domain. A pink bedspread covered the twin bed in the middle of the room, and red checkered curtains hung from the two windows. The wallpaper was full of tiny fairies, which seemed to dance freely over the walls. The sweet voice, which was at play, was just a squeak when it stopped to look at the man who stood with her grandparents.

He saw it, over the girls red sweater, unmistakably his, the ankh over her chest. He came closer, focusing on the shiny gold object, squinting, torn by the incredible possibility that it could be the same one that had belonged to him. This was the ankh and chain Liz gave him as a present many years ago, the one he had given back during the argument that split them up.

Instantly, Claude knew he loved her. As though he was one of the subjects in her kingdom, a feeling overcame him, difficult to believe because he had never seen her before. Never into kids, he felt overcome by a tenderness that came from within, pushing with the strong desire to hold her, to hug her almost to the point of squeezing her in his arms. Katherine was the missing piece to all that was inexplicable, to the bizarre rendition that had delivered him there.

He remembered another afternoon in Paris, not so long ago, when he and Natalie sat at the Emplanades by the Eiffel Tower, watching the children play. He would have sworn Natalie was here, now as an invisible presence watching them all together.

The young girl seemed unaltered by his company, as though he was a familiar face that came into the room. Her eyes twinkled with the innocence of her age as she looked upon him and her grandparents. Her biological age matched the time period when he had the affair with Liz and the cry inside his heart silenced all doubts, shouting that this was his daughter.

Looking at Katherine, he understood why Liz had to run away. She had to disappear to save Katherine's life, because in his anger toward the careless mistake, abortion was an appealing solution. No. He had to believe the termination of this life would have been rejected by him as an abominable mistake.

"Katherine, come. We want you to meet someone," said Lee, breaking through his thoughts.

At first the child was shy, staying where she was, then she obeyed, going toward Lee, who surrounded her with loving arms.

"This man has come to meet you." The grandmother forced a smile.

"Oh, you must be the nice man the lady told me about," the girl said, in a natural sort-of-way.

"What nice lady?" asked Claude, taken by the girl's words.

"Grandma knows, the lady who is beautiful and kind. She talks to me when my head hurts, and when she touches my forehead I feel fine."

"Up to today we thought that these stories about a lady who visits Katherine were either her imagination or the pressure growing inside the brain, as the doctors explained." Lee looked at Claude.

"We never thought . . . they could be real,"said Tim.

At that instant he understood the reason he was there was because of this small life. Katherine made him believe in the power of Heaven and the possibility of fate. Natalie had done well, as he understood the rare gift of saving a life. He had enough money to take charge of the situation.

"Are you brave, Katherine?" he asked, kneeling in front of her. He gazed into her eyes and he thought they were the same as the color of his eyes. They made him recall the color in his mother's eyes also. "You and I will go on a trip, to a place called New York."

"Is this the big city the nice lady talked about?"

"Maybe. We'll bring your favorite belongings, your doggie, some of the toys in your room. Grandma will pack a suitcase and she will come with us." Claude paused to exchange a glance with Lee. They made a silent pact as to what had to be done in order to get Katherine the care she needed. "The doctors will make you well again. Instead of a clinic, you will have a private physician, the very best I can get for you."

"I'm not scared," said the girl.

"Then you definitely are a brave child," he coaxed.

Looking at Katherine, she didn't appear sick at all. Her face was alert and her mind caught quickly what had to be done. She had no hesitation in accepting the future he proposed.

"My grandmother says I'm like my mother, a strong woman."

"You sound precocious for your years."

"And what does that mean?"

"That you are wiser than you seem for someone who is so inexperienced with life. How old are you?"

"I'll be ten in a week."

"That's a good age," he said, smiling. "I will come for you tomorrow morning."

He saw the stifled look on the McGuire's. They were simple people, and what had transgressed was as unusual as it had been intense.

"Do you suppose the tribulations of a life bring out the best in us?" Claude asked, getting up from the floor as he towered over the child.

"The Bible says life is a valley of sorrows where we come to purify the imperfections of our soul." Lee took a step forward, looking at her granddaughter.

"I don't read the Bible," said Claude.

"Elizabeth loved you," Lee's voice was just a whisper. "She died tormented by the love toward a man and a the child she was leaving behind."

"She made a mistake leaving me," his voice rumbled, staring at the child in front of him. "In a way we were a lot alike: she thought she knew me and I thought I had her all figured out. Instead we only knew ourselves. If she'd given me a chance, I would have done right for the three of us, but instead, our infatuation with our choices made a mess of it all. Read this. She left it behind"

From his pocket he took out the letter written by Natalie. He handed it to Tim who proceeded to read the note. When he finished, he passed it to his wife. As Lee read the piece of paper, her nostrils flared, her hands trembled.

"She brought you here, to . . . Katherine," Lee said. "This is Elizabeth's handwriting. I would know it anywhere."

"Natalie . . . or I guess Liz left it on my table before she disappeared." He walked toward the door, turning around to give one last look at the child. "I have been living in Washington for almost four years and I have known both of you for an equal amount of time. When did my journey start? Was it four months ago during a storm, or was it long before then?"

Whether Katherine was his child or not, he couldn't let her die, not now that he had met her. In the morning he would return as promised.

*   *   *

Claude stood over the granite boulders with the precipice below. Although the cliffs were a hundred feet above sea level, they seemed like a small step to breech, an escape route to banish the pain. The voice of the wind called him, teased with the thought of death. A large yellow moon hung low on the horizon, witness to the night. The mutilated emptiness inside his heart was more visible, alive under a sky full of stars, as though beauty made the ugliness of his life much clearer.

Reason had become chaotic and nothing made sense.

Cheated out of all he'd held sacred, robbed of the love of a woman who had disappeared from the face of the earth, he faced the supernatural. If it had been a scam to get him to pay for a child's operation, it had been well orchestrated, because he believed.

"Where are you now, Natalie? I'm in love with the ghost of the woman I killed." His wild and violent laughter delivered a mad man.

This had been the site of their idyllic romance, and now every word, every sentence she had spoken held a meaning.

"Did you trade me off in your barter with God, like you did ten years ago? Don't I have a say in this?"

He thought of his body, crushed and broken by the waves, mangling against the rocks, a kinder finale than the lethal wound that mauled his heart. The months with Natalie seemed like a foreign episode and now the end of a fantastic story.

"If you came back for me, then take me with you, because I don't want to live without your love. Let my arms embrace sweet death."

As he filled with the vertigo of his next step, the thought of Katherine stopped him. He couldn't jump. There was a promise to keep. Nothing but his money could save her life. Invisible hands reassembled the crippled spirit with an infusion of firm resolution. Death would have to wait.

His eyes burned with the tears filling, but he fought to hold them back.

"You have humbled me," he said with a visceral voice, more like a moan. "It's a lie that men can't have a broken heart, . . . that we don't cry. My life will be the emptiness of your forgetfulness, until we meet again, Natalie . . . my love."

*   *   *

On his way back to New York a small satisfaction rose within Claude, knowing that he was putting his money to good purpose. Katherine brought her toys and played with them in her seat during the flight. She talked to her Barbie doll, carrying an imaginary conversation back and forth, not bothering her grandmother and least of all him.

He paid no heed to the stewardess who flustered around him, offering her services most diligently. The only one who caught his interest was Katherine.

Watching her made him feel young again, refreshed, out of the hell that had become his life, and he envied that with her youth she could forget that her life was at stake, walled off by her fantasy world.

Finished with their meals Claude asked Lee to exchange seats with him. Katherine wasn't playing any more, stifled by a bored look on her face, and although he wasn't sure what he was going to say, it was probably the best time to attempt a conversation with the young girl.

"I like your hair in pigtails," he said by her side, in what was a childish manner. She looked at him with her big blue eyes, making him feel stupid that this was the only thing he could have found to say. "So do you go to school?"

"I used to," she replied, looking at him. "I stopped when my head began to hurt for hours during the day. The other kids made faces when I'd make a mess and I was puking almost every day in school"

"Does it hurt now?"

"No," she said, looking surprised that he didn't know. "She comes when I have pain — the lady. The teacher told Grandma I made other children uncomfortable talking to the lady, because nobody could see her."

"I believe you," he whispered.

Katherine looked at him. "They thought I was weird."

The noise of the motors filled the quiet of a moment.

"I like sitting next to you."

"And that surprises you?"

Claude smiled at her statement.

"I've never spoken to a nine-year-old. I guess I was your age once but I've forgotten what it was like. Yes, it surprises me that I would want to know so much about you and not know where to start, but this is good."

"I'm not so different from you, just younger. But remember," she winked at him, "I'll be ten next week."

He would have to get her a birthday cake.

Katherine was not obnoxious, and he was enjoying her proximity more than he imagined. He thought it would be easy to like her. Happiness was forever banned from living in his heart again, but this feeling would do for now.

"Do you like to fly?" he went on.

"This is my first time, but it's boring and too long. I'm glad I don't have to do it more often than this. I think I would prefer bicycle riding or even walking."

"Well, I think walking to New York would be a long walk, but why don't we get up and check out the back of the plane?"

Katherine smiled, filled with adventure. He took her hand and got out of his seat under Lee's scrutiny. The stewardess came up to him, offering the service of the restroom at the front of the aircraft for their convenience. He thanked her politely as he crossed through the blue curtain, which was drawn to separate first-class from coach.

"She's pretty, isn't she? She's been looking at you since you sat down."

Katherine had taken him by surprise. She had caught the attentiveness of the woman. The truth was that he had noticed the subtle flirtations of the woman without intending to respond to her advances.

"Not all trips are this long, but when they are, it's good to come in good company," he smiled.

They were standing on line for a water closet at the back of the aircraft.

"Do you travel often?" asked Katherine.

"Yes, I do, but I'm not crazy about it either. My job takes me out of town too often."

"People should never have to do what they don't want to do."

"That would be nice," he said. "You have a lot of small dogs. I saw you playing with them yesterday, when I was in your room. Do you like animals?"

"Oh yes. When I grow up, I'm going to be a ve-te-ri-narian." Her face lit up.

He laughed because she had a hard time pronouncing the entire word.

"I agree, people should chose a profession that makes them feel good."

"One day my grandma is going to get me a puppy. She said she would."

"Dogs make good friends," he smiled once more.

"Do you have many friends?"

"No, not too many. I lead a very lonely life, working most of the time." His words came out full of self pity, something he didn't want her to see, but it was too late.

"Then I'll be your friend. I'll ask my grandmother to be your friend also. She's very nice, you know."

"I'm sure she is."

The line moved up and it was her turn for the lavatory.

"Close the lock behind the door," he told her. Katherine smiled and he thought she knew better than he gave her credit. Anyhow, he waited outside her door until she was finished and then returned with her to their seats. He felt something close and intimate when the girl took his hand.

"Grandma tells me bedtime stories. Do you know any?" asked Katherine, sitting next to Claude once more.

"I guess I do," he answered, scratching his head.

"Do you have children?"

"Do you have children?"

He wanted to tell her that he thought she was his, but instead he just shook his head.

"Well, then you can practice on me," she replied, very matter-of-fact. "If you want, you can tell me the stories you know, and I'll tell you if they're any good. I can even tell you some of the ones I know if yours are very bad."

The girl had a contagious smile. He thought she was something else, neither rude nor mean, just a witty child. Carrying on a conversation with her was easier than he thought, and he loved that she was exhorting a calm in the pit of his misery.

During the trip, he explained to Lee that Brandon would contact her in the morning with instructions about the hospital. A pediatric neurosurgeon was informed of her condition, and emergency arrangements for Katherine's care were being made, even as they spoke, as he had arranged to have all the medical data transferred to New York.

When they arrived, he insisted on having them stay with him rather than in a hotel room, because he wanted Katherine near him. His apartment was large enough to accommodate them for the short period they would be in town.

"I have no words to thank you," said Lee before going to bed.

"I haven't done much."

"On the contrary, you have given my granddaughter a chance to live. I swear, Tim and I will repay your generosity."

"I assure you. It's unnecessary."

That night tucking Katherine in bed, Lee prayed with the child. Claude overheard them as he passed the guest room on the way to retiring to his own.

". . . And Lord, have with you my mother, protect Grandma and Grandpa, and oh Lord! Don't let Grandpa forget us while we're away . . . and, oh yes, please take care of Claude . . . because he's a nice man and let him like me a lot . . . and think of me as his friend. Amen."

29

Claude left for work early, covered by his business exterior. It was a week from his departure, but he looked like he had aged years instead of days. He hid behind determined foot steps, but the truth remained in the dizziness of his thoughts, functioning in an orifice of time without end.

He owned the world, but once again life was the hollow pursuit of power without the love which, unknowingly, he had conjured out from the mouth of death.

If this had been a ploy to convey the financial banking for these desperate people, the McGuires deserved to be praised for their elaborate plan, because he believe in the aperture between heaven and earth that had allowed love to transcend beyond the laws of possibilities and the scope of reason. He would find Natalie, perhaps not in Washington as she had promised in her letter, but through the gateway known as death. However, there was business to resolve before embarking upon such a journey.

Summoned at his command, the private secretary made sure to call Brandon Shearson, requesting his presence at Transworld first thing that morning. His lawyer stood in front of him before taking a seat.

"You look worn out." Brandon crossed a leg, squared off over the other. "Does it matter to you?"

"I imagine it's from the long trip, or perhaps . . . nights of pleasure. I hope whatever got you looking like this was worth it."

"It's nothing like that," said Claude with a rasp in his voice.

"Why did you call me?"

"Is the arrangement for the hospitalization set up?"

"It is," responded Brandon, releasing a mouthful of smoke into the air. "After I leave you, I'm meeting Mrs. McGuire at the hospital. I need to get her should any consequence avail brought about by your good will to sponsor medical treatment."

"Lee's not going to sue anybody if something goes wrong. Both grandparents are aware of Katherine's outcome without the shunt. What I mean is, did you make it clear that my estate will be the guarantor of the debt in case I have an accident?"

"An accident? Why are you doing this?"

"Katherine is my child."

"I tell you, Claude, no wonder you look ill." The lawyer straightened up in the chair. "I would keel over if a woman stuck a child on me. Is it supposed to be Natalie's?"

"Just know that the kid is mine," he said.

There was a silence between the two men.

"Do you want to run it through me?"

"Just tell me about the arrangements at the hospital. I imagine the neurosurgeon is top notch."

"He's the best, but remember I'm a friend and legal advisor to you. If you want to run the details before you step into shit, hell! Do it now, not when it's too late. You didn't get married or something like that did you?"

"No, I didn't." Claude's voice was a monotone.

"So why are you telling me Katherine's your child?"

"Because it seems that way."

"Well that's not enough," said the lawyer, cutting him off. "I thought you met Natalie a few months ago. How can the kid be yours?"

"I had an affair with a woman named Elizabeth Bates ten years ago."

"We can run tests."

"Maybe, we'll see. In the meantime the girl needs brain surgery and I want to pay for the whole procedure. Lee McGuire is her legal guardian. She has to review the consents, and sign the papers at the hospitals. I want no delays."

"I'm working on all of this." Brandon squinted as he leaned forward. "About the only thing that I agree with is that Natalie is beautiful, even captivating."

"You saw her?" Claude held his breath.

"No . . . , the paintings. I saw them at the gallery downtown."

"The gallery?"

"Yes, Pilar had a friend of hers take them on. The opening was on Sunday."

He remembered he had given Pilar all the paintings before he left.

"I didn't give her permission to . . ."

"I'm sorry," said Brandon catching on. "I figured you knew."

"I gave them to her, but I didn't think she was going to show them around."

Claude closed his eyes as he pressed over the temples with his hands.

"Natalie is not with you anymore, is she?" Brandon put out his cigarette. "You're going to hate me for saying it, but you look like you've been through a storm."

"Don't waste pity on me. You won't get very good returns on your investment."

"Are you kidding? You're the king with the Midas touch. Tell me the name of your new company and I'll buy it while it's penny stock. Even your paintings are going to make you money."

"What do you mean?"

"The critiques. You're an artist now according to this morning's reviews."

"Pilar . . ."

"Well, you know she has a mind of her own."

"My paintings are not for public viewing."

"I'll leave you to settle your differences with her."

"There's one more job for you, Brandon."

"What is it?"

"Change my will. Do it before the end of this week."

"Your will? Don't tell me you're thinking of killing yourself over Natalie?" said Brandon, smirking cynically. There was a long silence between the two men while the lawyer straightened up in his chair. "It was a joke in poor taste. Go ahead, shoot me. I probably deserve it."

"Maybe I should, but I won't because I need you. Katherine Bates is my sole beneficiary."

"Have you taken leave of your senses?" The lawyer stood up, leaning over the desk. "I should meet this invisible girlfriend of yours. She sure fried your brains!"

"End of discussion," said Claude with a burst. "Just be my attorney."

"For that reason I can't let you make mistakes. This may be a huge one," said Brandon, arching an eyebrow.

"Katherine is my daughter. Why can't I leave her my fortune if I die?"

"You've been suckered to believe a ploy by very clever people. Listen, now that she's going into the hospital, let's check this girl out. I'm sure she's going to have blood work. We can take a little extra for gene studies." There was a moment of silence. "Hey, guy! Go for it if she's your child, but if she happens to be an impostor, then you have no moral duty."

"Very well," he conceded. "I'll let you test me, but do it quickly. I don't want delays upon my plans."

"You scare me, Claude. I've never seen you like this, but by the end of the week I'll give you an answer. If she's your daughter, I'll write you a will."

30

Katherine went into a private room at Columbia Presbyterian. Money could fix almost every need, as Claude had discovered. When he walked through the door of the hospital room on Thursday night, Katherine lay in her bed. The room smelled of alcohol and medicines. The white sheets over the bed made the child look paler than he remembered her, and for the first time since they met she looked ill.

He wanted to stay away fearful of the effect she had upon him but he realized his heart was much stronger than his will. Katherine resurrected the memory of his own mother and his inability to safeguard her from death but more than anything else, Katherine reminded him of the family life that could have been but never would be, between him and Elizabeth.

He fought to stay detached, but it was a futile effort because his conscience compelled him to see her before the surgery scheduled in the morning. Shocked by the full blow of reality, he was taken aback when he realized Katherine's lips had forgotten how to smile.

She looked at him more like an old woman than a girl, saddened by the weight of her impending future. But her skin was soft, not marked by the lines that deepen and make for sags, no rough spots nor lentigines, the tell-tell signs of age. Katherine was wonderfully young and he was saddened with the thought of all the years lost away from her and the ones never to come.

Doctors and nurses had pestered over her, and the IV's infusing fluid into her veins were a silent anchor to reality. Her arms were colored purple from hematomas where sharp needles had drawn blood and missed. Dressed in her Winnie the Pooh pajamas, she looked angelical, and he wished he could have dance away with her, into a ball room where she was the princess and he, the king. If there were such a place, he would ban sadness from their hearts forever, and he would summon Elizabeth to his side and love her till the end of time.

Lee had dosed off in the chair next to the bed so she didn't see Claude come in, but like a guard dog parked by her master, she propped up with his presence and acknowledged him with a wave of the hand and a forced smile. He felt pity for the woman who, like him, was battered by the jaws of fate. Emotions had exhausted her, bringing an old woman to the edge of endurance. Brave women made this clan.

Claude realized Lee was surprised to see him there but she got up, making way for him to come closer to her granddaughter. The old woman had signed all the necessary papers and the consent for the surgery listing the risks of surgery: paralysis, infection blindness, coma and brain damage. Katherine could survive the procedure to live in a vegetative state, death being the most merciful alternative.

"Hi, Kat!" greeted Claude. "Do you think I can call you that?" Katherine nodded her head affirmatively as he sat by her bedside. "It's been a long day for both of us," he went on, trying to smile. "You look tired, and I'm sure I do too."

"I'm glad you came." Katherine let out a long-winded sigh. "Grandma said you wouldn't come, but I knew you would."

"You were right. I wanted to see you."

"Will you be here when they take me for surgery?"

"I'm going to try. Unfortunately, tomorrow I have a very busy schedule. It's difficult to push away responsibility, but I'll do my best," he said trying to be sincere.

"The nurse said she's going to shave all my hair in the morning," her voice trailed off.

"Your hair will grow back, stronger and much nicer than before. Don't worry about it."

"I'm afraid of dying," Katherine's voice died out, as she started to whimper.

Claude took out his handkerchief, handing it to the child, and she blew her button nose. Then he came to the edge of the bed and put his arms around her, patting her gently on the back, like he would have done when she was a baby and needed to burp. He looked back at Lee who was by the door. Then forgetting about her, he caressed the girl's head, hoping to comfort her. Not sure if she fully understood the idea of death, it was obvious there was something frightful in such thoughts.

"You won't die, Kat," he said, pushing his voice out of his throat. Destiny couldn't be that cruel.

Lee stirred behind him as she wiped off a tear falling down her cheeks. Both of them had one goal in common, the well being of the child.

"If I had a . . . father, I would want him to be like you," she said, smiling through her tears. "I always wanted to meet him. Grandma said my mother died when I was born, but she never said anything about my father. Are you him?"

"I would be a lucky man to have someone like you," he whispered. "Don't worry about tomorrow. Everything will be fine. When you come out of the hospital, I'll take you for a carriage ride around Central Park."

The girl's face lit up, but simmered quickly.

"They stuck a lot of needles in me today. You see here." She showed him, pointing over her skin. "And here and here."

Claude felt guilty, thinking that one of those black and blues had been for gene testing. He too had a venipuncture site on his arm, as a phlebotomist had taken blood earlier that day.

"They said her veins were hard to get," said Lee from the corner of the room.

"No one will poke you again." Claude's eyes offered a promise.

"I saw the nice lady today. She came to say goodbye after the last blood drawing."

Her words came without preamble forcing him to stiffen up. *Was this supposed to be Natalie? Why was this her last visit to the child? Was Katherine going to die?*

"Don't talk about her," Lee pleaded with a tremble in her voice.

"But she's so nice, Grandma." The child's face brightened. "Today her face grew sad when she said she wasn't coming back again. I want to be with her, I told her I loved her . . ."

Death as we know it was the end of life, but Claude was beginning to think differently. If he were to believe that Natalie was Elizabeth's ghost, then there was another plateau, some metamorphosis after death which preserved the recollections of this life and the bonds made between people. To believe in all of this meant that the conversations between Natalie and himself were leading toward a greater truth, toward the reality of a continuum. Everything exchanged between them was meant to prepare him for these moments.

"What else did the lady say?" he asked, wanting to know more. This girl was like water for the thirst in his soul.

"We talked about you."

"Did you?" he asked, caressing the locks of blond hair.

"She told me you were upset, that I should hold your hand and help you as you have helped me. I'm not sure what that means." She blinked twice. "Do you?"

"Perhaps."

"There was a message for you, but I don't remember very well, something about . . . Yes, she said to tell you: *Blind men can't see, but the light of love can overcome the darkness of their doubts.*"

Katherine stretched out her arms, engulfing him around the neck. She stayed there pulling on the IV's that fed her body, and he pulled the poles closer or she would rip the catheters from under her skin. A warm and tender feeling entered his soul.

The girl felt frail close to his much larger bulk. *Am I blind not realizing the truth is in this child? Why can't my mind accept what is so obvious to my heart?* Kat, as he called her now, had been conceived out of the union between himself and Liz.

"I'll be here before you go in tomorrow. I'll be right here, Kat," he promised.

"I will miss the lady," she said in a whisper, coming closer to his ear. She peaked over his shoulder to watch her grandmother. Then concealing her voice, bringing herself even closer, she whispered a secret only for the two of them to hear. "She's my mother, the lady who visits me. Grandma doesn't know, but it's her daughter. I will really miss her when she's gone because I love her and she loves me. I asked her to take me with her, but she said I had to stay with you."

No, Katherine could not die. She had a life time ahead of her.

"I miss her, too," he said. "But you must stay with your grandmother and me."

"Do you think she really won't come back?"

"Oh God, I don't know. I don't know, but you stay with us." His voice turned soft. "Your mother loved you. One day I will tell you much about her, but for now I think she has become your guardian angel."

"You knew my mom?" Just like a child, the girl had forgotten all else with this new found knowledge.

"I did."

"Tell me about her, Claude."

"Hmm, she was a lot like you, fun to be with, kind and loving. She loved life and she loved you immensely. She renounced being a woman to be a mother because she thought a man would kill you, the man who conceived you. She ran away from him to nurture the life growing inside her."

"Did you love my mother?"

He made a small silence. Then he spoke up.

"Yes, very, very much."

"And do you love me?" Her eyes searched inside of his.

"I love you, Katherine," he said, after a moment's thought.

The girl smiled.

"I know you, Claude. You would never kill anyone."

She couldn't know he was that infamous man. These were just words without true value, but she had discovered his thoughts. At that moment he felt like a murderer, and her words offered him the kindness of a second chance.

"You sound so sad when you talk about her," she said.

"Only because I miss her so much. Why don't you close your eyes and I will tell you a bedtime story? Sleep little girl, sleep," he whispered in her ear, then she lay down.

One day he would share all his secrets with Katherine. He pushed back the hair from her face, and he remembered his mother.

"My mother had eyes like yours," he told her.

"Your eyes are blue also," said Katherine smiling.

Their relationship was spontaneous, unrehearsed. To Claude's surprise, he had developed a great affinity for the child. He wasn't lying when he said he loved her.

He started the fairy tale and soon after, Katherine slept peacefully.

"I'll be here in the morning," he conceded almost to himself, looking at the child. He went toward Lee, and looked her in the face, the face that was buried under wrinkles and the silver color of her hair. Her eyes were warm, and no matter their tired look, he found a gentleness in their glance.

"Why are you so nice to us?" asked the grandmother. "I know you're hurting over the disappearance of the woman you love. You might even think we're swindlers after your money. Although her innocence touches you, Katherine's *beautiful lady* could be part of a hoax. I watched you . . . , you are genuinely concerned about the outcome, and despite my reservations I can't help but like you, Claude. This is why I don't have the heart to push you away from my grandchild. I like your nickname for her."

"She's become someone special," he confessed. "I'm not sure why. Maybe because she's the victim of fate. Maybe because I love the woman who brought her to me, or maybe because she's my child."

"There's a lot I don't know these days."

He thought Lee wanted the truth, the answers he didn't have.

"I had Katherine checked today for her gene compatibility and mine."

"I know," said Lee, crossing her arms over her chest. "I had to sign the consent."

"You don't mind?"

"I think all of us should know," she said. "I feel sorry, not just for my grandchild, but for you, for myself and for my own daughter who cannot hold the child she loves, even though I sense she's around us. Once again, thank you."

"Are you coming home with me?" he asked.

They both looked at the girl sleeping.

"No, I think I'll spend the night here . . . in case she wakes up."

"The recliner doesn't look very comfortable. I'm sure you didn't sleep well in there."

"I'll be fine."

As he faced the city streets on his way home, he wanted to believe in the greater purpose of all that had happened, and he smiled realizing how important Katherine was for Lee.

*   *   *

Claude was there as promised, very early that next day. Shocked when he saw Katherine's head shaved off, he kept his self restraint for the sake of not frightening the girl. The reality of brain surgery was eminent. Soon after, he heard the noise of a gurney coming closer, driven from the hallway into the open door of the room. His respiration grew into a shallow rapid quail when the transport apparatus drove through the doorway. A hearse driven by black horses would have made less of a muster.

Through the fog that numbed his brain he saw the nurse come in, gentle with her smile, offering Katherine a bonnet to cover her scalp.

"One of you may come to the operating room with the child," said the woman. Then the nurse unlocked the clasp of the chain around the girl's neck, handing it to Claude, the closest at her side. "You'll have to keep it for her. No jewelry's allowed."

The nurse's voice seemed to come from across the room, instead of where she was, right next to him. He felt as though someone had placed ether over his nose, and he floated with an out-of-body experience. Lee stared at the ankh in his hand, and he thought she knew it was his, that Elizabeth had given it to him, but it was impossible that anyone could know.

The Egyptian ankh was the symbol of eternal life. It represented the soul. He thought of hiding the jewelry at the bottom of a pocket, but instead he snapped the broach around his neck, tucking it under his shirt. Lee could have said something, but instead she kept silent.

"Can I take Wuff with me?" asked Katherine naively about her favorite toy.

"Yes, sweetie," said the nurse, smiling at her.

Claude looked at Lee once more.

"You go," said the grandmother."I don't have the guts to follow her into surgery."

The paraprofessional started to push away the stretcher, together with the orderly. Claude took her fingers when they searched for his, squeezing them, hoping to reassure the girl that everything would be okay.

"You'll be fine, Kat." His voice was like a note off key.

Suddenly, he had forgotten about his own plight, wishing to hold the small hand for as long as God gave him life. Crossing through the hallway, into the elevator, they stopped on the fifth floor, reaching the double doors of the operating room. His shirt was wet from the sweat pouring out of his armpits.

The walls were too white, the lights awfully bright. Too many people were dressed in baggy clothing, the color of apple green. The nurse asked Claude to put covers over his shoes and dress in a yellow paper gown over his street clothing. He had to wear a head bonnet to conceal his hair, all of which he followed like a zombie. They could have said, touch your toes and walk backward and he would have done it, but instead, he followed the nurse into the O.R.

Another nurse inside reviewed the data on the chart, looking for the medical clearance with the results of electrocardiograms, x-rays, and blood work.

He wanted sunglasses for Katherine to shield her eyes from the two halogen lights that were over the field of surgery like two blazing suns. He thought, *How is it that doctors, haven't figured it out yet, that pre-op patients should leave their rooms wearing dark visors over their eyes?*

Claude's focus was on the girl, who held onto Wuff and his hand. The anesthesiologist floated over the girl with a mask. The neurosurgeon stood on the side, waiting in the ritual anteceding surgery. The instruments were laid upon a Mayo stand, surgical steel blades lined up at the end of the tray.

"Fourteen, fifteen, sixteen." Counting to the beat of a metronome the nurse went through the four-by-four pile of sponge gauzes that would be used during the operation. "Seventeen, eighteen, nineteen . . ." At the end of the surgery and before the sutures were in place, the count of these gauzes had to match because on rare occasions a piece was forgotten in the mess of blood and guts.

Nothing unnerved Claude more than the saw on a silver tray. The doctor had explained that they were going to separate the cranium by the suture lines into five pieces to access the site of the blockage. Afterwards, they would glue the bones together the same as they had been before.

"I'm going to place this over your nose and mouth, Katherine . . . Breath into the mask and don't be frightened," said the anesthesiologist, with the indifference of eyes that stared over the surgical mask. "There's air in   here . . . Don't be scared."

Even though she had been peaceful, the girl's eyes opened wide, afraid of suffocating because it felt so strange to breathe inside the gadget. She struggled as he held her arms. Then Katherine closed her eyes. The toy fell onto the impeccably clean tiled floor of the room. Mechanically, Claude bent over to pick up her dog. The anesthesia had taken effect as the child lay still, so immobile, seemingly dead. He remembered his black and white dream, sure he was standing upon the same earth. He couldn't see Natalie and Katherine dancing together because he was the outsider on the other side of the circle of trees.

"Now you must wait outside," said the nurse who had accompanied them.

As he walked away, he turned around one last time and saw how they transferred Katherine to the operating table. Pentothal must have escaped into the air as his knees quivered and he felt doped up, but he realized it was probably the fear inside him, more than any anesthetic, that made him quiver.

For the first time in his life he dealt with the raw edge of fear and he wished more vehemently than ever that Natalie was there, watching, taking care of Katherine. Nobody could see her, because it wasn't meant for them to see, but he sensed her ghost was there. She left him her secrets, the knowledge that she could stand on water and be everywhere she chose to, because spirits moved much faster than man's clumsy protoplasm. Physical restraints were for people, not for spirits.

The initial feeling back in Washington when he first met Katherine had transferred into a stronger, more lucid sentiment. More than just the compelling thought of doing an altruistic act of compassion, today he walked out of the O.R. knowing he left his daughter behind.

31

The waiting room was a nauseating bubble gum pink, with rows of gray vinyl chairs lined against the walls. Claude paced back and forth, waiting for the outcome of the surgery. The hospital, the doctors, everything was the very best, but too many things could go wrong. His phone rang, he paused, answered, talked, and then hung up. This exercise took place three or four times during each hour.

"It's taking forever," Claude thought out loud."

Lee sat, twisting rosary beads between her fingers.

"Why don't you go for breakfast?" she said.

Two hours had passed in the endless wait. He knew it was ten o'clock, having looked at the Rolex on his wrist innumerable times. Food was the least in his mind.

"I would prefer knowing how long we'll be here."

"I pray to find comfort, . . . and to pass the time as well."

"Maybe waiting is more difficult because I'm not focused into the reality of time," he said, making sense only to himself. He was sounding a lot like Natalie. "We count days from the moment of our birth. Why must we measure age instead of wisdom? "

"There's no choice. We're given certain rules."

"Rules? Don't you think the rules have been re-thought? Natalie told me but I didn't realize it then. Lightning is electricity and currents can alter matter. She was a spirit until a blast of energy gave her more density, enough for me to feel her. Her spirit had traveled to the grave of Elizabeth Bates with a latent wish, the wish to be human, to get a chance to redeem a mistake because I was meant to help my child all along but she forfeited a continuum when she made her choices. Could this be possible or am I trying to make sense of what has none? Today is Katherine's birthday. It's today isn't it?"

"You know?"

"I feel like an expectant father in the maternity ward. I know because I saw it in the hospital documents, and she told me in the airplane."

"I promised her a birthday cake after she's better," said Lee.

"I'll be there to see her blow out the candles."

"You really think Elizabeth came back, don't you."

"Yes, Lee. Natalie is Elizabeth. She told me about four states of matter, it's just that I'm so black and white. But I'm learning about possibility."

Lee couldn't understand him because he had stopped making sense when he was touched by a miracle. Life had become a different concept.

"Faith in the impossible has guided men of wisdom and knowledge."

"Natalie left me the answers, the oars to navigate through life. All I had to do was listen," he said.

"I have faith all will be fine. God is with us."

"And what is God?" He looked straight into her eyes.

"God is understanding and love."

"I fell in love with the strength that forbids me to forget. She said I would remember her in the life of a child, and she promised that I would be a good father. Did she mean this about my experiences with Katherine?"

The old woman shook her head. "I heard your restless walking in the apartment the first night we got here, and I realized you were like a spirit without a place to rest."

"I haven't slept a full night in two weeks."

"You care about my grandchild with a strength that is uncommon."

"Because I loved the woman who brought me to her."

"My daughter knew pain and disillusionment." Lee looked up at him. "She loved a man, and if you were that man then it's about time I told you that Katherine is alive because my daughter couldn't kill the seed of love between the two of you. Katherine was her sacrifice."

"I understand."

"She said that with this child, what lived between you would never be forgotten and that one day this child might bring you together. Maybe she has." Claude dropped on one knee.

"You must believe I didn't know she carried a child of mine," he said with a trailing voice. "I would have done anything to keep her from dying."

"You drove her away."

"I was a fool blinded by misguided values, but I know she forgave me when she chose to come back, although I don't know if I can ever forgive myself."

"She never had a harsh word about you, but she suffered in silence and I hated you with every day that passed. You were the culprit of her dilemma. You denied her the support she so desperately needed. In her death bed, she made me promise not to blame the baby for the faults of a man and a woman. I thought it would be impossible, but I love my grandchild more than my own life."

His silence gathered the feelings that choked the words inside his throat.

"I fed hatred on a stranger," said Lee. "Now the devil has a face, but it's very hard to hate you. You've done a lot of good . . . and if Katherine survives, we will owe you her life. How ironic, don't you think?"

"No one could hate me more than I do."

"Katherine asked you to be with her this morning. Aren't you here, Claude?" Lee smiled at him compelling him to get up. "It might have been more comfortable to use your money without getting attached. I'm an old woman, but life is still teaching me about people and things."

"Elizabeth will never walk out of here by my arm but Katherine might. I want to believe in a woman's love and in the child who anchors this overwhelming experience."

"Don't let the experience of living destroy your life."

Claude sat next to Lee.

"I'm here because I found hope in the form of a child." Claude swallowed, displacing his eyes to the far wall of the room. "If it weren't for Katherine, you would have read about me in the papers. My promise to help her stopped me from . . ."

"Dear God! And now, are you still thinking of it?"

"I went through a desperate moment, close to madness when Natalie was lost forever. Too cruel to be a joke, don't you think?"

"We would never play such a trick on you."

"Even if you thought I was the devil, as you just called me?"

"No matter who you were," said Lee with a steady voice.

"I have to admit, love is the light that pushed me through the threshold of my disbelief."

"Then you're convinced Katherine is yours?"

"Even before the result of gene compatibility. There's no doubt in my heart that she is my child," he said, standing up. "I knew as soon as I saw her. Her physical appearance is a lot like my mother, her eyes, her hair, the smile on her face. I consented to the paternity investigation for the sake of all involved, including your grandchild. Nobody should take away her birth rights. I'm one of the richest men in the world."

"It scares me — "

"My wealth should be her inheritance and my family name, her name. I'm the bastard, born out of wedlock to Marie Aumont. Katherine will be different."

Lee kept quiet. She clasped her hands together while her eyes averted his face.

"I have forgotten my losses to look at the needs of a child," he said. "I have come to love beyond the confines of my life to fill my heart with the surrender of a father and the acceptance of the impossible. May your God help me to live on."

"You're an interesting man."

"Don't flatter me, Lee."

Lee resumed her praying. After ten hours of surgery, the neurosurgeon appeared in front of them. All had gone well, and although Katherine had to go into the surgical ICU, the expectations were optimistic for her convalescence. Lee couldn't stay in the hospital that night so Claude took her to dinner for a decent meal. At first she refused, trying not to spend more of his money, but what she didn't understand was that all the hospital costs — as steep as they were going to be — resulted in an insignificant sum of money for him. Producing money came easy; but how complicated to develop lasting friendships and deeper commitments. *Could it be possible to learn how to live all over again?*

They stopped at a church on their way home because Lee wanted to thank God for delivering her grandchild safely through the surgery. Claude sat in the pew, while she prayed on her knees. He looked at the altar, at the saints in the small chapels quartered on the sides of the building and he felt the presence of an omnipotent power, of a being wiser than any of them could ever imagine, not a chastising God, but one full of love and forgiveness for anyone who sought Him out. Claude found himself less lonely knowing Him there.

Later at home, Lee went to sleep right away, but he went out into the balcony seeking a breath from the autumn night. Forty-two floors above ground level, the wind blew powerfully at this time of night. The lights inside the penthouse were dim, and the quiet of night went undisturbed by the noises of the city below. Claude looked down at the drop to the street realizing his obligation for Katherine was fulfilled, but was it really? It could be that it had just begun. Suicide crossed his mind again, but it wasn't an option anymore.

He flipped the lapel of his suit while he wrapped the jacket across his chest, overtaken by a frigid chill. The drop in temperature forced him to go back inside. The white see-through curtains tangled when he closed the sliding doors, making him look like a specter in the dark. Without any warning, a shadow cut across one side of the room. The confluence of a body moved through the limelight.

He held his breath as his senses keened because there was a presence in the room. A strange sensation came over him, inexplicable, but fantastically real. It wasn't his imagination — Natalie was there. The subtle scent of her perfume flared inside his nostrils. He felt her stronger than ever before. His eyes swept around the open space, remembering she said that spirits moved faster, making it hard to grasp their form.

In silence he stood, taking brief steps enveloped by the dim light which came from the hallway. The apartment was cold from the open doorway, or was it because Natalie was there? He wanted to touch her, to see her, to tell her how much he longed for her, but there was nothing except the sound of his heart beat.

Perhaps his mind was playing tricks on him, but he looked around once more. Then he stood still, immobile for what seemed a lifetime. The dining room table was there and farther away, the furniture in the living room. Tall columns rose like giants sustaining the roof before collapsing, crushing him in rubble. No, the ceiling wasn't going to come down, and his senses were denying her presence, but an unspeakable feeling was taking over, crying out that the ghost of the woman he loved was there with him.

His body didn't have the ability to perceive what was not human because it was like trying to focus upon microscopic particles with the naked eye. The encounter was brief, yet it filled him with her presence.

She was here.

Two different states, but here, together in one space.

Katherine came to mind, the key to unlocking two universes. He wasn't sure why the child was taking precedence over all his other thoughts, over his immediate need to find Natalie, but she was. As though a message lingered, trapped in invisible waves and uttered by lips forming no words, he searched trying to hear, perhaps bypassing the input of his ears, instead sinking deeper inside, into an untapped portion of the mind. His mouth parted, wanting to say anything, but he was stopped by silence. There were no lips to speak, no words to hear, but he was receiving a message from the space around him. His heart galloped.

And then, out of nowhere he understood, as though he had been struck by lightning. His thoughts formed into lucid sentences, and the purpose of all this was the silent message from the beyond. Without words, the central idea was reaching his mind as through a telepathic trance traveling in a wireless system. The child's importance, which had been growing in his heart like a mountain in the midst of a valley, suddenly was clear.

He was here for Katherine and she for him, because the girl needed a father, and he needed to form a bond with the woman who was gone. His daughter was the bridge uniting life and death. She was the innocence lost from his heart — the truth between Elizabeth and himself. Just as imperative, he had to see her grow up, imparting purpose in tomorrow. Living with Katherine would dissipate a lot of loneliness because she would bring meaning to the journey of life.

The child was a part of the woman who was gone, a part of himself; she was the union of two halves. A magnificent realization shook him from the feet up. For the first time in his life he was able to see, not with his eyes, but with the faith that rooted from his soul.

Claude remembered the love which had grown almost like a secret between himself and Katherine, and here was the chance to form a family with her, a purpose for his empty wandering.

"Oh, God!" he whispered, looking for air to fill his lungs.

The revelation was unmistakable as his mind had listened to a message sent from Heaven. Guessing that Lee would want to hold on to Katherine, he would argue that neither of them had to give her up. Katherine could enjoy the affection and the care of all her loved ones, as the love of many people could only enrich her growth. Peace, even a subtle contentment replaced desolation, as though a hand had reached to save him from inside the black void.

The storm had marked the opening of a gate. The power of a Supreme being used nature for a unique opportunity at the exchange of leaving Natalie unenlightened about her origin in the trade off. But as Natalie fulfilled her quest, she returned more and more back into the spirit form, an thus to recall, rebelling against the inevitability of who she was, because of the love fastened to this life.

Without turning on the lights, he walked into his room lit by moon beams coming through the open curtains. Like a cat relying on other than his senses, he got around wanting to walk among the shadows. His eyes were the ones which kept him from seeing her, his ears from hearing and his hands from touching the woman he could not cast out. A strange sensation told him she was there with him. The instruments were wrong. His mortal mind was stumped by the way Natalie came around this time.

Throwing himself on the bed, without removing his clothing, he just lay there feeling her seep inside his body. Without a doubt his Natalie was there, with him, existing side by side. He remembered words which came from nowhere. He wanted to dream, hoping to perceive that which his senses kept away from him. Dreams were the tools she left behind. Natalie, Elizabeth they were one and the same. Now he was so sure. His mind drifted as sleep relaxed his body. There were no more barriers between himself and the impossible.

32

Peace brought resignation and greater depth to his beliefs. A week after the surgery Claude showed up at the hospital with a large birthday cake and the nurses flocked around Katherine's bedside to sing her Happy Birthday. The child insisted on passing a piece of cake to the other beds on the floor, if their health allowed, and soon a slew of patients marched by her room, curious to meet the child who had become so popular.

During Katherine's hospital stay, Claude went every day to see her at rehab and sat like any other parent through the hours of waiting, mindful of her progress. Many times they sat, not like a man and a child, but like two friends who need to talk about their work, the progress with therapy and the adventures of the mind. Katherine entered the empty cavity left with the disappearance of his beloved, and like her surgical wounds, he began to mend with the magic of a child and her love for him.

Lee watched in silence, sometimes stepping away to give them time alone because the thirst to be together became obvious, so obvious that the nurses, the doctors that came and went, those who had a chance to watch them interact were made to understand how easy and uncomplicated true contentment could arrive. On the day of Katherine's discharge, he could have asked Lee to take care of it, but with the enthusiasm of someone who wins a prize, he cancelled work to see her home with him.

That evening, at the end of his work day, Claude stayed behind with Brandon, sifting through some of the documents distributed during a meeting in the board room. He was immersed in the business at hand when his lawyer put a hand on his shoulder and looked him in the eyes.

"I got the results of the blood test we ran on you and Katherine," he stated. "It took longer than expected because we had to exhume the body in the grave, and the permits from the county had to come before proceeding further, but here they are — " Brandon gave him a piece of paper. "The two of you are compatible."

Although Claude expected the results to come through as such, the news caught him with the weight of legal confirmation. He read the document, then folded it into his pocket, his face reflecting the understanding living for many days now.

"I double checked the results myself, and there's no doubt. Katherine is your child. It seems like she's going to be one of the richest girls in the world. Would you mind telling me about the mystery behind this girl?"

Claude stood up, forcing a smile.

"You wouldn't believe me even if I told you, but I thank you for the work you did. You know what I want, my will."

"I knew you'd say that." Brandon was taking out other papers from his briefcase. "Here it is."

"It's done?"

"You said you wanted it redone, didn't you?"

Claude took the papers that were his, a detailed legal document listing his assets and one heiress.

"You leave me intrigued with the mystery of the woman I never met, and the woman dead in Washington, mother to the child which is yours."

Brandon loaded his briefcase with his belongings ready to leave the building having concluded all business at Transworld but not before Claude shook his hand and exchanged a glance without words. Both men walked out together, Brandon back to downtown and his firm, Claude to his office.

That evening when Claude walked into the streets of Manhattan, he had a sense of self-awareness, having confirmed what his intuition had cried out. Dressed in his black wool gabardine coat, he passed a pet shop on his way home. He walked by there often but today he went inside. His purpose was to buy a dog for Katherine. The girl would be leaving for Washington very soon, having finished with her convalescence, and he would miss her the rest of his life.

The thought of ending his life was as far removed as the thought of losing her.

The excitement of the surprise settled with a flutter when he walked into his home. Almost with childish intent he called her name, knowing she would come to greet him like always, with a kiss and a hug, showing off the love that had grown unstoppable. But today he would share her with the new addition to the family. He smiled inwardly, thinking about the expression on her face.

Just as he thought, today was no exception: the child ran toward him, happy to have him in her life, wearing the knitted cap Lee had made for her bald head.

Taking the dog out from behind his back, in one hand he had the ball of fur.

"For me?" she gasped, stopping in front of Claude at the sight of the dog.

"Yes, for you Kat," he said, laughing.

"Oh thank you, thank you, Claude." She took small leaps into the air, and her arms flailed at the sides. Then she took the puppy. "Grandma, Grandma! Claude got me a real Golden Retriever just like Wuff!"

He followed the girl who ran off. He saw Katherine throw herself on the living room floor, allowing the small animal to climb over her and play carelessly. Lee came out of the kitchen, wearing an apron. She had been fixing dinner. They saw each other, and she smiled with the indulgence of his gift.

"You didn't?"

They both stood for a moment looking at Katherine with the puppy.

Pleased with the choice of his mood, he went to hang his coat. Then he motioned Lee to meet him in the kitchen. The flavor in the smell of her cooking floated in the air, making him hungry. Why couldn't life go on just as it was now? Lee could take care of them, but he knew she had a husband and another life waiting in Washington.

"Will you sit with me a moment?"

She followed his gesture, taking a chair next to him. There was an envelope in his hands.

"My lawyer brought the results of the testing." He handed the papers to Lee. "She's my daughter."

A silence rose. The woman took a moment to see what was in the content of the documents.

"So you're asking me to accept the fantastic story about my Elizabeth?"

"It's important," he said in a deep voice. "You have lived part of the experience with me. Don't you believe? "

"I know you want Katherine," she said. Her face contorted into a painful mask carved out of fears.

"I love her, but I won't use my money to take her from you."

"You taunt an old woman. You're rich, we are not. Men like you buy everything that stands in their way."

Claude took back the document. The dorsum of Lee's hand was covered by age spots, the veins of her hands blue under the thin and wrinkled skin. She had a black sweater that covered her arms and most of her neck, but it couldn't cover the harshness in her words, nor the wounds left behind by the perils of life.

cover the harshness in her words, nor the wounds left behind by the perils of life. She was his housekeeper in Washington and Tim the gardener who lined the beds with Impatiens for spots of color in the spring. They had chosen to work at his employment to give Katherine more than they could afford.

"Katherine could have a better lifestyle raised by my side, but my money can't buy happiness if I cast away the love she feels for you and Tim." His voice was warm. "I have grown wiser thanks to the experience of knowing a woman, your daughter, and I'm certain she wanted me to find Katherine, Tim . . . and you."

"I can't give up my grandchild." Lee clutched her chest.

"I don't want you to give her up. No, not at all. What I would like is to share her with the two of you."

"Let her get the best of two worlds, is that it?"

The female voice raced into his ears, loud beyond the comfort level, but he knew it was because she was threatened by the facts.

You will always be her grandmother, but I would like to be her father." He had the right to hold on to the child who was delivered to him through supernatural means. Now that she was in his life, he needed her there.

"I can't live without her."

"Vacations will be yours, but let her go to school in New York."

Lee kept quiet.

"Talk to Tim. I'll bring her to you when she's off from school and if you want to visit us during the school year, I'll pay for the expense. There's plenty of room in my home for the two of you." He thought for a moment. "The ideal situation would be for the two of you to come and live in New York. I would offer you my unconditional help."

"I don't want your generosity in exchange of my grandchild."

"I didn't mean to offend you. Don't take it the wrong way."

"We're not into fancy apartments or the money you throw around."

"I could get very used to the way we're living now but . . . I understand, you have your pride." His voice was a coarse note. "Pride gets in the way of many things. Don't take her away, please. Give us the chance to know each other."

"You realize you have no experience as a parent."

"Then I will learn like all the other parents, by trial and error and the use of my judgement and my instincts and . . . my love for her. I can give up my freedom, decrease my hours of work in exchange of parenthood, but it's not all sacrifice because Katherine gives much more in return."

"It's not as easy as you think," she lashed out.

"I will do what must be done to become the father she needs. No dreams nor false expectations. Elizabeth took away my chance at fatherhood when she ran off to Washington many years ago. Don't do the same thing now that she's given it back. I love my daughter. She's a part of me."

Lee got up and turned her back on him, making herself busy, cutting up the salad. The noise of the knife over the cutting board was a blunt rebellious snap. She shredded to bits the cucumber she was slashing. The pressure cooker over the stove let out a whistle that startled her and she flinched as the sharp edge of the blade cut her finger. Blood dripped over the granite counter top as she applied pressure with the other hand.

"Let me see that," he said rushing next to Lee.

"I'll be okay." She covered the wound with a hand towel, continuing pressure to stop the bleeding. "I've gotten cuts like this before."

"I'm sorry, Lee. I've upset you."

"It's not the cut that hurts, it's the thought of not being next to her every morning at breakfast before I see her off into the school bus. It's the thought of forgetting her smiles and being with her when she needs to share the events of every day. I'm the only mother she's known."

"I like you, because you have the same strength that Elizabeth owned and the same perseverance that lives in Katherine. The three of you come from the same breed of women, you survive against adversity with the strength that comes from the love inside your hearts.

"Baking pies at the crack of dawn can't pay for her needs no matter how much you care about her. On the other hand, all my money can't buy her love.

"I respect you for the pain you have endured, for the loss of a daughter and now for having to deal with the man who seemingly takes away the grandchild that has lived with you so long.

"I swear to you by the love I hold so sacred that I won't keep her to myself." He paused to catch his breath. Here he was, pleading for his life. "Katherine will be fine, no matter who raises her, but I would like to be a part of it. Let her choose, and if she wants to leave with you then I will follow her to Washington. You see, I can give up everything for my daughter."

Lee looked into his eyes. "I believe you really would."

"I can be content anywhere in the world if she's near me, but I can't renounce her, not now that I know her."

"You ask for a lot, Claude." Lee walked away.

"I ask you for the right which is mine," he said, getting in front of her. "Don't let her grow up in the absence of a father."

He knew about the misery of missing someone. He knew about the mess which selfish people make out of life. He also knew his money could pay for the law to give him custody, but he didn't want to do it that way.

"I can't promise you anything," said Lee, walking out of the kitchen. "I'll discuss it with Tim, but I can't promise more than that."

Katherine ran toward her grandmother when she saw her. The puppy followed, wagging his tail as he wobbled against her legs when he caught up.

"Can I sleep with my dog, Grandma?"

"I don't know. We'll see, we'll see," said Lee, eyebrows lifted.

"I'm going to name her Pudding. Do you like that name, Claude?"

"I like it, yes. It's a good name."

"My favorite desert is vanilla pudding, and she's my favorite dog in the world, so she'll be Pudding."

Claude looked at Lee once more, as he left her behind, going toward his bedroom to change out of his work clothes. He thought Lee wanted to be fair but her feelings were getting in the way.

After dinner, Lee called Washington, just as she did every night. Tim's voice came from the receiver.

"He showed me the legal papers that confirm his paternity."

"We're getting older," said Tim on the phone. "It's not easy to raise a child by ourselves. He seems to care about her, very much from what you've told me."

"I don't know," answered Lee at her end. "We've managed with Katherine all these years. I would miss her very much."

"It's a wonderful opportunity for her to stay with Aumont. He's a generous man, and he has a good heart. There was no obligation on his part to do anything, but he did, and all he had was a feeling and a bizarre story. He placed the well being of a child he didn't know over his own personal disaster."

"I know, Tim, but still, how could we live without her?"

"I will miss her, too, but he says we can come as often as we choose. Let's give it a chance, at least for her sake. If it doesn't work out, we're still her legal guardians and she can come back to us. Don't they seem to get along?" asked Tim.

"I have to confess, they do," Lee admitted. "He's very good with her, and I know he cares."

"Then give them a try," replied Tim through the phone. "Elizabeth brought them together and Katherine is his daughter." There was a brief silence, then he went on.

"Aumont is giving us the choices. That's unusual for a powerful man."

"All right, I'll try to see where this takes us."

"Have faith, Lee. Have faith . . ."

"Oh, Tim, I wish you were here."

"I'll see you in a few days, Sweets. Just hold on a bit more and we'll be together. I know it's been rough for you."

"You're right Tim. I'm not as young as I used to be. I need to come home."

"I miss you, Lee."

33

Father and daughter walked into F.A.O. Schwartz. The magic of the toy store entered their bodies as Katherine's dreams of childhood defused into Claude's soul. Every time she laughed, it was like a ray of hope for his day, instilling the stamina to go on living for her sake and his. Katherine walked through the store, excited with the fantastic display of toys. The life ahead of them was filled with the adventure of living.

The McGuires agreed to leave her in New York for the school year, to see how the relationship would fare, but Claude's goal was to live the remainder of his life with his daughter. He liked that Katherine had never been a pampered child and that she had the self restrain to walk out of the establishment without a fuss when he decided to leave without a purchase. Claude thought her grandparents had taught her well, but the toy store would see them again, and the next time he would surely buy her something, but he didn't want to spoil her, something which would come easy given his wealth.

Horse-drawn carriages were parked at the corner of Fifth Avenue and 59th Street. Claude had promised Katherine a coach ride the night before the surgery, and this was the Saturday he had chosen on a bright day of Indian summer at the end of October. Katherine loved all animals, and this was a new adventure.

Her golden hair was just getting long enough to style in a bob. In her denim overalls and a red jacket she looked like any other child, but for him, she was a miracle.

The desire to tell her about his paternity had dwelt in him for many weeks. Lee had left him the choice of when and how to do it. The hoofs of the horse over the pavement made a rhythmic coupling, and now seemed as good a time as any.

"There's something I want to say," he whispered, changing into a serious tone.

"What is it, Claude?"

Her eyes looked up.

"It's very important for me to tell you that you have become the most precious part of my life." As he put his arm around her, he was careful with his words, measuring that each one was the perfect one. "When I asked Grandma to let you stay, it was because I couldn't bear the thought of continuing in the loneliness I lived. When your mother came into my life, she reminded me that living should not be centered around my work."

"My mother?"

"Your lady came to visit me also." He smiled with her memory. "I loved her very, very much. She taught me . . . not to take love for granted, as it can easily be lost. You fill my heart with that love and I will cherish you as my most blessed gift from God."

"You said she came to you." The girl giggled. "Why did she visit you? You weren't sick."

"You make such sense with your questions." He paused a moment, then took her hand. "In a way, I was sick. The important parts of life had escaped me, I thought money and status could buy me happiness but now I understand that life without love, without . . . you is an empty void. She helped me find you, Grandma, and Grandpa . . . and even to believe in the greater power above us. For years I thought God didn't care. Now I know better"

His words were taking him forward.

"Pudding is important, too. Don't forget her," Kat reminded.

"Yes, I guess she's important to us both." He smiled at her childish outbreak. The carriage pulled through the park, the foliage tinting the sky with the hues of fall. "I knew your mom before you were born," he ventured on. "We were younger, maybe . . . silly with some of the things we chose to do. When I was growing up, my parents were very poor, and I promised myself l was going to make more money than I could spend in all my life. My mother died when she couldn't afford the medical cost of tests that would have saved her life, and that made money seem very important. I forgot that everything needs to be balanced. Otherwise, it ends up choking you."

"Why did it take you so long to find me?"

"Oh, Katherine!" he sighed. "Sometimes life is very complicated. I was younger, adults make mistakes. I let your mother get away with you. She needed me, but I wasn't there. Then, well . . . one day she came back and taught me how to look at myself, how to discover the feeling that was always there. She brought out, I guess, the man that was buried in his self-made grave. Through her I found you and I'm convinced she watches over you . . . and maybe a little bit for me."

"Am I going to stay with you forever?"

"Forever is a long time, but I hope you stay with me for many, many years." Invaded by raw emotion, his voice cluttered. "One day a young man will come and you will want to be with him, but until then, I want you to be my very best friend."

Natalie had saved his soul by leaving Katherine as the extension of their love.

"She told me about you," the girl said, in a tone more grown up than her age. "I knew that you would find me . . . even before you came, just as I knew that you would be that very good friend. She told me."

Her words drew a special feeling. There was nothing more magnificent than the love of his child and the memory of the woman he would love forever.

"I wish I could become like . . . a father to you."

"You would want to be my father?" she asked. "Is that why you asked Grandma to let me stay with you?"

At the end he wasn't sure why Lee agreed to his proposal but he was happy the end result was Katherine's living with him. This was the moment he had feared but at the same time hoped for. Her hand felt small inside his own, but it made him feel brave.

"I'm your father, Kat. You're an irrefutable part of me."

"You're my real father?" Her pupils widened as Katherine held her breath in disbelief. The child threw her arms around him. "Can I call you Dad?" she asked, looking up through her large blue eyes.

"You can call me whatever makes you comfortable but yes, I would like it very much, if you called me . . . Dad."

Feeling the same contagious happiness in the demonstrative outburst of his daughter, he felt whole for the first time in his life. He couldn't help but to imagine the happiness that would have been given the chance to father Katherine ten years ago. But this is what was, and the future that would be.

"Dad," she repeated with music and warmth in her voice.

Here he was content hearing such a simple word, and he knew that through Katherine he could redeem part of the past.

"One day when you're older I'll tell you how I found you, facts which I don't fully understand but which brought me to this point. These were events which should have left me crippled if it hadn't been for you. Not only do I want to be your best friend . . . but your father also," he said.

She pulled out the chain from around her neck.

"Can you help me take it off." The gold ankh Elizabeth had given him had been returned after the surgery to Katherine.

"It's yours," he said.

"No, it's really yours . . . I just kept it safe until you found us."

He didn't ask how she knew. Taking it off her neck, he placed it around his own, continuing their ride through Central Park. Together with his daughter, he would never be alone again.

Later that day, Pilar telephoned from Amelia Island in Florida. She was on vacation but wanted to remind him about the art exhibit. The media was doing a television exposé of his work.

"Thank-you, Pilar," he said on the phone.

"For what? For making sure you're there? I know you weren't happy learning I displayed your paintings, but I knew they weren't for me. You were hurt and sometimes we say stupid stuff without meaning it. I told my friend at the gallery they were on loan. They are yours to sell or to keep. You're appreciated as an artist, and you'll have more time on your hands after December. You might want to paint some more."

"Thanks for being my friend, for working with me all these years." There was a small silence on the other end. "Listen, I decided about the man to replace me."

"You did?"

"It's you." He heard her gasp. "I was going to tell you after you came back from vacation but you might as well savor the next two weeks knowing you'll be busier than ever on your return."

"Thank-you."

And so he had ended the business of his firm.

After checking that Katherine was tucked away in bed, he left her to the tutelage of the woman who had come to live-in. The nanny was not meant to replace his affection, just some of the hours until he came home from work. Lee had helped to choose her.

Clarita was a kind and helpful Spanish immigrant who raised four children of her own. His plans to settle down were almost there — on December thirty-first he was stepping down as CEO — but it was good to have a woman close to Katherine because Lee was right, his daughter was going to grow up fast, and there were things more easily said between women.

"You look handsome, Mr. Aumont," said Clarita with a thick Spanish accent as she handed him his coat. Next to him she was a tiny woman, with café-latte color skin, who grew a natural flush over her cheeks every time he smiled at her. She was a vegetarian, keen on organic foods and antioxidants, and he never thought he would enjoy the experience until he tasted it.

"Take care of her, Clarita."

He wrapped the scarf around his neck.

"Oh Señor, you know I will." She smiled reassuringly. "She sleeps like a little angel that she is. Enjoy your evening. I will do good care of your daughter."

He knew she would.

34

The guests filled the gallery at Soho, crowding the hallways to unexpected capacity. Natalie had led him to the artist, and Pilar had sought his recognition as one. How bizarre that all of this would unfold. People stood glued to the floor, looking at the public display of his art work framed upon the walls. A more realistic picture of those days came into his mind, although every once in a while he wondered if he had been involved in a great hallucination that brought him by coincidence to his daughter. How much more insane to believe in the specter brought forth in the storm, involved in some metaphysical crossover, spirit over matter for the sake of uniting him to Katherine.

No, even if no one else believed, Natalie was not a figment of his imagination, and at moments such as now, looking at her pictures all over the gallery, he immersed in her memory as he touched her with his thoughts. He felt luckier than most, understanding the limits of his mortality and the far reaching magnitude of love surviving death. These paintings brought him to the edge of memories.

The night was cold but, inside the guests enjoyed their cocktails and the soft music which came from a group of musicians off in a corner. People had cornered him the entire evening.

"Your paintings are amazing, Mr. Aumont. Can't stop looking," said an art critic. "You cast a melancholic spell, drawing into the drama of a feeling. I look forward to viewing more of your work in the future."

"Thank you," he said.

"Agony and pain — " cut in Brandon with a subtle smile. He had pushed through the multitude of gatherers to reach his friend.

Claude looked at Brandon, knowing he knew his ache. They were standing in front of a landscape scene where Natalie appeared running through a field of red poppies, her hair blowing in the wind, her face alive with the experience of living.

"I'm so pleased you let us represent you," said the gallery owner. Leopold's hands had a flair, and his voice was too soft. Claude realized the man was gay. "I must thank Pilar again for bringing your work to me."

"It's too bad she couldn't be here." Brandon drank his martini. "But I imagine she'll catch the reviews in the morning papers."

"I have many offers from clients who want to buy your work," said Leopold.

Claude smiled at all of them because they were filling his ears and he wasn't used to this much flattery. He wasn't sure if he could paint again, although Katherine was there to recharge his spirit. The idea entertained his mind. Life was open to many possibilities, some so unexpected. He walked away with Brandon to a space that seemed secluded on purpose for them to stand alone in front of the last painting of Natalie. This was indeed his very best.

"It's still there, isn't it?" Brandon asked. "The feeling, the memory of a woman, I can see it in your eyes."

"She was my perfect counterpart."

"She should be here tonight."

"You are so right, my friend. I miss her, unlikely that I will ever forget her — " Claude sipped from the fluted glass of champagne.

"You must go on with life, Claude."

"I assure you that I have."

"Will you ever tell me what happened?"

Claude's answer was his silence. He was staring at the face on the picture.

"She left you because of Katherine, didn't she? Tell me, how did the mother die?"

"I wish it was as simple as you want it to be, Brandon. She's gone from me. Forget about her and the mystery which will surround her name."

In silence, as though the two of them were burying her body, they stood before the gallery walls where her memory was alive.

"I noticed how that chick back there was eying you, the art critic? I bet you could convince her to do a great piece on your art work."

"She's not my type"

Brandon would never understand his loss.

"I'm going to walk over to Cindy," Brandon said, with naughtiness in the tone of his voice. "She's been waiting for my company all night. I see her looking this way . . . Why don't you join me? Her girlfriend looks like such a slice. I guarantee you. We could do doubles tonight!"

"Go, Brandon. I'll stand here just a little bit longer," Claude said, as he looked at the ladies waiting at a distance. "I'll probably go home in a while. The evening has been a pleasant one, something most unexpected."

"I'll be around a while longer. Change your mind and take me up on my charitable offer to entertain you even further with the ladies. I doubt you'll be disappointed."

"There's no need to find further amusement for me. I'm okay."

"Suit yourself, but think about it. If you change your mind, the night is young." Brandon was ready to walk away. "A man like you can have any woman he chooses."

His friend was wrong. He could never have Natalie.

Framed, he saw her image captured in time, reaching up with one arm, yearning, searching for the same miracle he wanted, making his longing for her much worse because he knew she had wanted the same things he did.

"Natalie . . . ," his lips betrayed his silence. "If only you could cross into this world again. You left me Katherine, but I miss you so much."

Life was sustainable with the thought of their daughter, but as a man he longed for more. There was nothing stronger at that moment than the thought of the woman he still loved and the yearning of the union he had known.

The pungent memory of his desire filled his soul while his eyes clouded with the sting of this heartache. He bit down on his jaw so hard that he thought his teeth would crack. Then, as quickly as a breath, the shiver of that cold autumn night entered his body making his hair stand on end. His blood flowed too rapidly, as his heartbeat took a jolt. The warmth of long, soft fingers caressed the back of his neck, the way she used to come, the way Natalie gently filled him with desire.

Unsure of why he felt compelled to close his eyes, he did. He held his breath, afraid of disconnecting from this moment. The people from the room vanished; the noise became a silence. The lights dimmed as the external world unfocused from his senses. The perfume of the woman long desired, the ruffle of her body against his own, time had stopped and she was there. Once again, like the night in his apartment after Katherine's surgery, the shiver up his spine announced the window between two separate dimensions. And then, he felt Natalie's lips upon his own, the ones which were unmistakably hers, moving over his, prying with unmistakable familiarity. As authentic as the woman on the canvas, this was the physical manifestation of the woman he knew.

Like fingerprints, he recognized her touch. He pressed against her, allowing for the want in his longing. Then he heard her voice, but knew there were no words to be heard.

"I'm here . . . I haven't, nor will I ever leave your side. I love you,

Claude . . . with all the might of what has always been." Her voice was a whisper over his lips, entering his soul and staying there, burning with its strength. *"I live in you and you in me, so you will find me always . . . as I will be with you and Katherine through many lives . . . for I will love you until the end of time."*

Claude didn't want to open his eyes, but a dizzy spell took his balance away for a few seconds, enough to force him to open them, afraid of falling to the floor.

"Stay with me," he begged, knowing he had broken off the moment.

He stood alone on the floor in front of her painting, having felt her touch, tasted her caresses, even heard her voice. Where had she gone? He turned around to look for her, but there was no one like Natalie at the exhibition hall. He could have spotted her among a million people, among the many beautiful women in the building, but none of them was the right one. It had been she, an angel come to life. He was so sure.

His chin trembled with the thought of love. A tear fell down his face. The feeling was there, suffocating with its intensity.

"It's you, I know it was you," he said in a very low voice. "You were here, everywhere, inside me, around me . . . I will never stop looking for you, and one day, one day at the end of my journey I'll find you again. I believe, I believe in you and in me, and if this is madness, then in that, too. I love you, I love you also forever."

No one was really looking, nor hearing nor touching him. He was talking to himself, and if someone had caught a glimpse they would have said it was his eccentric genius. They were all focused on what the senses perceived. Natalie had become the phoenix, the beautiful bird of plumage from his dream and like the phoenix, from her ashes she would find life again.

They were the alpha and the omega, the beginning and the end.

With the knowledge that he had obtained life for the purpose of learning, of taking out more wisdom than when he entered through the gate, he would go on living. Finished with business at the gallery, it was time to leave. It was midnight.

He went for his coat, putting on his gloves and wrapped the scarf around his neck. With one hand he combed the silver over his sideburns. Winter was right around the corner. The cold wind cut his face as his hands hid inside the pockets when he stepped outside. Nobody there really noticed or missed him, involved with themselves.

That night he knew he was a better man than when he first began his journey. A special woman had rescued his soul. When he saved her life in the woods, she returned his own. Natalie promised a life for a life, and she had delivered — his.

Contentment merged within with the thought that life was there for the taking. Feeling alive, he smiled, knowing Katherine, his daughter, was waiting for him at home.

The end.

❖   ❖   ❖

I wrote this novel before 9-11-2001. I debated keeping the scene at Windows on the World, World Trade Center. Some of my friends have expressed the concern that this would be distracting to my readers, but at the expense of sacrificing my novel, I opt to keep it in the content as a tribute to those who passed away there.